S0-BIW-507

Magic, Lies, and Deadly Pies

Magic, Lies, and Deadly Pies

A NOVEL

Misha Popp

NEW YORK

This is a work of fiction. All of the names, characters, organizations, places and events portrayed in this novel are either products of the author's imagination or are used fictitiously. Any resemblance to real or actual events, locales, or persons, living or dead, is entirely coincidental.

Published in the United States by Crooked Lane Books, an imprint of The Quick Brown Fox & Company LLC.

Crooked Lane Books and its logo are trademarks of The Quick Brown Fox & Company LLC.

Library of Congress Catalog-in-Publication data available upon request.

ISBN (hardcover): 978-1-64385-995-8
ISBN (ebook): 978-1-64385-996-5

Cover design by Trish Cramblet

Printed in the United States.

www.crookedlanebooks.com

Crooked Lane Books
34 West 27th St., 10th Floor
New York, NY 10001

First Edition: May 2022

10 9 8 7 6 5 4 3 2 1

To everyone working to dismantle the pastry-archy in their own way

Chapter One

The first time I killed a man with a pie, it was an accident.

But only the first.

That was a lot of pies ago, and this is most definitely the on-purpose kind.

It's not fancy, but it doesn't have to be. It's just a buttery Oreo-crumb crust filled with rich peanut butter mousse, drizzled with salted chocolate ganache and dusted with crushed peanut brittle.

Okay, maybe it's a little fancy.

I can't help it.

The pie is tucked into a custom wooden carrier with *Pie Girl* burned in a looping script above a silhouette of a steaming pie. The box is absolutely adorable, received on barter at last year's farmers' market, and its elderly maker would probably die if he knew where I was bringing it.

Which he never will.

No one knows I'm here, parked in my dad's old truck across the street from the Sigma Kap house, which is less because I'm stealthy and more because I've gotten used to not telling people what I'm doing. Seven years of living alone will do that to a person.

I perk up as the front door opens and two guys come out, laughing and shoving each other, both laden with bulging gym bags and protein shakes. They drop onto the sagging front steps, toss their bags to the ground, and simultaneously pull out their phones like some sort of modern-day synchronized dance act.

Neither is the one I'm after.

I check the dashboard clock and swallow a curse. Tomorrow starts the farmers' market season, and I'll be baking all night if these piss-gibbons don't leave soon.

Plus I don't want the peanut butter mousse to get too soft.

I'm not strictly opposed to marching up the steps between them, but I'd prefer not to. Pie has a way of making people social, and this isn't a pie I want people interested in.

The booming thump of bass from an approaching car vibrates the truck's windows as the two guys stand and gather their things. Finally.

They climb into the car, and it's all I can do not to fly out of the truck. Now that it's go time, my heart is racing and I feel exposed. So instead of rushing, I take five minutes to scroll through the articles I have saved on my phone.

Kevin Beechum: It Wasn't Rape
Victim Impact Statement Leaves Court in Tears
Light Sentence for Turnbridge Baseball Star Angers Many
Slap on the Wrist for Turnbridge Baseball Hero
Kevin Beechum 'Thrilled' With Outcome, Says Justice Served
Judge's Ruling Sparks Outrage
Anna Hargrave Breaks Silence: Light Sentence a Sign of 'Dangerous Things to Come'

Kevin Beechum deserves this pie.

Magic, Lies, and Deadly Pies

I hop out of the truck and smooth the floral fabric of my dress. It's one of my Nana Fleur's creations, full skirted and fitted at the waist, stitched together with her own version of the Ellery family magic, a special blend of self-confidence and courage sewn into each seam. I can practically feel the threads humming with it as I heft the pie box by its pink strap and set off toward the house.

For a split second, I consider leaving the pie on the *Welcome Bitches* doormat, but I don't—for two reasons. First, I'm not giving up the box.

I ring the doorbell.

Second, I want him to know who it's from.

The door opens to reveal Kevin Beechum, bare-chested and sleepy-eyed the pungent funk of cannabis wafting out around him.

Perfect.

I paste a cheery smile on my face and tilt the box so he can see the logo on top. "Hi, I'm Daisy, the Pie Girl. You were entered into a drawing for a free pie, and I'm pleased to say you've won."

He scratches at his naked chest. "Seriously? I don't remember entering anything like that."

I up the wattage of the smile. "Seriously. It's a weekly promotion, and anyone could've put your name in. It's like having a secret admirer in pie form."

He grins that lazy grin that has charmed so many lawyers and reporters. "Sweet. What kind?"

I slide the lid off so he can see. "Peanut butter and chocolate."

"Oh fuck yeah," he says. "That's my favorite."

I want to say I know, but I don't. It was a detail I'd picked up while researching him, part of a Meet the Team Q&A the campus paper did. Favorite candy: Reese's Peanut Butter Cups. It was too easy.

"It's a new recipe," I say, and even though I've made peanut butter chocolate pie a hundred times, it's not a lie. This particular version is new. "If you want to try it now, I'd love to hear what you think."

"Sure, come on in." He steps back to let me in and leers as I step through. I feel his eyes do that thing, the up-and-down assessment like my body is a racehorse he might bet on.

I swallow my disgust and keep smiling. After all, guys are always telling us to smile. Truth is, they should be really nervous when we do.

Every surface of the kitchen has been taken over by piles of crusty dishes and empty beer cans, so I clear a place on the scratched table. He crowds me as I pull the pie out of the box. I should be scared of him, but I'm not, even as he presses up against my back. The urge to elbow him in the balls is real, though.

"Do you have a knife? I'll cut you a slice." I keep my voice flirty and light, airy as my dress.

"Maybe that isn't what I want a slice of anymore." His breath is fetid against my ear. I roll my eyes. This fucker has no idea.

With a giggle, I spin away from him. My skirt twirls around my legs. A dance of death.

"Maybe it's what you want a slice of *first*." I wink at him, and his lips stretch into a lecherous grin. I want to slap it off, but I don't. My eyes land on a battered knife block that's sure to be cultivating more bacteria than a CDC research lab. Knife blocks are utterly disgusting, but beggars can't be choosers.

Besides, it's not like I'm eating any of the pie.

"I like this housewife routine," he says, leaning on the table and letting his eyes wander. "Seriously. Are there more of you? You do parties?"

I pluck a water-spotted chef's knife from the block, test its edge against my thumb. Duller than the dude in front of me.

No matter.

"It's just little old me," I say. I slide the knife into the pie, and the layers of mousse and crust give way easily beneath the wide blade.

"That's too bad."

"Probably for the best." I hold the slice of pie out, the cookie crust firm enough to support the slice without a plate.

"That looks amazing," he says.

"It's to die for."

He doesn't take the slice from me or get a plate, simply leans in and bites it in half. Crumbs rain down onto the floor as he chews.

I hold my breath, waiting to see if the effect is immediate. These pies are tricky sometimes.

He groans around the mouthful of chocolate and peanut butter, and his blue eyes roll upward. "Holy shit," he says after swallowing. "That's fucking bomb."

He staggers to the fridge and pulls out a half-empty gallon of milk and pops the top. He chugs it, drops it on the table near the pie, and rifles around in a drawer until he finds a fork.

"Definitely a cheat day," he says. I want to take a picture of him, standing there half-naked with a pie in one hand and a fork in the other, milk dotting his upper lip. A souvenir of sorts. But I don't. I never do.

He eats like he's starving, but three-quarters of the way through the small pie, he starts to slow. "The pie coma is real." He drops into a chair at the table and stabs another bite. "But it's like I have to finish it."

"I'm glad you like it," I say, and some part of me even means it. At its core, baking pie is about making people happy. The world can be going to complete shit, but a freshly baked pie is a reprieve, however slight. Even these pies.

"I'm gonna need to nap for like a week," he says. "I thought sugar was supposed to make you hyper. I feel like I could die, but in a good way. Do you have a store or something where I can get more of these?"

His words are slow and slurring, and I know it's almost time. I say, "This was one of a kind."

"You could make a fortune on that." He nods drunkenly. "A fortune."

That's the irony of these pies. The ends are usually, although not always, like this: peaceful and happy and satiated.

The very opposite of what is deserved.

"Would you like to go lie down?" I ask.

"Mm-hmm."

I take his arm and guide him up from the table. He leans into me, mumbling incoherently, as I guide him to the living room. I don't like leaving them in kitchens. Dining rooms are okay, beds and bathrooms too, but kitchens are sacred. Even the gross ones.

He collapses onto the sofa like a felled tree. His breathing is shallow now, but he is content.

I kneel down beside him. He doesn't deserve content.

"Kevin," I say. "Kevin, try to look at me."

His eyes flutter open, find mine.

"That's it. Pay attention. Your heartbeat is slowing down now. That's from the pie." His face contorts in fear, but I hold a hand up. "No, shh, there's nothing you can do. Just relax into it. But the pie, Kevin—you weren't a random winner. This is important. It was a special pie, just for you. Courtesy of Anna Hargrave."

Chapter Two

Going to church is weird for me, and not just because I kill people with pie. It's more that I can't think of a worse place to hold support group meetings.

Seriously. Most of these groups promote themselves as secular, or at least nondenominational, yet they hold their meetings in church basements because, ostensibly, they're cheap. They're also depressing as shit.

It's insulting because, really, if you're at a low enough point in your life that you're showing up to tell a group of strangers every bad thing that's happened to you, chances are you've given up on God by then. And if you haven't, you need more help than a support group.

The domestic violence group at Saint Stan's is my favorite. I know that sounds weird, but it's a big group in the city, and the members are constantly changing. I've found this is true with most domestic violence groups, but Stan's in particular.

The gathering is usually big enough to hide in, which makes it good hunting ground. I learned the hard way that small-town meetings are only good for dropping off strength pie donations. Staying to observe when there are less than ten people in the room is a recipe for having to contribute, and the only thing I care to contribute is dessert.

I'm not myself when I come to meetings. Instead of my usual froofy dresses, I wear baggy jeans and oversized hoodies. I put on makeup, but not to look nice. I smudge it under my eyes so I look more tired than I am. I leave my hair down, something I never do during the day, and comb a bit of shortening through it so it hangs lank and greasy around my face. I become invisible, save for the pies.

I bring cutie pies, miniature bakes the size of large cookies, which I leave in a plain white box on the refreshments table. The flavors rotate, but they're universally cheerful: raspberry lemon, cherry vanilla, triple-berry. I cut starbursts of steam vents in the top like sand dollars and sprinkle them with piles of crunchy Demerara sugar. Way more than most people need, because these aren't most people. These people need the extra.

Every single pie gets taken, every time. If they're not eaten, they're squirreled away into purses and pockets, wrapped in paper towels to be nibbled on later or shared with children.

When people ask what the secret ingredient is that makes them so addictive, I shrug and say I don't know.

But I do.

It's not the vanilla bean or the dash of almond extract. It's not the double dose of sugar or the European butter.

It's power.

The pies for these meetings, regardless of flavor, are infused with as much strength and hope as I can cram into each one.

I have no way of knowing for sure, not without getting super stalky about it, but I like to think the pies are responsible for the evolving cast of members. My goal is for them to eat enough that they build up an excess of mental strength and can get away from their situations. I know it's not always that simple, but it can be, sometimes. Of course, once there was a woman who was particularly smitten with a batch of cinnamon peach cutie pies who ended up taking a frying pan to her abusive husband's head, but that was extreme. She'd wanted to do that long before she ever tasted my pie.

And if the pie pushed her over the edge, well, good on me.

The chairs are set up in concentric circles, spiraling out to fill the room. Many are already occupied. I choose a spot by the door, on my own, where I can watch.

It's funny how people's bodies can tell you more than their words. If I didn't have a higher purpose, it would feel wrong being here, taking in all this pain and suffering like some sort of vampire. But I have a cause.

It's the ones who don't talk that worry me most.

The ones who are talking are safer. They're articulating, to themselves as much as to the room, that there is a problem. There's a reason the cliché says the first step to solving a problem is admitting you have one.

It's the silent ones, like the woman across the room who hasn't raised her eyes from the floor a single time since she sat down, that I worry about.

It's probably her first time. It's the first time I've seen her, for sure, because I would remember someone that striking. She's different than most of the women here. Younger, for one. Maybe midtwenties, hardly older than me. She's dressed well in a high-collared pinstripe blouse tucked into a navy pencil skirt. Her highlighted hair is swept into a neat chignon, and small pearl earrings dot her lobes. She could be sitting in a work meeting except that her high-heel-clad feet are crossed too tightly at the ankle and her clasped hands are not as still as they appear. She's using a single manicured thumbnail to rake into the web of her opposite thumb—small movements but enough to leave crimson furrows in their wake.

One foot twitches back and forth like a manic metronome beneath her chair.

The group leader, an aging therapist who has embraced her hippie persona wholeheartedly, welcomes everyone to the meeting and opens the floor for sharing.

As women stand to share their struggles and triumphs of the week, I watch Pinstripe. Her angular jaw is set like concrete. Beneath it a fog of bruises shows along her collar where the fabric has rubbed away the makeup. If she senses me noticing, she doesn't show it.

The group leader says, "I see we have several new faces tonight, and I want to thank you all for coming. It was very brave of you to take this first step. This is a safe space. We know how hard it is because we have been where you are. Some of us are still there." Murmurs of agreement pepper the room. "If anyone would like to introduce themselves, I encourage you to stand up. You only have to share what you're comfortable sharing."

A petite Black woman with immaculate locs stands up and says, "I'm Angela. This is my first time here. My sister's the one who told me about it. I left a bad relationship a month ago when I found out I was pregnant. It's one thing for him to put hands on me, but not if he's endangering my baby. That's my line. But he keeps calling and coming around. Says he wants to be in the baby's life, that he has rights. Well, I have a right to protect myself and my child, you know?"

The group leader offers up a list of resources, and several other women chime in with advice and commiseration.

The entire time this goes on, Pinstripe's eyes never leave her knees.

Mine never leave her throat.

"This week we're going to be discussing the importance of future-thinking mindsets," the leader says. "Is there anyone else who would like to say anything before we get started?"

When Pinstripe stands, I almost fall off my chair. I'd have bet my oven she wasn't a sharer.

"Yes?" the leader says encouragingly.

Pinstripe shakes her head, eyes still glued downward as if she can't bear to see where she's wound up.

And then she bolts.

There's a commotion in her wake, and the therapist looks torn between following the fleeing girl and her duty to the women still in the room. She stays as sympathetic murmurs ripple through the crowd. This isn't the first time there's been such an exit.

I get up, swipe a pair of cutie pies from the box, and dart into the hall. I can hear the machine-gun rattle of high heels above me as I book it up the stairs.

I catch the glow of streetlights as the heavy wood door swings shut, and I curse myself. This is risky. Too risky.

But I'm already rifling around in my canvas purse, searching until my fingers close around a cool metal disk. I shove through the door and pull the object out, scanning the street. She's already a block away, moving quickly with her head down.

"Hey, wait," I call after her.

She ignores me.

I run.

"Wait," I gasp as I catch up to her. Pie baking is not good cardio. "Wait. Please. I can help you."

"I don't need help. That was a mistake." Tear tracks streak her pretty face. "You shouldn't have followed me."

I reach for her arm but stop before I touch her. She's had enough people touching her without permission. The button I'm holding clinks to the ground as I drop my hand. She stops, automatically bending to retrieve it as I do the same. She pulls her hand back first as we rise together. I hold the button out to her.

"I can help," I repeat. "Or I know someone who can." I curse myself for the stupid disguise. Irrationally, I want to be myself right now, not another victim.

She snorts when she looks at the little button, a kitschy slice of cherry pie swathed in a *Pies Before Guys* banner.

"Look, I know this sounds crazy, but there's a pie maker." I hold out the hand pies. She doesn't take one. "The pies can take care of what's happening to you."

She looks at me like I've escaped from a locked psych ward, and I suppose that's fair.

"What, the way to a man's heart is through his stomach? What kind of fifties housewife bullshit is that?" She takes off again.

"No, not like that. Well, actually, yeah, kind of exactly like that, but not how you think." God, this is a nightmare. There's a reason I don't do this kind of recruiting. I take a breath. "Look, I'm not explaining it well."

"I don't care. I have to get back to the office. I'm supposed to be there late. He's picking me up at eight. I have to be there." Fear makes the words sharp, and she speeds up like she might have already missed him.

"*He* meaning the one who did that?" I ask, pointing to her neck.

She tugs the ruffled collar higher. "It's nothing."

"Bullshit."

"Why do you even care?"

Because it's what I do, I want to say. Maybe pie can't save the whole world, but it can save *some* worlds. It can save hers.

"Keep the button. There's contact info on the back," I say. "Message it, say you're from Saint Stan's. If you can't leave, you can get a pie that will fix it. You'll be safe."

"Fix it how?"

I shrug, decide to level with her. "Depends on the case. It'll kill him or cure him. But based on the fact that he's already tried to strangle you, I think the former is more likely."

She touches her neck. "You sell poisoned pie?"

I shake my head. "No, not me." *Lie.* "And not poisoned. It's, well, magic. For real. Untraceable. It'll look like a completely natural death." *Truth.*

"I don't believe this."

"You don't have to believe in something for it to be true."

We walk in silence for several blocks until we come to a high-rise office building. She pulls a key card from her purse but doesn't swipe it.

"How much?" she asks, voice hoarse as if the words are betraying her.

I point to the button. "You pay it forward. The only price is passing along the pie maker's info to someone else who needs it."

"That's it?"

"That's it."

"I'll think about it," she whispers.

Chapter Three

The lights at Frank's Roadside Diner are still blazing, and the diner parking lot is dotted with cars when I finally make it home.

Friday is fish night and one of the only days Frank stays late. I pull around back and park next to Penny, the gleaming pink-and-white vintage RV I inherited from my mother. I'll rehitch in the morning, when I can actually see.

Through the thin door, I hear the scrabble of Zoe's nails on the checkerboard floor, and I call a greeting to her as I unlock the van.

Once I'm inside, she immediately launches herself at me with the full force of a creature who was convinced she'd never see the person who fills the food bowl ever again.

"I wasn't even gone that long," I say, dropping down so she can jump on me.

Zoe squirms all fifty-five pounds of herself into my lap and covers my face with doggy kisses. I let her, with minimal protest, because it wouldn't be a stretch to say I owe the silly brown-and-white pit bull my life. When things went bad with that first pie, I could've lost it, lost her, lost everything. But I didn't.

"Okay, quick walkies, then it's pie time," I say. She bounds around my legs as I get the leash and barely sits still long enough for me to clip it to her collar. "We're going, we're going."

As we cross the back lot, I catch the cherry-red glow of a cigarette near the back door and wave.

"Hey, Pie Girl," Juan shouts. "Ovens on tonight?"

"Please!" I call back.

"Better leave me something good," he says.

"You know it," I promise.

Juan is second-in-command in the diner and will probably take over when Frank dies, since the old man is far too stubborn to ever retire. He was as surprised as anyone by the arrangement Frank and I struck—pies in exchange for parking and electricity. According to Juan, Frank did favors for no one and figured I must be magic.

If only he knew.

The diner pies are fun to make because they're simple. Or maybe classic is a better word. Sky-high apple, cherry, chocolate cream, and lemon meringue, each infused with the barest hint of a nostalgic magic so they feel like home and happiness. I occasionally rotate other options in, specials for the week based on what's in season or striking my fancy, but the diner isn't the place to experiment.

That's what the farmers' markets are for.

Well, yes, okay, first and foremost the farmers' markets are for money, but the reason I can count on selling out is because I don't bring the kind of pies you find by the slice at Frank's diner.

I hustle Zoe along, get her back in the RV and fed, and grab the green apron from the hook by the door on my way out. When the diner is empty, I let her come in with me, but not on Fridays.

Frank doesn't take health code violations lightly, and fifty pounds of pit bull is definitely on the health inspector's no-no list.

The smell of frying fish hits me before I even reach the back door. I pick my way around the battered milk crates that are the official break-time seating of restaurant staff everywhere and let myself in.

"Where've you been?" Frank barks, wiping his hands on a threadbare white apron.

"Uh, pie delivery?" I don't mean for it to sound like a question, but I'm still not used to accounting for my whereabouts, least of all to Frank.

"You had a visitor," he says.

"I did?"

"Some guy on a bike nosing around your trailer. Dog was barking her fool head off at him, only reason I even saw him. Chased his ass off, but you got yourself some kind of trouble I should know about?"

"It was probably someone from the college. Did he leave a name?" I appreciate Frank's watchfulness, but the last thing I need is him scaring away paying customers.

"Didn't ask. Smarmy bastard couldn't even take his damn helmet off so I could get a look at his face, but I told him if he wanted pie, he could come inside and buy a slice like a normal person, otherwise he had to git. Didn't like the way he was peepin' in your windows like that."

Neither do I, but I try to shrug it off. The guy probably just wanted to place an order, but still, it's weird that he'd show up behind the diner. I take regular pie orders when I'm parked at the campus or the markets, and all the other ones come through the Pies Before Guys account.

"Well, he can always come to the market tomorrow," I say, disappearing into the walk-in cooler to fetch the slab of pie dough I prepped yesterday.

"You make sure my pies get done first, hear? And none of that fancy edible-flower shit either."

I bite back a smile. One time I did that, just one, but he's never letting it go. "You got it, Frank."

"And eat something, will ya? You're getting too thin."

That is hardly true, but I know he can't say something just to be nice.

Juan winks and slides a stainless-steel bowl across the prep table at me. Inside is a steaming mound of hand-cut fries, sparkling with flakes of sea salt. I inhale the sharp scent of too much malt vinegar and grin. Just the way I like them.

"You're the best," I say, shoving three in my mouth and instantly regretting it. It's like eating lava and I gasp for breath, steam billowing out of my mouth like I'm a demented dragon. "Oh shit, that's hot."

"Every time." Juan shakes his head, laughing. "You do it every time."

I pluck out another fry and blow on it. "Patience is overrated." I poke my pie dough to see if it's soft enough to roll yet. It isn't. "Except where pie is concerned."

"Speaking of pie," Juan says, drawing the words out. He gives me his best begging-puppy face, which is pretty good thanks to the fact he has the kind of lashes that would make a Kardashian jealous. "In exchange for scorching your mouth, can I get a special pie? Pretty please?"

I point a fry at him. "You destroy my taste buds with fiery, salty, malty goodness, and you think you deserve a reward?" I swallow the fry. It really is perfect. I nod. "Okay, yeah, fair. What do you need?"

He drops a batch of fish fillets into the fryer and has to wait for the sputtering oil to quiet before he answers. "It's Eric's birthday."

"Ooh, birthday pie is nice. Doing anything special?" I unwrap my dough and use a bench scraper to portion it. There was a time I had to weigh it, but that was a lot of pies ago. When Juan doesn't answer, I glance up to find he suddenly looks bashful, younger than the midthirties he is. I raise my eyebrows at him.

"Staying home." He draws in a breath and dumps the rest of the sentence in a rush, beaming. "And filling out adoption papers."

"It's about time," I say, laughing. I'm already concocting the magic in my head: love, luck, and a heaping dose of strength.

Juan and his husband have been talking about adopting a kid since I came to Frank's, but it's never been the right time, they've never had enough money saved, they've been too scared. That last one is the stupidest thing I've ever heard, which I've told Juan a hundred times at least. They already have a zoo of pets, so I doubt adding a kid to the mix will be that much more work.

"You guys are going to be great dads."

"I hope so." He pulls the basket of fish out of the fryer as Frank reappears.

The old man grabs a pair of metal tongs from the hanging rack and clicks them at us. "I'm not paying you two to shoot the shit."

"You're not paying me at all," I say sweetly, draping a round of dough into a deep-dish ceramic pie pan.

"Damn good thing," he says, loading up a pair of plastic boats with fish and fries.

"You'd miss me if I left."

"Bah," he says, and slings the tongs onto the prep table and bangs through the door to the dining room, muttering about his lack of servers.

"He would, you know," Juan says. "Miss you. I would too."

"So would everyone else when he went back to serving frozen pie," I say, giving an exaggerated shudder. But here's the thing: I do know. When I struck the deal with Frank, I was only looking to find an out-of-the-way place to park Penny for a while. I didn't expect to find a family. But I sort of have.

Chapter Four

I'm jolted awake in the dark hours of the morning by Zoe losing her absolute shit.

She's in the tiny stairwell, barking loud enough to rattle the pie tins.

I slap around for my phone, find it, and see that's it's barely past four. I can think of zero people who would be visiting at this hour.

Or any hour, really.

"Zoe, shut it," I call. My alarm is set to ring in an hour and I'd really like to spend it sleeping. "Come on. Snug time."

She ignores me, her barks echoing in the small RV.

I groan and roll out of bed. Maybe it's Frank, but I can't guess what would be so important it couldn't wait until after oh-god-thirty. Then I remember what he said earlier, that someone had been snooping around, and I go still. I creep to the kitchen and peer out the window but can't see anyone there. Zoe whines one more time, then trots up the stairs into the kitchen. I pet her and point to the bed. "Go."

She does, content that she's scared off whatever was outside.

Probably just a cat.

Or the wind.

I'm sure of it.

Yet I pull a chef's knife off the magnetic bar on the side of the fridge and inch toward the door, holding it close to my side. I hear nothing apart from my own beating heart. Fuck it.

I throw the door open, leading with the knife, and step outside.

Nothing.

No cat, no wind, no prowling intruder. Just an empty back lot, lit by the sallow glow of distant streetlights.

When the door slams behind me I jump, whirling with the knife up, but there's no threat. Just an envelope, taped to the door.

An envelope that wasn't there when I went in for the night.

Frank was right.

Zoe was right.

Someone has been lurking outside.

I pull the envelope down, scanning the dark for signs of motion. Nothing. I crouch down and check beneath Penny for any hidden monsters before going inside.

I'm too wired to sleep, but I take the envelope to bed with me anyway. Zoe climbs over me, curling into a ball between my legs before I even get the bedside light on. I have to stretch to avoid disturbing her.

The envelope is white and completely generic. *PIE MAKER* is written on the front in sharp capitals.

Inside is a single sheet of typewritten paper.

Centered on the top, in caps, it says *ORDER FORM*, but it's not my order form.

It's not even a form at all. It's a note.

I know who you are and what you do. If you want me to keep your secret you'll do for me what you've done for them.

My gut feels like I've taken a rolling pin to it, but I keep reading.

I require a pie for each of the following:

Kerenza Vallery at 1608 Lakeside Drive—Citrus preferred, NO stone fruit. (Allergic, will not eat.)

Brittany Cline at 11B Morgan Ave—chocolate

Emma Rogers at 212 Crable Street, Unit 8—any flavor

Deaths can be slow and agonizing or quick and painless. Your choice. Payment will be tendered in the form of my silence. I assure you that is more valuable than money.

You owe me.

There is no signature.

The paper shakes in my hand, and I force myself to breathe steadily. I tell myself it's just an adrenaline dump, a fight-or-flight response triggered by the threat of exposure. I will not panic.

I grab my phone and check the Pies Before Guys account. No messages. All murder-pie orders come through the app, no exceptions. Even the support groupers I talk to personally have to go online because, as far as they know, I'm not the Pie Maker, just a satisfied customer.

I reread the note slowly, attempting to channel an inner Sherlock I don't have. It's so wrong I don't know where to begin. First of all, Kerenza, Brittany, and Emma are obviously women, and I don't kill women, no matter how much they deserve it. There are already too many men out there slaughtering the female of the species. It's a line I refuse to cross.

I read again.

There's no referral. All murder-pie requests have to come with a referring sender. Pies Before Guys is strictly a word-of-mouth service, and a referral is literally the only way anyone can even find out murder pies exist. It's not like I take out billboard ads.

And there's that comment about money, which is something I refuse to take for murder pies. It's another line I won't cross. It was one thing for my foremothers to profit from their cheerful, harmless magic, but I'm not just whipping up coiffed confidence or love bouquets. There's a difference between being an avenging pie maker and a hired gun, at least to me. My services can't be bought, only earned.

I know who you are and what you do.

But they don't, not really, because if they did, they would know I can't choose whether the death is fast or slow like they suggest. I can only set it in motion.

But they know enough.

They know where I live, and that's a violation I cannot abide.

I take where I live very seriously, because Penny isn't just my home, she's my legacy. She has held generations of Ellery magic and is the last link I have to my mother.

When I was fifteen and Mom got too sick to work, a man came to tow Penny from our driveway, and I watched her roll away with tears streaming down my face and an ache in my heart that had as much to do with the van as with my mother. In my head, the two had become inextricably linked, and I knew deep down that once Penny was gone, Mom wouldn't be far behind.

I was right.

It wasn't until my seventeenth birthday that I realized neither of them was truly gone.

I was in the kitchen, weaving wide strips of pie dough into a desperate wish-laden lattice. I knew there would be no cake, no candles to carry a wish now that Mom was gone, so I was baking it into my own birthday pie. The spicy scent of cardamom wafted up from the sweet apples as I worked the pastry strips over and under each other, trapping the magic between the crusts. The movement was soothing, the pattern just complicated enough to keep the worry at bay. I crimped the edges into deep scallops and brushed an egg wash over the top. I considered a sprinkle of sugar, but Dad never liked pies that were too sweet, so I just slid it into the oven and set a timer.

The stranger arrived just as the pie finished baking, as if lured by its scent. The firm knock had Zoe up in an instant, barking like the world was ending. I set the pie on a wire rack to cool and shushed the dog.

I slung my dish towel over my shoulder, arranged my face into a semblance of cheer, and opened the door.

And almost fell right over.

A familiar, heavyset Latino man stood on the porch, holding a fat envelope. But he wasn't what threatened to take my legs out. Behind him was a pink RV.

Penny.

"Daisy?" the man asked.

I nodded dumbly.

He smiled, the corners of his eyes crinkling with merriment as tears flooded my own. "You look just like her. Happy birthday!"

"What's going on?" I asked. It had to be an apparition. A trick. "How do you know it's my birthday?"

The smile widened. "I'm Aramis, a friend of your mom's. Or rather, the son of a friend of your mom's. She did my mom's hair when she was at Cedar Grove. My mom looked forward to those appointments all week. They really helped keep her spirits up at the end."

"Oh," was all I could manage. None of this was making sense.

"When your mom got sick, real sick, I mean, she came to me about a surprise she had planned. For you." He held out the envelope.

I took it shakily and opened the flap. Inside was a set of keys and the title for the RV, showing the transfer to me. Penny was mine. "But how?"

"I build tiny houses, a lot of them on wheels, and when your mom said she wanted help sprucing up this old girl, I was all in. Interiors are the fun part, and plus, I felt like I owed your mom for being so good to mine. She was a good lady, your mom."

I stared at the title and brushed a finger over Mom's familiar looping signature. "She planned this? Back then?"

He nodded. "You want to look inside?"

I followed him in a daze down the front steps. As we got closer I saw that the pink paint was the same, but cleaner. All the scratches had been buffed out, and the white trim shone in the late-autumn sun. I unlocked the door, feeling like I was moving underwater, and climbed inside.

The smell of perm solution was gone, as were the adjustable salon chair and huge mirror.

The black-and-white checkerboard floor was still there, gleaming like new. The main window had been enlarged to let in more light, and the wood paneling on the walls had been painted a crisp white that made the RV seem bigger than it was. The hair-washing sink, with its deep cutout and adjustable sprayer, had been replaced with a stainless-steel basin and high-necked faucet. White subway tiles decorated the backsplash. I trailed my hand along the edge of the counter and over the black knobs of the four-burner range. "This is amazing," I whispered, noticing the pink KitchenAid mixer tucked into the corner near the refrigerator.

"She wanted to combine the amenities of a professional kitchen with the coziness of home. Check out the bottom cabinets."

I pulled the magnetized doors open to reveal shelf after shelf of pie pans. Every size, from every era, in glass, metal, and a rainbow of ceramics.

"She bought all of them herself," Aramis said as I stared. "Before she got sick. This is a surprise that's been a long time in the making."

"Did my dad know?"

Aramis's face twisted with conflicting emotions, and I knew.

"He didn't," I say, so he doesn't have to betray my mother's confidence.

"She wanted it to be from her and her only," he said.

But I knew it wasn't just that, and my heart broke anew.

My mom had been diagnosed with cancer, but she hadn't died from it. She didn't have a chance to. Instead, she'd had to watch my dad fall apart while her body failed, losing himself in bottles until he was so far gone that he lost her too. I'd tried to tell myself that she didn't know, that his facade had been enough to keep her from worrying, but obviously it wasn't if she had hidden something this big from her husband.

I refused to let his weakness ruin this moment, though—not for me and not for Aramis, who had put so much work into it.

I opened more cupboards to reveal storage bins awaiting flour and sugars, a fold-out spice rack, and a pile of Nana Fleur's frilled and faded aprons. "You're like my fairy godfather," I said.

"It was my pleasure," he said, and I believed him.

Later, in the tiny bedroom, I found the letter, sealed in a Penny-pink envelope, my name written across the front in a handwriting I knew as well as my own.

My dearest girl,

This letter is in case I am not there to see your face on your seventeenth birthday. I hope I am, but you know the treatment hasn't been easy and this disease is unpredictable.

I wish I could see the person you're becoming and I pray you have not been swallowed up by grief. I don't think you have been though, because you're stronger than that. Ellery women always are.

Your dad is going to need some of that strength, but make sure you keep enough for yourself too. You have to be your first priority, always.

I wish I could give you riches or the secret to the universe, but I can't. What I can give you is freedom. Choices. A place of your own.

Penny isn't the grandest of RVs, but she has been good to the Ellery women. Take her and make her your own.

The weight of your gift will not always be light, but if you stay true to yourself, you'll always be able to bear it.

I know you're going to do great things.

Ellery women always do.

Love,
Mom

So whoever is threatening me may think they know me, but they don't. If they did, they would know better than to violate my home like this. I almost feel sorry for this mystery man, because he has no clue what he's messing with.

Chapter Five

"Hey, I know you!"

I whirl, startled by the closeness of the male voice behind me, and swing the awning pole up like a sword before I have a chance to think. The guy backpedals, hands raised and eyes the size of pies.

"Whoa, sorry, sorry," he says. "I didn't mean to scare you. You're that pie maker, right?"

I lower the pole but don't drop it, not completely sure I won't still be using it to take his head off. My mind flashes back to the note, and I think there should be a law about how many times in one day strangers get to claim they know you. Unless this flannel-shirted farm boy is my midnight postman.

"From the college?" he says. "My cousin goes there, says there's this girl who makes the most amazing pies. In a pink van."

I relax a fraction. The lack of sleep is making me paranoid.

"Yes, I'm the Pie Girl." I gesture to Penny, where the logo makes it perfectly obvious who I am. Cheery pie girl by day, murdery pie-sassin by night.

"Cool. I'm Noel." He reaches out a hand, and I shake it because I may be a monster, but I'm not rude. His fingers are long and thin, same as the rest of him. "You need help with that?"

I follow his gaze to where my pink-and-white-striped awning flaps from its single pole. "No, I got it," I say. To prove it, I take the pole, fish it around the corner of the sun-bleached fabric until I find the pocket it slots into, and plant the pole in its base.

All around the common, vendors are erecting their own tents and laying out wares. I flip out the legs on my table and turn it right side up, dragging it close to Penny's side so I can pop in and out as needed to restock. I open the door to fetch the tablecloth, but before I even get inside, Zoe rockets out, zooming around the dewy grass before crashing into Noel's legs. He laughs and leans down to scratch her ear.

"Zoe, leave him alone," I say.

"I don't mind," he says, and because Zoe is now sprawled at his feet, legs waving so he has full access to her belly, I believe him.

"Her name's Zoe. She usually has manners." I spread the tablecloth out and start arranging the pies and tarts.

"Looks like we're gonna be neighbors," Noel says, and even though I didn't ask, I find I don't terribly mind listening to him. Or, to be honest, looking at him. "This is my first year doing this. My uncle says it's stupid for an orchard to be here this early in the season, but I don't know. I think if we're going to survive, we have to do more than sell apples in the fall."

"You have an orchard?" Potential pie ingredients always get my attention.

"Well, technically it's still my grandfather's until we settle some things, but yeah, Hollow Hill. It's mostly apples, but we have a few peach trees, some berry bushes." A grin splits his face, sending starbursts of crinkles out from his eyes. "You've never had raspberries until you've had our raspberries. They're super tiny, but the best thing you've ever tasted in your life. Like eating sunshine."

"That sounds amazing," I say, dismissing him as my midnight murder-pie seeker. No one could be that in love with berries and also want to kill a woman.

"They show up in July. You should come to the orchard, try them fresh off the bush. There's really nothing like it."

"You don't even know me," I say, and laugh because the understatement is real.

He shrugs. "You make pie. I make fruit. What else is there to know?"

He has no idea.

* * *

By ten o'clock I'm too busy to think about the note or raspberries or anything except how many pies I have left. The market is crawling with customers, mostly lone women but plenty of couples and families to round it out. The white gazebo at the end of the common houses a teenage boy with a guitar who is providing a rather impressive soundtrack of nineties alternative covers.

I have a line five or six people deep. They seem content to wait as they bask in the scent of baking pie that drifts out of Penny's open door, petting Zoe as she weaves between their legs.

I cash out the guy I'm serving, a hipster who leaves with the last white chocolate pomegranate tart, and excuse myself to go pull a batch of cutie pies out of the oven. While I don't go through nearly as many here as at the college, I've found the mini pies are perfect for kids to eat while their parents shop, plus their aroma is as good as any advertising I could pay for.

When I come back out, I'm surprised to see Farmboy behind my table, a paper cup in hand.

"Honey spiced cider," he says, before I can ask. "Made from my own bees and my own apples."

Trading among vendors is pretty common—as the bundle of rhubarb sitting on Penny's counter that I paid for with pie can attest—but not in the middle of a rush. I remind myself that this is his first time out and smile at him. "Smells great," I say, already turning to my next customer. "What can I help you with?"

I almost fall over when I realize who it is. Pinstripe. From the meeting. On her arm is a clean-cut blond guy whose Captain America vibe doesn't quite hide the hardness in his eyes. Or maybe I just know to look for it.

"We're getting married in July, and I was wondering if you did weddings? We're having a hundred and fifty guests, and instead of cake, we thought a pie buffet would be fun and more summery."

I swallow my shock and try to work out whether she knows who I am or not. But she doesn't, not when my hair is up and I'm wearing a swingy dress with tiny lemons printed on it. I'm too out of context, out of character.

"Sure," I say. "I can definitely help you. Can I just get through the rest of the line, then we can chat? The Hollow Hill booth next door is sampling cider if you want to wait."

"Goes great with pie," Noel says, leading them back to his booth.

I go through the rest of the line, cashing out pies and taking a handful of orders. I retrieve the cooled cutie pies, arrange them under a glass dome on the table, and wonder if I got it wrong. Maybe it's not the same girl.

I put on my cheeriest of smiles and wave the couple back over even as my heart sinks.

It's definitely her. The highlighted hair is the same, and even though she's dressed in leggings instead of an office skirt, she carries herself the same way. Like a dancer or a gymnast.

A gauzy scarf swirls around her neck like ice cream.

"So, what are we thinking?" I ask her, because I can't bring myself to speak to him.

"Well, at first I was thinking about having a buffet of regular-size pies, but those are adorable," she says, pointing to the cutie pies. "And those might be easier to serve."

"You could also do mini pies, in four-inch tins," I say, showing her the size with my hands.

She looks up at her fiancé and beams. "That could be cute too."

"Doesn't matter," he says, looking bored.

For just an instant she looks crestfallen, but she covers it quickly.

I lift the dome off the cutie pies and hand her one. "On the house," I say. I wonder if this is going to connect the dots for her, the sight of me offering her a pie, but it doesn't. She takes a bite and moans in delight. The dark blueberry filling is mixed with vanilla sugar and a hint of lemon zest, and the crust shatters around it like a fine croissant. Captain Douchecanoe takes it from her before she can get another bite.

"The diet," he says simply, and finishes it without comment.

She touches her scarf, embarrassment darkening her cheeks, and I will the pie to turn to murder in his belly. But the magic doesn't work like that. You can't put it in after it's baked.

As much as I want to scream at her for making the mistake of marrying a guy who's grabbed her by the throat, I don't. I know no amount of telling someone they're wrong will change their mind. They have to get there alone. And so we go through the details of the order, working out flavors and quantity and pricing while her worse half plays on his phone.

"Lot of money for dessert," he says when I give her the quote.

"It's less than we'd pay for cake," she says.

"Whatever."

I meet her gaze and ignore her scarlet cheeks. "We can always tweak things when it gets closer if we need to," I say. She thinks I'm talking about saving money, but I'm not. I'm talking about saving her, eighty-sixing the whole order and subbing in a murder pie. "And I would be happy to arrange samples of any flavors you're not sure about. Can I get a name and contact number for the order?"

"Jackson Vance," the fiancé says, and rattles off his number.

"And?" I say, looking at Pinstripe expectantly.

"And I'm the one paying for it, so any communication can come through me," he says before she can answer.

I smile, but I know it doesn't reach my eyes. "All righty. In that case, the last thing I'll need is a fifty percent deposit to hold the order." I actually don't need it, but I'll be damned if I let him just walk off like he's in charge.

He grudgingly hands me a credit card, which I swipe through the reader attached to my phone. I tap on the *Create Customer Profile* tab and hand him the phone. "If you could just fill that out so I can add you to the wedding folder."

He does, because why wouldn't he? We live in an age where it's second nature to enter your name and address into online forms and it's perfectly plausible that a baker would have a separate folder for wedding orders.

I don't.

But I do know where he lives now.

* * *

Even though I sell out well before the market closes, I leave the striped canopy up and sit on Penny's bottom step, watching Zoe sleep and wondering just how it is that the universe has seen fit to deliver me a mystery midnight pie order I have no intention of filling and a girl who desperately needs a pie she has no intention of ordering all in one day.

I pull up Jackson Vance's address on my phone and stare at it for a long time. It would be crossing a line to bring him a pie without her asking. An important line. The serial killer line.

There's a difference between helping someone who asks for it and deciding on my own, from the outside, who the world would be better off without. The exception to this is cases like Kevin Beechum, whose misdeeds were so highly publicized and who was so, so smug about getting away with it that there was no doubt of the right thing to do.

But to meddle in the private lives of ordinary people is different. The answer never comes from outside. But as much as I know this, I can't erase the image of the bruises smudged around Pinstripe's neck or the desperate, hopeful look in her eyes as she tried to plan for a wedding that may very well be the death of her. I can't decide if it's worse to step in now, take the choice away from her with a surprise pie at his door, or to let it play out and risk him killing her before she decides she deserves better.

"Thinking deep-dish-pie thoughts?" Farmboy asks, jarring me out of my reverie. I didn't even notice him sidle up beside me. A glass bottle dangles from his hand, an inch or so of cloudy amber liquid swirling in the bottom.

"Always," I say, with a sunny grin that belies my dark thoughts. "Good first day?"

"Awesome. Went through all my samples and sold more than I expected, especially honey, so I can't complain." He holds the bottle out like an offering. "Thought you might like this, so I made sure to save you a taste."

I take the bottle and look up at him—miles up, it seems, from my low perch—and give it a cautious sniff. It smells like sunlit orchards and the uncomplicated sweetness of a summer day.

"It's safe," he laughs. "Been sampling it to customers all day."

"Why do you keep bringing me stuff? I've got nothing left to trade."

He shrugs, narrow shoulders swallowing up his ears. "I reckon a pie maker probably spends a lot of time feeding other people. Seems right that someone should return the favor."

"You reckon?" I cock an eyebrow at him.

"I do," he says. "Come on, tell me what you think."

What I think is that I am overcome with jealousy of this simple farm boy, with no worries bigger than his apples, but I don't say this. It's not his fault he's so pure. Instead I swallow the cider, expecting a repeat of the morning's honey-sweet offering, but this is nothing like that. The spiced cider was pure cozy comfort, but this is bright and lively, like being punched in the taste buds by an apple tree in the best way possible.

"So?" he asks, anticipation bright in his brown eyes.

"Farmboy, I think this is amazing."

The grin that splits his boyish face stirs something in my chest, and it's impossible not to smile back. "Yeah? I think it's gonna be the answer, you know? To saving the orchard. Apples alone won't do it, but alcoholic apples might."

I should ignore it, the squeeze around my heart and the warmth I want to blame on the late-spring sunshine and the spiked cider, but my head is too full of other nonsense to remember the rules. Right now I don't want to think about wronged women or murdered men or threatening letters. Right now, just for a minute, I want to be the pie girl this farm boy believes I am, simple and sweet as apple pie.

I scoot over on the metal step, making space for his gangly body, and gesture for him to sit. The fabric of my skirt rustles against his jeans as he adjusts his long legs, and I'm distinctly aware of the contact. It sends an unexpected flutter through me that is in no way unpleasant.

I drain the rest of the cider in one pull. "Tell me more about this orchard."

Chapter Six

By Monday, Farmboy's situation has officially added itself to my list of imminent problems, a fact as inexplicable and irritating as it could possibly be.

It's my own fault, I get that, but telling myself so doesn't help as I set my sign out or turn the oven on to start the day's cutie pies. It's a distraction I don't need, not now, because on top of my mysterious stalker, I'm going to be up to my eyeballs in stressed-out college students in a matter of—right now.

"Pie. Please," sighs a weary student at the window. From the bedraggled look of her, she's been up all night, can barely stay on her feet. In the run-up to finals, this spot outside the Turnbridge University library is a goldmine. Before noon I'll have a line of anxious students snaking around the building like junkies needing a fix. They couldn't tell you why they crave pies so much during finals, but for some, the extra energy and focus baked into each crust is the only thing getting them through.

"Apple, triple-berry, or almond?" I ask, grabbing a bag. "I'll also have cherry, maple, and chocolate hazelnut in a bit."

"Both," she says, rubbing his eyes. "I mean all. One of each."

I throw three pies into the bag, size her up, then add an extra triple-berry. "First customer of the day gets the buy-three-get-one-free deal," I say, not because it's true, but because she looks like she can use a win.

"You're a lifesaver," she says, handing over payment. "I'll be back later for hazelnut."

I make a mental note to set some aside and to up the energy level in that batch. I check my hazelnut stash to see if I have enough to try something new, wondering if I can work in something destressing that won't counteract the energy or focus ratios.

"Yo, can we get that deal too?"

I turn to see a trio of dudebros standing at Penny's window. They're fresh faced and musclebound, the kind of glossy student-athletes who are obviously here more for their prowess on the field than their performance in the classroom. "Negative, Ghost Rider," I say cheerily. These are the kind of guys who've had everything handed to them on silver platters. No way in hell they're getting free pies. "First customer only."

"That's not fair," he complains.

"Nor is life." I smile to show I might be joking. "Plenty of pies available, though. What can I get you, boys?"

"Your number?" the shaggy blond one asks, nudging his sidekick with a laugh.

It's so predictable it hurts.

"Fresh out of stock." I say it without rancor, but as any woman knows, this is the point where these interactions can get real ugly real fast. Lucky for me, this isn't one of them.

He takes the rejection with a good-natured shrug. "Had to try."

Part of me wants to interrogate him about this, figure out why he thinks spotting a woman in his path means he "has to" try to make things awkward. But I refrain. Barely.

They each leave with an almond pie, either not noticing or not caring when I charge them three dollars more than I should.

The dudebro tax is real.

The hours sail by in a flurry of customers and pie prep, but through it all my mind is pinging between Pinstripe, my midnight letter writer, and Farmboy's failing orchard. Each issue is vying for top spot, and even though the order of priority should've been obvious, I find myself returning to the orchard issue more often than necessary. Maybe because it's the only easy one to solve. I don't like feeling helpless, and while I can't save Pinstripe from herself and I can't unmask my mystery man, I can daydream the hell out of some ways to save a cute guy's orchard, and only one of them involves a murder pie.

Noel's issue is simple. His father and uncle inherited the orchard from his grandfather, and neither of them wants it. But Noel does, and that's the only thing keeping his father from selling out to the uncle. Noel needs to get the orchard turning a profit so he can buy his uncle out. Of course, a pie delivery to said uncle would take care of things, but I'm already grappling with one possible noncontracted murder pie; I really don't need to throw another one into the mix, no matter how charming said Farmboy might be. Murder can't always be the answer.

By the afternoon lull, I'm more than ready to stretch my legs. I'm about to put the *Be Back Soon!* sign in the window when a bespectacled man steps into view. He's not one of my regulars, but there's something familiar about him. A professor, probably. Who else would wear a tie with a short-sleeved button-down? I peg him for business or accounting, maybe computer sciences.

"What can I get you?" I ask.

He takes a long time studying the chalkboard sign listing the available choices before asking, "You make all these yourself?"

"Sure do. All from scratch, with local ingredients whenever possible," I say. He's still looking at the menu like it might tell him his future. "The maple's been popular today, and the syrup is from right in town. Branston's Sugarshack."

He takes a few more moments to ponder the offerings and apparently life, the universe, and everything else before saying, "I'll take a maple."

"You got it." I package it up, and he hands me a five.

"I don't need the change," he says, already turning away to pull the pie out.

"So not accounting then," I say to Zoe, who thumps her tail in agreement.

I put out my *Be Back Soon!* sign, slide the window closed, and freeze, puzzled. The guy is still out there, a few yards away now. He's examining the maple hand pie like it's an alien artifact. Without warning, he drops it into the red trash bin, brushes his hands off, and walks away.

"Well, that was rude," I say, grabbing Zoe's leash. If there's one thing I've learned from working in food service, it's that people are weird. "What do you say, Zo, once around the pond?"

And no, talking to my dog does not count as weird.

I lock up and we head out. Scores of students are taking advantage of the sun, sprawled in the grass and on benches with books or phones in their hands, and Zoe basks in their attention as we pass. I wonder what it would be like to be them, worrying about finals and not the literal fate of the people who need me. It would be easier, sure, but I don't think it would be better.

We're barely halfway to the pond when someone crashes into me from behind, sending me stumbling. Panic flares, thoughts of midnight stalkers flooding my synapses. Zoe lets out a surprised yelp, and I whirl around to face my attacker.

But instead of my mystery man or even my unhappy pie guy, a striking purple-haired girl in a battered motorcycle jacket and combat boots is backing away, hands raised in apology.

"Shit, sorry," she says. "I'm a moron. I was running to catch up with you, not kill you. My bad."

I take a breath, adrenaline still sparking through me. "I was just taking Zoe for a quick walk. Did you need a pie?"

She loops an arm through mine. "Perfect, I'll join you," she says, pulling me along. She's half a head taller than me, and where I'm soft and mostly squishy, she's solidly muscled in the way life-long athletes are, although she doesn't strike me as sporty. "Nice day for it, right? Horrible to waste it inside. Cute dog, by the way, and I'm not even a dog person."

I stop, forcing her to do the same. I want to ask what kind of monster isn't a dog person, but I refrain. "Who are you, then?"

"Melly," she says, like it's the most obvious thing in the world. "I wanted to talk to you, but not while you were busy. So I waited."

Even though she's obviously nothing like my mystery man, the idea of her watching the van creeps me out.

"Sorry, that sounds weird, right? I wasn't being a stalker or anything." She swings her messenger bag around to the front and fishes around in it. The flap is covered with pins and patches, among them a smiling pink uterus emblazoned with *Grow a Pair* over the ovaries, an angry cat holding an *I Grab Back* sign, and a

Never Again coat hanger. In the corner are a pair of glittery buttons that read *Roller Derby: Make Friends and Hit Them!* and *Hell On Wheels*. "I need a favor."

She hands me a photocopied flyer advertising a rally outside the dean's office on Thursday.

"So if you haven't been paying attention, this dickweed"—Melly jabs a finger at the photo of a stodgy older white man in a run-of-the-mill suit and tie—"the so-called champion of liberal arts education, has not-so-secretly been posting all kinds of men's rights propaganda on his Twitter account. He claims it was supposed to be on his private account, not the college one, but let me tell you, that private one was worse. Racist and homophobic jokes, sexist manifestos, the whole lot. Who wants someone like that in charge of a school? Where women go? Where trans people go? Where immigrants have been welcome? We don't need that kind of hate here."

I was no closer to guessing what favor she could possibly need from me. "You know I'm not a student, right?"

"But you're a human! With a brain!" She gestures at my dress—pale blue with a white collar—and matching Keds. "Or is this whole housewife schtick for real? Are you really content to just make pies all day and ignore the world around you? Because if you are, then I was mistaken, and I don't like making mistakes, so you better tell me I'm wrong."

She marches off, bag swinging in her wake, and I follow her because, while this may not be how I intended to spend my walk, there's something magnetic about this girl and I want to know more. Know her. Part of me even wants to tell her more, tell her what I see, week in and week out at domestic violence meetings, that I know exactly what kind of consequences the dean's hate speech can lead to. I want to tell her that I actually am content to make pies all day, because making pie is not nothing, making pie is revolutionary, and it may not change the whole world, but it can change individual ones, and that matters. And even if I never made another murder pie, it would still matter, because pie makes people happy, and there is nowhere near enough happiness in this world anymore.

But all I say is, "You're not wrong."

She turns, a mischievous spark in her eye, and loops her arm back through mine. "Knew it. So you want to come? Set up the pie truck? I don't want this to be a flop, and if we keep people fed, they'll stay longer."

"You want to bribe them with pie?"

"I want to bribe them with your pie," she says. The way she leans ever so slightly into the *your* makes my stomach twist. I can't decide if it's a good or bad twist, whether it's me she's interested in or just the pie. I can't decide which I want it to be.

Hell on wheels indeed.

Chapter Seven

On Wednesday night I make my rounds to the meetings, delivering strength pies to three different church groups, but I don't linger at any. Not tonight.

I have Jackson Vance's address pulled up on my phone and a head full of bad ideas that I let GPS talk me right into.

His house is invisible from the road, a steep and winding driveway lined with neatly trimmed hedges the only sign it exists. I curse. Of course this wasn't going to be easy.

I drive by slowly, trying to catch a glimpse of the house in the fading light, but the curve of the driveway is too sharp. The road is empty and I blow an awkward U-ey, tires scraping gravel at the edges. I do another drive-by, but the view is no better from this direction. I consider just driving up it, claiming to be lost if I'm caught, but I don't.

I pull over, frustrated, although I don't know what I was hoping to gain by seeing where he lives. Even if I actually caught him in the act of threatening Pinstripe, it's not like I can just rush in to save the day. I don't have pie, I don't have a weapon, I don't have any kind of real plan.

I don't have any right to be here, meddling, but here I am.

Suddenly headlights illuminate the driveway and I scrunch down in the seat. The car, a hulking SUV that can only be Vance's, doesn't stop, doesn't signal, just swings out into the road and accelerates with a roar.

I let him get some ways ahead and ease the pickup into gear and follow.

I know I should be back at the diner, prepping pies for tomorrow, but I follow the SUV all the way to the highway and into the city. My hands are sweaty on the wheel, and I watch my rearview like I'm the one being tailed. It's easier than it should be, following someone like this.

It's the kind of line I have no business sidling up to. The lines are important to me; they have been since I started Pies Before Guys. I know something happened with me, with my magic, that makes it different from my foremothers', but I keep it in check. Without my mother's guidance, my grandmother's legacy, I might've turned into a real and proper monster, but I haven't. Not yet. Thanks to the lines.

The list of lines I won't cross can always get longer, but never shorter. So far it includes:

Never choose a mark for personal gain.
Never kill a woman.
Never accept money for a murder pie.
Never divulge the identity of anyone seeking a pie.
Never reveal myself as the face of Pies Before Guys.
Never get in too deep to get out.

I probably need to add *Never meddle in the affairs of others* at this point, or maybe *Never follow unsuspecting people like a weirdo*, but that's a decision for Future Daisy. Present Daisy is too busy navigating the exit ramp and sticking with the SUV through a horrifically designed intersection. Enough horns are blasting that I'm not bothered if one or two are meant for me.

After a few minutes of driving with only one car between us, the SUV pulls into a crowded restaurant parking lot. A gray-suited Jackson Vance gets out, handing the keys to the valet. Shit. There's no way I'll get away with that.

I drive by, snag a spot on the street, and hop out, backtracking to the restaurant. I'm wearing my usual meeting clothes, jeans and a hoodie, and I don't draw attention as I move down the bustling sidewalk. I slow as I near the restaurant, watch him walk to a table on the patio. A woman, elegantly dressed in a figure-hugging blue sheath, rises to meet him. It's not Pinstripe, but that doesn't stop him from kissing her lingeringly on the mouth. She touches his cheek, says something I can't make out, and they sit. I'm not aware that I've stopped walking until someone jostles around me, muttering a huffy *excuse me*. I hurry on, not wanting to be caught staring, but given the way Jackson and the girl are looking at each other, I think there's little danger of them noticing anything except each other.

I continue up the street, mind whirling, and duck into a coffee shop. I don't need the caffeine on top of my buzzing brain, but I order an iced mocha to go. It gives me something to fuss with other than my phone when I pass the restaurant on my way back to the car, making it less obvious that I'm getting pictures of the two lovebirds, heads close together over their wineglasses.

The shot isn't crystal clear, not from this distance and not in this light, but it's clearly Vance, and that short Afro is clearly not Pinstripe's. I don't have a plan for the photo, not yet, but I learned a long time ago that it's better to have evidence in the face of liars than to rely on your word.

Still, taking the covert picture makes me feel like a bit of a creeper. It's a realization that pulls me up short and floods my brain with thoughts of the guy who's been nosing around my van. I tell myself this is different, that I'm only engaging in some light stalking for the greater good, but still, the ease with which I move through Jackson's periphery chills me. My mystery man could just as easily be doing this to me and I would never know. I chase the thought away with a vow to be vigilant. If he's following me, I'll find him. I won't be as oblivious as Vance.

I nurse my mocha on the drive home, the plastic cup leaving rings of condensation on my jeans. The fact that Vance is cheating on Pinstripe shouldn't surprise me, but I'm angry on her behalf. Part of me wants to drive straight back to their house and show her the photo, but I know I have no right to do that. It's one thing to act on someone's behalf when they ask you to, but it's a whole different ball of beetles to bust into someone's home uninvited and tear their world apart.

* * *

The parking lot at Frank's is mostly empty when I pull in, and I'm relieved. I need to start prepping pies for the rally, and the quieter the kitchen is, the better. I take Zoe out to pee, then slip her in the back door with me, knowing Juan won't mind if she hangs out in the back.

I call a hello, going straight to the walk-in to get my butter. I don't even see Frank standing at the sinks until he's stomping out toward me, a steaming spoon pointing at Zoe.

"What's the damn dog doing in my diner?" he barks.

I jump, cheeks reddening. "Sorry," I say, letting the walk-in door close with a hiss. "Wasn't thinking."

I hustle over to Zoe, where she's happily following Frank in hopes of a snack, and grab her collar. "I'll put her back."

"You do that. Only reason I'm still here is waiting for you anyway. Where have you been? You better not be letting my stock get low."

"Nope, you're full up. All the usual, plus a couple of strawberry rhubarb coming out tonight." Frank's gruffness is part of his charm, and I know better than to take him seriously.

He harumphs and says, "Your little friend was poking around again today. Would've seen him yourself if you'd been here like I expected you to be. You gonna start having boy trouble at my establishment, we're going to have to rethink our arrangement, missy."

I stop, hand still on Zoe's collar, and stare at him. The look on his face says I'd best be taking this part seriously. "Boyfriend?"

"The guy I was telling you about the other day. Persistent bastard, he is. Asked for you by name this time, like you was familiar, but the rude little shit couldn't even take his bike helmet off. There a compelling reason he can't just call you up? Don't you all got the cell phones?"

I curse myself for my stupidity. Here I've been following Jackson Vance like I'm on some kind of mission, and all I've done is miss the chance to see who's been following *me*. So much for being vigilant.

"I'm sorry Frank. I'll sort it out, I promise."

"You do that," he says. He turns back to the stack of dishes he's been scraping, finds a leftover bit of steak, and flips it at Zoe. "Dog can stay. Just this time. Better than listening to her bark her head off."

I try not to smile as he goes back to grumbling to himself. Zoe can win over anybody.

It bothers me, though, what he said about rethinking our arrangement. I know the grumpy-old-man act is mostly just that, an act, but the fact is, I get more out of our arrangement than he does. If he doesn't want to worry about who my van is attracting, he has every right to send me packing. I could go anywhere, of course, if I had to. Every state in the country has women in need of pies, and I could set up shop in any of them, but the truth is, I like it here. I didn't plan to put down roots, but I like the diner, I like the banter of the kitchen, the predictability of Frank's moods and Juan's infectious enthusiasm. I like the college and I like knowing the best meetings to hit up to help people. I like that I'm on my second year with the farmers' market and already have a loyal following. It may not be home in any traditional sense, but it's a life that works for me, that I enjoy. I won't let some stranger jeopardize that. I can't.

Chapter Eight

No night is as long as one spent awake with nerves. Every time I drift off to sleep, I wake with a start, sure someone is lurking just outside the van. Even Zoe gets sick of my restlessness and abandons the bed around three AM in favor of the more peaceful kitchen floor. I try not to take it personally.

In the morning, the desire to inject caffeine directly into my brain is real. I'm eating a study buddy cutie pie as I drive, hoping a smidge of the energy and brainpower I've baked in will wake up my synapses, but I know it won't. That's one of the quirks of my gift: I can't use it directly on myself. The effects just fizzle. The only boost I'm going to get is from the sugar.

The day, at least, has the decency to reflect my weary state. Clouds hang heavy in the sky; a weak wind barely has the force to rustle the leaves. It would be an insult to be so drained on a perfect sunny day.

I park at the library and find the tired girl from Monday waiting on a bench. She jumps up when she sees the van and is at the window before I've even parked. I stumble out of the truck, holding the door open for Zoe, who trots over to the girl for scratches.

"Sorry to ambush you," she says. "Please, please tell me you have hazelnut again today. Those were amazing. I swear, they're like eating a hug."

So the tweaked recipe was a success. Interesting.

"I do, but they're not warm yet," I say, climbing into the van. "You want to wait? It won't take long."

"Doesn't even matter. I'd eat them as popsicles if that's all you had. Can I have six? Is that ridiculous?" She giggles. "I'm not eating them all at once or anything."

"I don't judge," I assure her. "Glad you like them."

"You're seriously a lifesaver. I don't think I'd get through finals without these babies." She pays and leaves with a cheery wave.

I stay parked there until the lunch rush clears out, then I head back to the diner to pull my back stock out of the freezer. I'm in and out before I can get hung up with any of the kitchen crew, but not before happily accepting an apple-and-cheddar panini from Juan. Even the Pie Girl can't live on pie alone.

I put the first batch into Penny's oven before I even leave the diner so they'll be ready to pull out when I get back to campus. I've thought long and hard about what specific concoction to put into the rally pies and settled on a blend of clearheadedness and commitment, with a pinch of passion thrown in. Not enough to sway anyone into a frenzy, just enough to raise their voices.

It's still overkill.

The chanting is audible from a street away. Zoe sits next to me on the truck's worn bench seat, head cocked in interest. As we near the administration building, throngs of people block our way, signs held aloft. I drive slowly, barely moving, and let people clear out. The smell of baking pies has heads turning as we make our way through the parting crowd.

I have no idea where I'm supposed to park. There must be close to two hundred people here, and it's obviously just getting started. Someone slaps a hand on my window and I jump, but when I turn, it's only Melly, purple curls wild around her freckled face. A sign is propped on her shoulder and her eyes sparkle behind black-rimmed glasses. The sky may be overcast, but she is radiant.

"That way!" she shouts, gesturing with a megaphone toward the flagpole. I nod, and she slaps the hood of the truck twice in farewell as she lets herself get swallowed up in the crowd.

The flagpole is planted on a grassy island ringed by a driveway, and I tuck in as close to it as I can. The parking lot sprawls out on my left, and I have a perfect view of the makeshift stage the protesters have erected to the right. Almost immediately a line starts forming around the flagpole, and I'm glad I had the foresight to already have pies in the oven.

Any exhaustion that clings from the night before is chased away by the energy of the crowd and the almost unending stream of customers. The stockpile of pie dough I keep in Penny's fridge dwindles as the afternoon wears on, and the last few batches go into the oven with no more magic than a sprinkle of hope baked into them. This crowd doesn't need anything more than that.

Melly is a master at this, almost to the point where I wonder if she's working her own magic. She leads the group in chants and hops on and off the stage to introduce a smattering of speakers while a gawky kid trails her with a video camera. A light drizzle has begun to fall, but still the crowd swells, signs and voices raised as one.

When she takes the stage herself, a hush falls across the crowd, and I find I'm as captivated as the rest. With my oven cooling and my stock down to crumbs, I have no reason to stick around, yet I can't bring myself to leave yet.

"Students, staff, and fellow supporters," she booms into the megaphone, "your courage in standing up to this administration is commendable."

The crowd cheers and thrusts their signs skyward, but she doesn't bask in their fervor.

"In the past week it has come to light that Dean Matthews is not the man we thought he was. Through his very own tweets, he has offered us irrefutable proof of that. Post after post of hate, of homophobia, of xenophobia. For many of us, these statements remind of us one thing: the dark days of the Donnelly White House." She pauses to allow a cascade of jeers to pass before continuing.

"When we voted him out, we proved that we are united against hate. We are united against tyranny. We are united in building a brighter future for ourselves, for each other, and for our nation," she shouts. "So that is why I call on you now, to stand *again* against oppression, against violence, and against fear. Hate had no home in our capitol, and it has no home on our campus."

Goose bumps cascade up my arms as more cheers erupt. It seems impossible that this power is coming from the purple-haired girl prowling the stage like a panther.

The drizzle turns into rain, but still no one leaves. Such is her hold that I don't even acknowledge the telltale ping on my phone that signals an incoming message for Pies Before Guys.

"Today we call upon the university president and the board of trustees to do the right thing. Stand with us and prove that hate has no home here. We believe in the rights of women to make their own choices. We believe in protecting the weak, helping the helpless, and fighting for what matters. We believe that human rights are human rights, no matter where you come from, who you love, or what your pronouns are. Because Dean Matthews has proven that he does not believe these things, he must go. He must go!"

She stands, fist held to the weeping sky, and lets the crowd carry the chant for a few moments. When they quiet, she continues, softer now, and everyone leans in to listen. In the hush, the trilling ding of another message hitting PBG is like a fire alarm, but I ignore it.

"College campuses are meant to be havens of learning, safe spaces to explore new ideas, challenge preconceptions, and thrive. We cannot allow someone who engages in hate speech to hold power over the lives of so many students. We are a campus of women, of queer folx, and of immigrants. We deserve better."

Her voice rises.

"We deserve to study in a nonhostile environment. We deserve the safety and security of knowing that our campus administration sees us as human beings, worthy of existing. Dean Matthews has made it clear that he does not."

Boos and hisses swell like a crescendo. On the counter behind me, my phone chimes again. I barely notice it.

"Education is about opening minds, not closing them. The students of Turnbridge University deserve respect. We deserve equality. We deserve an administration that cares! We *demand* an administration that cares!"

She drops the megaphone to the stage and jumps down amid a thunderous chorus of *He must go!*

The air crackles with something that, if I didn't know better, I might call magic.

Chapter Nine

After her speech, Melly gets lost in the crush of bodies, and when my phone chimes again, I shake myself, breaking the weird trance I've fallen under. Four new PBG alerts. That's high. I tap the notification icon and pray I haven't been found by spammers.

The messages list in reverse order, so the newest are at the top. The first three are showing the same username, RememberRemember, which doesn't follow the rules. The fourth, the first message to come in, is from Marissa06906. That fits. First name—real or made up, I don't care—and the zip code where the pie is going. The zip code part has to be real. I can't make any determination if I don't know where I'm going.

I start with that one.

> *Judith06119 gave me your information. I need help. I have no one to turn to and the police won't help. My brother-in-law is on the force and he knows what Mark is like, but he doesn't care. I can't risk him getting involved and making things worse. It could get me killed. If Mark finds out I'm even sending this email I could be killed. Please, I don't know what else to do. I have no money of my own and no family. I've attached evidence. He doesn't know I have the phone or the photos. He'll kill me if he finds out.*

I download the file and am faced with what should be the contents of a police file. They're all selfies, mostly taken in a full-length mirror. I start with the first, ignoring, for a moment, the worst of it, zooming in until I can see the edges of the mirror's reflection. Visible in the space around her body are bits and pieces of a sparkling, sterile bathroom. The expanse of marble screams money, and everything is sharp angles and bare surfaces. There is nothing comforting about the space. Such details can matter.

Armed with that scrap of context, I zoom back out and take in the whole. Marissa is clad in a matching red bra-and-panty set, which is another detail I file away. Most women, on normal days, don't match, no matter what Victoria Secret would like you to believe. Sharp hip bones jut out above the waistband of the silk knickers, and every rib is visible. There is nothing healthy about this level of leanness. More context.

The galaxy of bruising across her torso doesn't need context. The purples, blacks, and greens swirl together in the worst kind of constellations. Kick marks, lots of them and of varying ages. My jaw clenches, teeth grinding, and I flick through the rest of the photos. More of the same: bruises, mostly below the neck in places that will be hidden. A split lip. An awkward shot of the back of her head, bloodstained platinum hair parted to reveal an angry V-shaped gash. It's enough for me. I send a reply, explaining exactly what I need in order to move forward, half ready to start driving tonight.

A sharp bark from Zoe alerts me a split second before Penny's door bursts open, ripped aside by a gust of wind. I spin around, reaching for a rolling pin as I go.

"Whoa, whoa, whoa! Jumpy much?" Melly says, hands raised. She shakes her mop of dripping curls, splattering my entryway with rainwater. Zoe goes over to give her a sniff, but Melly barges past her into the tiny kitchen, absolutely filling it with her presence. “Man, I’m glad this held off as long as it did. Would’ve sucked being out there in a monsoon.”

She plunks her forearms on the counter and leans in, broad shoulders dancing back and forth with barely suppressed excitement. “Did you see that? Fucking incredible, right? Way better turnout than I expected. Hey. What’s the matter?” She cocks her head the same way Zoe does, eyeing my phone. “Something bad happening?”

I stuff my phone in the pocket of my dress. I forgot I was even holding it when Hurricane Melly came sweeping in. I’ll deal with the other messages after. “What are you doing here?”

“Celebrating! Decompressing! Seeing how pie sales went and whether you had a good time.” She punctuates each declaration with an arm wave, as if these reasons are the most obvious things in the van.

“Shouldn’t you be seeing to your adoring public?”

“Psh, they’re long gone now,” she says, and when I look out the order window, I see she’s right. The rain is falling in sheets now, and the empty stage is the only sign the rally even happened. “You were still here, so I figured you were fair game. Maybe you wanted company. Maybe you were broken down. How do I know?”

God, how long was I lost in Marissa’s photos? Melly doesn’t give me time to dwell on it.

“So, questions, comments, compliments? What’d you think?”

“I think you’re pretty good at what you do,” I say, putting the kettle on for tea.

“Good? I’m fucking great,” she says. “I was born for this. Drives my family abso-fucking-lutely crazy. Bunch of repressed

Republicans. It's embarrassing to even be associated with them. I swear, I must've been switched at birth or something. My father actually thinks things were better when Donnelly was president. I can barely speak to him. And my mother's just as bad. As long as she's getting her fancy clothes and weekly manicures paid for, she doesn't care. My father could say they were going to start killing puppies for fun and she'd just be like, "Yes, dear, whatever you want, dear." Ugh. Parents, right? What about you, Pie Girl? Any crazy family?"

I freeze, wondering for a split second if I should lie. This is exactly the problem with getting to know people. They, in turn, want to know about you, things you can't tell, and you end up with a mile-high-pie stack of lies. I know I should invent a fictitious fake family, because it's the safest answer, but instead what comes out is, "Not anymore."

Melly cocks her head again, and her brows furrow. I can see a question forming on her full lips, but something stops it and she lets it go. I almost collapse with relief. The last thing I want is to walk down memory lane right now.

Melly rattles on about the rally, speculating on the number of attendees and whether or not Dean Matthews—"the damn coward"—was in his office for the whole thing, while I wonder exactly what this force of nature is doing in my van. And it's not that I don't want her there. She's fascinating, sort of like a peacock or a rare parrot, but her presence is akin to seeing such a creature at the dentist's office: utterly inexplicable.

"So, Pie Girl, tell me about your day," she says. "We're all rained in; might as well enjoy it."

Something about the twinkle in her eye when she says this last bit makes my skin flush, and I turn to busy myself getting tea bags into mugs. For one thing, I have no idea how to answer that, because I can't exactly tell her that my day began before dawn, thoughts of stalkers disrupting my sleep, that it led to this parking lot and being captivated—spellbound—by her performance, her passion, on that stage, and ended with a murder-pie contract.

But the weird thing is, I want to.

"It's been a day," I say, leaning down to scratch Zoe's ears, keeping the truth off my face.

"Pretty lucrative though, right? I was watching; I saw how busy you were. I knew looping you in was a good idea."

I'm not used to being the object of anyone's attention. In fact, I mostly live my life trying to avoid that very thing, but the idea of her looking out for me while she was so busy with the protest warms something in me.

"It was fun," I agree, letting the worries of Pies Before Guys slip away, just for now. "Thanks for inviting me. If you have another, I'd love to do it again."

"Hell yeah," she says. She studies me for a moment and I feel uncomfortably like the little furry things that always end up getting eaten by carnivores on nature shows. "So, Pie Girl, are you seeing anyone?"

I stifle a surprised giggle at her lack of subtlety. "Ah, no. No, I'm definitely not."

"Last one that bad, huh?"

I can feel heat creeping up my face and wish I could will it away. "Not really a last one to talk about."

Something in my tone must convince her it's an avenue not worth going down because she abruptly changes course, something I'm starting to think is just her normal conversation style.

"So how come you're just a pie girl and not a student? You're my age, right?"

"Twenty-three."

"Close enough. So what is it? Bored? Kicked out?"

Her directness is jarring but not unkind. I take a risk and match it. "No money." It's not the whole story, but it's not a lie either. I'm getting the hang of these almost-truths.

She nods sagely. "Fucking capitalism, right? Education should be free, that's what I say. I guess there are worse things than making pies for a living. But you don't want to do this forever though, right?" She stops talking long enough to look around the van. I wonder what it looks like through her eyes. It's odd having someone else inside. Penny might cater to the public, but the public stays solidly outside. I can count on one hand the people I've invited inside, and they were all from before my mother died, while the van was still a salon. Since then Penny has been my private sanctuary, a shell as much as a home. Something about this realization, or maybe her question, makes my skin flush.

"There are worse ways to make a living," I parrot back, unable to keep the defensiveness from creeping in.

She laughs. "Touché. I like you, Pie Girl. Maybe pie won't change the world, but that's okay. I can change it enough for both of us."

From the depths of my pocket, my phone beeps again, and I wonder what Judith06119 and Marissa06906 would say about my ability to change the world.

Chapter Ten

In the end, I wish the remaining three messages on the PBG account *were* just spam. Or that I'd never opened them. Anything to keep me from seeing what's in front of me: official requests to have pies delivered to Kerenza Vallery, Brittany Cline, and Emma Rogers.

It shouldn't surprise me. If he knew enough of who I was to leave that note on Penny, then he knew about the Pies Before Guys program. Simple as that. The Pie Girl is on social media to update people about where I'll be parked on campus or which markets I'll be at, but PBG operates well off that radar. At some point, my mystery man has crossed paths with someone who was able to lead him directly to me. Not just Pie Maker me, but real-life, living-in-my-van me.

The thought is a parasite eating at my brain, and it takes an effort to keep it from leaching into the pies. Normally I can jump back and forth between projects with ease, but tonight I work in batches, concentrating hard to keep focused. No matter how much I want the truth, I have to wait. It can't interfere with the pies.

I do Frank's pies first. The simple, straightforward fillings are a balm to my buzzing brain, and Juan's banter with the dish boy is just enough to keep me present in the kitchen and out of my head. I fall into a rhythm, the solid *thunk-thunk-thunk* of the knife against apples as steady as a heartbeat. These pies will be perfect.

When I pull the last one out of the oven, the kitchen is winding down around me. Juan mops the floor, filling me in on the latest adoption news while the dish boy returns pots, plates, and silverware to their proper homes. It's different than the nights Frank is around, more relaxed. It's good. I try not to remember his threat of eviction. One of my do-not-cross lines, *Never get too deep*, works only when I have people around me who remind me that I'm normal. These people do. Frank, too, for what it's worth.

The servers finish with their side work—salt and pepper topped up, ketchup bottles filled—and disappear into the night, the dish boy trailing after them. Juan lingers in the kitchen, swinging his keys around his finger.

"Everything good, Pie Girl?" he asks.

"Always," I say, slapping a sunny smile in place.

He raises a skeptical brow. "Liar."

I sigh. "Long week."

"Don't I know it," he says. "But what else?"

I keep my eyes on the crust in front of me and pinch the crimps with surgical precision. I don't want to lie to Juan, but there's no way I can tell him what's on my mind either.

"Let me guess," he says. "You're worried about Frank."

"I'm not *not* worried," I admit.

"Frank's a blowhard. He'll talk like he's gonna chase you out, but he's not. He's more likely to shoot the guy poking around your trailer than he is to kick you out."

"I don't know. He seemed pretty serious."

"I'll believe it when I see him follow through. Which he won't." Juan leans across the counter and swipes a blackberry from its carton. "Is it the guy you're worried about?"

I wave my rolling pin at him as he reaches for a second. "Out of my fruit!" He takes it anyway and pops it in his mouth, waiting for an answer. "Sure. Yes. Maybe."

"I'll take that as a hard yes."

"Wouldn't you be creeped out if some guy was poking around your house?"

"Depends on the guy," he says with a cheeky grin. Once again, the rolling pin makes a handy threat. "But no, that's fair. You're a young girl on your own. That's gotta be scary as fuck."

I slide a piece of parchment into the crust and dump enough sugar in to fill it to the brim. This is my secret, the nonmagical magic of my pies, and I let Juan see me do it.

Normally when pie crusts get blind-baked, or precooked, they're filled with beans or rice or actual weights made especially for that purpose. Not mine. Mine get filled with sugar, which slowly roasts as the crusts bake until they're full of toasty, caramelly goodness. That sugar then sweetens the fruit, the custards, and the streusels of other pies. It's not a huge difference, but it's enough that people can't put their finger on it, and that's why I do it. My pies aren't good because they're magic. They're magic because they're good.

If Juan realizes he's being let in on a secret, he doesn't show it. Typical guy. "I'll be fine," I assure him. "I have Zoe."

He laughs. "That marshmallow isn't exactly a security system."

"People don't mess with pit bulls. Even the sweet and squishy ones."

"You're right, you're right. But seriously, if you're worried, you can always camp at ours. Eric won't mind."

A sudden lump makes it hard to swallow, impossible to speak. I busy myself with chopping almonds, and it's their teardrop shape that I focus on when I say, "You guys' kid is gonna be so fucking lucky." He has no idea what he'd be inviting into his home, no idea what I am beyond the Pie Girl, but he doesn't care. He's happy to open his home to me without knowing who's on my tail or what I'm capable of, and I find it impossible to look at him in the silence that follows.

"Well yeah, obviously," he says, after a beat. "But seriously, you're totally welcome. I mean, Eric might charge rent in pie, but you can't really blame him."

"I appreciate it," I say, which is a lie. It's not even close to what I feel, but I don't quite have words for that.

I do, however, have a pie for it.

After he's gone and my farmers' market pies are cooling on the rack, I make two more. One packed absolutely full to the top with gratitude and another filled with hope.

* * *

Another night passes without sleep.

Part of it's Melly, as much as I don't want to admit it. I have spent the past six years of my life on a crusade to help women live better lives by killing the men in their way, but somehow this purple-haired college girl has made me question whether that's enough, whether I should somehow be doing *more*.

It bothers me, because I know there are only so many pies I can bake and so many people I can help, but I also think that should count for something.

After the rally, I may have stalked her a bit online. Only a little, only to see exactly who it was that had gotten under my skin so much. And what I found was someone who was absolutely, one hundred percent committed to her cause. All of her social media accounts were public and they all had the same messages: Equal rights for all genders. Protect the unprotected. Be the revolution you want to see in the world.

She was practically a one-woman crusade.

I'd like to think we're different sides of the same coin, but I'm not sure she would see it that way. I may be helping individual women, but Melly would probably say the micro level isn't where real change happens. She exists solely in the sweeping macro save-the-whole-damn-world-at-once realm that I can't hope to touch even with a whole army of murder-pie makers.

And as if that weren't enough to keep me awake, there's the issue of my mystery man. I'm hoping he'll show tonight. At this point, I'm itching for a confrontation.

While I wait for him to appear, I dig into the lives of the women on his list. If I can figure out how they're connected to him, maybe I can figure out who he is.

I start with Kerenza Vallery, a fairly easy find given that she doesn't have the world's most common name. As PBG, I pay for several deep-web search services, and I'm able to narrow it down to two possibilities. One shows Vallery as a maiden name, unused since the early 1990s, so that leaves me with the other, who has to be my Kerenza Vallery, twenty-four, of Brookhill, Massachusetts. She has a private Facebook account with an impossible-to-identify profile picture of a tank-topped woman climbing a massive boulder, a private Instagram, and a public LinkedIn. This last one reveals that she graduated from the University of Massachusetts with a master's in public health two years ago and has been working in that field ever since, first in Worcester, then in Cambridge. I note the name of her most recent employer and Google it. She's featured on the company's staff page with a photo and a short biography that tells me about her policy work and little else. But I have a face. She's pretty in an all-American kind of way: chin-length blond bob, pale-blue eyes, and tortoiseshell glasses that may or may not be there just to make her look more serious. I screenshot her photo.

Brittany Cline is harder to track. The address I was given, 11B Morgan Ave, doesn't have a Brittany Cline living there. It did last year, but when I attempt to trace her, the best match I get is a Brittany Cline, age twenty-five, living in Seattle. That doesn't seem right. If this guy knows who I am, he knows I can't teleport a pie across the entire country to do his bidding.

Or maybe he doesn't.

Maybe he doesn't know as much about me as he wants me to believe. The thought pleases me.

I try to follow this Brittany Cline down a rabbit hole but am stymied by a complete lack of social media accounts. Not just accounts with the privacy settings cranked up to the max, but none at all. That's odd. Even people who hate social media tend to still use it. It's how they know they hate it.

All I manage to find is one reference to Seattle's Brittany Cline, a direct quote from a news article about the volunteer work she does at the women's shelter and the need for donations. I note the name of the shelter, search on it and Brittany Cline together, but get nothing further.

So.

Even if I were inclined to help my mystery man with his problem, it wouldn't be easy. Short of a forty-five-hour road trip to a girl who might not exist, it'd be impossible.

That leaves me with Emma Rogers.

There are no less than six of them in Massachusetts, but only one is based right here in Turnbridge. She's twenty-six, the oldest of the trio, but if profile pics are to be believed, she doesn't look a day over twenty. Her public Facebook says she works at Galen and Harris Law and has for the past four years but reveals little else beyond relationship status—in one—and birthplace–Salem. I scroll through her posts, but it's mostly year-long gaps punctuated by annual flurries of birthday wishes.

I click photos and, again, find little. But I don't need it. Her profile picture has already told me plenty.

Emma Rogers is Pinstripe.

Chapter Eleven

Saturday morning's clouds are pregnant with impending rain, and the air feels like a harbinger of fall instead of summer.

But I can deal with a rainy market day.

What I haven't figured out how to deal with is what I'm going to do if I see Pinstripe again. No, not Pinstripe. Emma Rogers. I know who she is now, she has a name, and I know someone wants her dead.

What I don't know is what to do about it.

When I get Penny parked in our allotted slot and the awning out, I'm glad I didn't bail. All around the common, tents are going up, wares are being arranged, and the sheer normalcy quiets my brain bees.

Noel arrives before I have my awning up, and he's out of his truck and helping before I can even say hello.

"I thought we decided last week I didn't need help with this," I say, but there's no ire in the words. "You have your own booth to set up."

He grins at me, the morning breeze sending his brown curls flopping in his eyes. "Yeah, but rainy apples aren't the end of the world. Soggy pies, though? No one's going to buy those."

He's not wrong, but I'm saved from admitting it by Zoe's bark. She has her paws on the dashboard, nose pressed against the window. I open the door and she bounds down, twining herself around Noel's legs. He drops to a crouch and scratches her all over until she's sprawled on the dewy grass, belly up and tongue lolling.

"She's playing you," I tell him as I set up my table, weighting the cloth down with empty ceramic pie plates in case the wind picks up. "Marked you as a sucker from the moment she met you. She's going to start expecting this every time she sees you."

"Fine by me."

I leave him there, baby-talking to my meatball of a dog, and start getting pies out. I stack the orders from last week under the table in alphabetical order, names clearly written on the sides of the white boxes. Each one is tied with a pink-and-white string and stamped with the Pie Girl logo.

I go back inside and slide the first tray of cutie pies into the oven. When I come back out, a trio of pies balanced on each arm, I see that Noel has ripped himself away from Zoe and is getting his tent up. Zoe is nosing around the back of his truck, which is nearly as beat-up as mine, and I whistle for her. Traitor.

She trots over and settles herself in front of the table, where she'll be one hundred percent in the way and thus ensure maximum attention once people start showing up. She is many things, but dumb is not one of them.

The scent of baking fruit and spice drifts out of Penny, and I pop back in to check the cutie pies. Perfect. I pull them out to cool, setting the tray near the window for optimal scent advertising. Pies smell like home, it's just a fact, and that makes people want to buy them. Or at least, pies smell like the homes people dream of. If the platonic ideal of home is a freshly baked pie on a windowsill, that's something I can provide.

I take two of the cutie pies—a strawberry rhubarb and an almond—and wrap them in a paper towel. I wait until Noel's busy at his truck, with his back to me, then slip over and leave them on his apple scale.

The smile on his face when he finds them is as warming as the beam of sun that's fighting through the clouds.

We're hit with a surprising rush right when the market opens. I have a line five people deep within minutes, all picking up ordered pies and grabbing cutie pies to go. Nearly all mention the weather, talking about wanting to beat the storm, and can you believe this weather, and boy, don't we need this rainy spell? I smile and nod and send them on their way with pies, all the while keeping my eyes peeled for Pinstripe.

Around noon, the sky darkens and the common empties of shoppers. I drop onto Penny's steps, cursing the sky gods. I have too many pies left for this nonsense.

Noel picks this moment to sidle over, and I find I'm automatically scootching over to make room for him on the step.

"So I have an idea," he says, handing me a paper cup of cider and sitting down. "And I want you to hear me out before you shoot it down."

"That's maybe not the best sales pitch ever," I say, taking a sip of the cider. Unexpected bubbles dance on my tongue, chased by a honeyed sweetness. "Whoa."

That lopsided grin comes back. "Test batch," he says. "Nonalcoholic sparkling cider."

I raise the paper cup in a mock toast. "Test passed. This is what apple juice wants to be when it grows up."

"That might be its tag line."

"I expect royalties," I say, taking another sip.

He chuckles. "I might need to pay them in apples."

"I might need to put them in pie, so that works for me."

A low rumble of thunder is the only warning we have before the sky opens. All around the common, people scurry for cover, the few remaining shoppers ducking in with vendors under their tents and crowding the guitarist in the gazebo. Zoe gets up, comes around the back of the table, and flops down with a sleepy sigh.

Noel and I don't move. We don't have to.

Rain sluices off the front of the awning in a wall, making it hard to see beyond those few feet. It's like being ensconced in a private bubble, and even though we're outside in a storm, there's something cozy about it. We both watch the world close in for a few minutes as the rain batters the market.

"Okay, so, my idea," Noel says. The pinging of rain against Penny's metal body forces him to lean in close to be heard. "And I know I have no right to tell you what to do, but the pies you left me this morning, they were magic. Seriously, I have never tasted anything that good. And wait, before you say anything, I grew up on an orchard, so I've eaten my fair share of pies, and yours are in a whole other class."

He shifts away for a moment to work his phone free from his pocket, and I'm struck by the sudden chill where his body was nearly touching mine. I didn't notice it was there until it was gone. Stupid.

He fiddles with his phone, clearing notifications and opening his browser. He leans back in as he types, so it's like we're conspiring, although about what, I have no idea. Finally, he hands the phone over.

On the screen is a headline: *My, My, Miss American Pie!* Below, a smaller font reads: *Presented in cooperation with The American Bakers Guild, FoodTV Media Group, and local sponsors.*

"There's this Miss American Pie contest," he says. "It's a big deal. Statewide, and all the states are doing one. The winners get ten thousand dollars and their recipe included in the official cookbook. Like not a church cookbook, but a real, professional, find-it-in-Barnes-and-Noble cookbook. Almost like being famous."

The patter of rain shifts, softens. I stare at the phone, thoughts whirling.

"I think you could win it," he says, reaching over to scroll through the page as the rain slows further. "Look. The first round doesn't judge until next month. You have plenty of time. You could be the most famous pie girl in the state."

Birdsong starts to fight against the flagging storm, driving it out, but I pay it no mind. I'm too wrapped up in what I'm seeing on the screen and considering what he's saying. Ten thousand dollars is a lot of money. I could fund a serious amount of shipped murder pies with that. I could stop turning down the women I can't reach in person. I could save more of them.

But more than that . . .

I glance over at Noel, and my mind whirls with possibilities. The orchard. Frank's diner. Those things wouldn't be hurt by a little fame. Far from it. Maybe my pies could do good in more ways than just killing bad men. Maybe one good pie could help two good men.

The first round of competition is only three weeks away, and the final rounds are July third and fourth. I have time, sure, but not much. But, perhaps, enough.

I scroll through the rules: Pies submitted at the county level must be accompanied by written recipes and must be presented as full nine-inch pies. The statewide contest is to be judged in Boston, semifinals on the third, finals on the fourth. The semifinals will be a showdown among the winners of each of the fourteen counties, with the top three pies moving on to the finals. There are no restrictions on pie flavors, but preference will be shown to those that reflect patriotic or state-specific origins.

I click through to each page on the contest site without saying anything, and Noel doesn't interject. The part of my brain not consumed by pie-contest thoughts wonders if he knows how rare a skill that is. I don't even realize the storm has passed until I look up from his phone, see the sun is shining, and say, "Yeah. I think I'm in."

Chapter Twelve

Marissa06906 takes long enough to return the contract that I wonder if she's having second thoughts, but it arrives with an apology for the delay, citing her lack of a chance to access her hidden phone. There's nothing legally binding in it, obviously, but the contract provides an overview of what both parties can expect during the transaction along with questions for gathering the information I need to make the pie work.

In Marissa's case, she has agreed to personally take delivery of the pie from "one of my agents" (a fancy way of saying me) and will serve it herself. Some women like this personal touch, while others prefer the surprise delivery approach I took with Kevin Beechum. Because the magic in the pie is tailored specifically for its intended target, there is no danger of having the pies in the women's houses. They could eat as much as they want and still be fine.

It's part of what makes it so effective.

A naturally suspicious bastard might question why his wife or girlfriend was serving him something she herself wasn't touching, and while the dieting excuse works for some, my way ensures they never risk drawing such attention in the first place.

I've wondered more than once how many women who serve the pies themselves actually sample them, though. It must take an extraordinary leap of faith to believe they'll be safe, but maybe some of them don't care. Perhaps a pie-induced death feels like an acceptable alternative to their situation. If I could double-dose the pie, I'd let the women taste hope and freedom, but I can't risk muddling the magic.

Murder pies are made in the van, no exceptions. It's one thing to make magic market pies in Frank's kitchen, but murder pies are different. I suppose that's another line: *Never let anyone see the process.*

Which is a stupid line, because from the outside it just looks like making pie, but from the inside it's the most private thing possible.

I leave this pie until evening, after Frank's pies are done and the diner is closed. I don't bother prepping study pies, because I'll be spending most of the day on the road. I'll have to remember to post something to social media so I don't end up with too many disgruntled students.

There's something relaxing about doing murder pies that I can't put my finger on. I think it's because it's one of the few times I'm making only one pie at a time, for one person, instead of dozens for everyone. PBG pies are bespoke in a way that the Pie Girl can't compete with.

I review the contract before I start, to help ground myself in the situation. The target is Victor Layton, forty-seven, a hedge fund manager who commutes to New York City from their home in Stamford, Connecticut. The photo, a corporate head shot pulled from his firm's website, shows a white man with salt-and-pepper hair and hard gray eyes. The smile, presumably an attempt to look friendly, makes him look like a predator.

The age difference between him and Marissa is enough to be gross, so yeah, predator fits. In more ways than one.

I start with the dough, using a process most professionals would be horrified by. I start by measuring out two and a half cups of flour into a bowl. That's the only official measurement I make. I add a generous sprinkle of sugar, a smaller one of salt, and roughly chop up two sticks of butter. Then the part that would make the pros cringe: I chuck it all into the bowl and mix it by hand.

Most pie dough recipes go overboard talking about keeping your butter cold, not overworking the flour, and sacrificing your firstborn to the pie gods in hopes of getting something flaky and delicious.

It's bollocks.

I squish the butter into the flour until the world falls away and every ounce of my awareness is between my fingers. I pour all of my intention and will into the dough, mixing until flattened flakes of butter almost disappear into the flour. A drizzle of apple cider vinegar, a glug of ice water, and my hands are back in, kneading in the magic so it's as incorporated as the butter.

I wrap the dough and set it to rest in the fridge while I work on the filling. She requested cherry, which this time of year means frozen sours from Michigan, but they work just fine.

I heat them with sugar on the stove until their juices spill like blood. With the tip of a paring knife, I cut a long slice down a wrinkled vanilla bean, scrape its innards into the pot, and save the split pod to add to a canister of sugar.

I stir gently until the cherries are thick with magic, then set them aside to cool while I prep the crust.

I grab a handful of flour from the bin and flick it across the counter so it settles in an even layer. There's nothing magic about it, but the motion feels like spell casting.

The dough yields easily beneath my rolling pin, each pass adding intent and sealing the magic inside. I hum a bit as I do this, a cheeky murder-pie ditty I would never sing out loud because that would definitely be crossing the line. But it makes me smile all the same.

I drape the first round of dough into a tin pie plate and add the cherries. The remaining dough gets cut into strips that I weave into a lattice over the crimson filling. The weaving adds another layer to the magic, and I seal the whole thing with an egg wash and a dusting of crunchy Demerara sugar.

It's a thing of beauty.

Doesn't hurt that it makes the RV smell amazing as it bakes either.

I figure it has a solid hour in the oven, which gives me plenty of time to shower and look into the pie contest before going to bed. I don't have to be on the road too early tomorrow, so in a way, it feels like a day off.

To call my bathroom small is an understatement. Tacked onto the bedroom, it's roughly the size of a public toilet stall and holds the toilet, a minuscule sink, and a coffin-sized shower. But it could be worse—at least I have hot water.

I pull the curtains in the bedroom, undress, and step into the bathroom. The concertina door is more hassle than it's worth, so I leave it open.

I hear Zoe moving around the kitchen and expect her to come in any minute and stick her head into the shower. She does it almost every time I'm in here, like she's worried I'll disappear forever behind the curtain. But she doesn't show. I finish up, turn the water off, and dry myself in the stall. From the kitchen, the blinds rattle and a low growl follows.

Goose bumps erupt all over, having nothing to do with the cold. I pull the towel around me and ease out of the bathroom. I have no rational reason to tiptoe, but I do anyway.

In the kitchen, Zoe has her paws up on the serving window, a spiky ridge of fur raised along her back. Her nose is pressed to the window, the growl still rumbling in her chest.

"Zo, it's okay," I say, patting my leg to get her attention. She turns to look at me, drops to the floor, and whines. She doesn't come to me, and that makes my blood run cold. She goes to the door, sniffs at the bottom, whines again.

"Zoe, come," I say again, trying to keep the stress out of my voice. Even though the curtains are all drawn, I feel horribly exposed in just my towel, kitchen lights blazing. The thought of turning them off doesn't make me feel much better.

Zoe goes back to the serving window and jumps up, nosing aside the curtains again to survey the dark. My heart is racing and I have that feeling I used to get as a kid in the basement, that irrational urge to run away from unseen things. Without giving myself time to think about it, I flip the light switches, plunging the van into darkness. Zoe is just barely silhouetted from the faint glow of streetlamps outside. Pulling the towel tighter, I join her at the window, running a hand down her back. Her muscles are coiled tight, ready to launch her at whatever is out there.

I'm convinced that when I pull the curtain to look outside, I'm going to be face-to-face with my mystery man. Or a monster. Or one and the same.

The cherry vanilla aroma of the baking pie is overwhelming, a cheerful scent diametrically opposed to the stranglehold of fear around my heart.

Deciding it's better to know than not, I move the curtain and look. A human-shaped shadow stares back and I jump, heart racing. The shadow does too.

My reflection, nothing more. Stupid.

I search the darkness beyond the window. Puddles of light from distant streetlights reveal nothing out of the ordinary. My heart starts to slow, fight-or-flight giving way to reason and rationality.

I leave the lights off, the only illumination coming from the oven, dress quickly in my pajama shorts and a faded tank top, and slide my bare feet into Keds. My eyes have adjusted to the dark, and I find the rolling pin with ease, taking it on my way to unlock Penny's door. Zoe hovers at the top of the steps, ready to join me. "Stay."

She looks on the verge of disobeying, so I say it again, and this time she sits. It's one thing for me to go out in the dark and risk my own flesh, quite another thing to risk hers.

I ease the door open, slip out, and close it as quietly as possible. I immediately drop to a crouch, checking under the RV first. Years of horror movies have taught me there is always something waiting to slice your Achilles.

But not tonight.

I stand, check the outside of the door for a note. Nothing.

But still my skin prickles with the sensation of being watched.

Keeping the rolling pin at my side, I creep around the RV, staying close to its side. My head is on a swivel, alert for any signs of movement. The far side of the van, where it's closest to the diner, has the most places to hide, with its hulking dumpsters and stacks of boxes needing to be broken down, but I find not a single sign of life.

I start to wonder if Zoe was imagining whatever she saw or if it was nothing more harmful than a stray cat. But I trust her. And I trust myself. Something felt off.

It's when I'm back around to the door, ready to go inside, that I spot it. Hardly anything, really, just a smudge of motion at the corner of my eye. The rolling pin is up before I even process what's happening, and I turn, searching the dark. A person, crouched low, darts across the rear parking lot.

"Hey!" I shout, shoving away from Penny in reckless pursuit. The person sticks to the shadows, avoiding the streetlights, so I have no idea who I'm chasing. I chase anyway.

It's stupid and potentially dangerous, but I push into an all-out sprint, desperate to catch them. Again I'm reminded that baking pies is not good for cardio, and I'm gasping for breath within a minute, my legs on fire within two.

I lose sight of them at the corner, but an engine revs and I go in that direction, lungs screaming for a break. A motorcycle blows by, the rider's face obscured by a helmet, but I know it's my guy. Without thinking I whip the rolling pin at him, but he's gone before it has a hope of connecting.

Chapter Thirteen

The next morning I bring Zoe along for the delivery, for distraction as much as anything. I'm still spooked by last night and more than a little pissed. The indignity of having to hunt around in the dark for my rolling pin hasn't helped improve my mood either.

GPS announces that in a quarter mile, our destination will be on the left. I snort. "Not in Kansas anymore, Zoe."

The neighborhood screams money. Houses sit behind elaborate shrubbery, protected by long driveways with gates at the tops to keep the riffraff out. The cars cruising by are all luxury brands, worth more than my truck, van, and let's be honest, childhood home.

Definitely not in Kansas anymore.

Marissa's driveway is gated, but it's open, and I put my blinker on to turn in. As I slow, a thundering growl splits the air as a motorcycle races by, its black-clad rider crouched low over the black bike. Adrenaline spikes when I clock the signature red and royal blue of Massachusetts plates, but he's out of sight before I can register the numbers. *Coincidence*, I tell myself. It has to be. There's no way it's my mystery man, not here. I would've noticed a motorcycle following me. And even if it is, it's not like I can go after him, not when I have a pie to deliver.

I pull in slowly, following the winding slope down to the huge white house at the bottom. The driveway loops around a stone fountain and I circle it, parking so I'm facing out. This is a far cry from most of my deliveries, but that's the funny thing about shitty men. They're in all income brackets, from all lines of work, and I would bet my van that there are more of them living like this than most people expect.

I retrieve the wooden pie box from the floor of the truck and scratch Zoe's ears. "Be right back."

The front door is open, the woman I recognize from the photos peering out through the crack. She looks scared, pulled in on herself, but also defiant.

"Pie delivery," I say cheerfully, hoisting the box. She pulls the door wider, and I step into the gleaming marble foyer. A crystal chandelier hangs from an impossibly tall vaulted ceiling, scattering rainbows on the white walls.

"Thank you for coming," Marissa says. She leads me through to a kitchen large enough to house four pie vans. I fight to keep my jaw off the ground.

I set the box on the granite island, slide the top off. Marissa peers inside like she's expecting to find spiders instead of a cherry pie.

"You're sure it's going to work?" she asks.

"One hundred percent. If for any reason you change your mind, just throw it away."

She nods, more to herself than me, as if steeling herself. She turns, bends to look in a cupboard, and retrieves a black ceramic pie plate. "Will it fit in this?"

I slide the pie out of the box and drop it in. The silver tin of the disposable pan disappears below the rim of her dish like it never existed.

"I want to pretend I made it," she says, somewhat sheepish.

I smile. "Take all the credit you need."

She suddenly grabs my hands in both of hers. "Thank you," she says, eyes bright with tears. "You're saving my life. I know how it must look, a house like this, a husband like him, but—"

I cut her off. "I know." I hold her gaze, and something passes between us. "I understand."

She sniffles, nods. The tears stay put. She retrieves a purse from one of the stools. "Please, you must let me pay you for this."

I shake my head. "No, really. That's not how it works." The look on her face almost makes me feel bad for not taking her money, but I hold firm. I pull two pins from my dress pocket and hand them to her. "You're part of Pies Before Guys now. The only payment accepted is that you pass along the Pie Maker's information to another woman who might need it."

She stares at the pins like they're talismans, then buries them in the depths of her purse. "Thank you," she says again.

"My pleasure."

* * *

On the drive home, I spend as much time watching my mirrors for motorcycles as I do watching the road, but aside from a leathery-skinned couple on a Harley, I don't see any. Zoe lies across the bench seat with her head on my thigh, and I tell her all about what's happening with Pinstripe, and with the PBG requests, and with my burgeoning plan for the pie contest.

Zoe is a good sounding board for things, and she's used to listening to me prattle on. For a long time, most of those first couple years, she was all I had to talk to. Sure, I talked to customers, but in the beginning I was constantly moving, always worried that first pie was going to catch up with me. But it didn't. It wasn't until I landed at Frank's that I let myself believe it, though. I dipped a toe back into the world of humanity. I talked to people. I had work friends. A regular schedule. A normal life for a normal girl.

And okay, sure, I occasionally kill bad people with good pies, but no one's perfect. Perfect is boring.

"And now," I say to Zoe as we trade the highway for the back roads, "it's like all the monkeys are hurling their wrenches right into the middle of it and I kind of want a bit of the boring back. I don't even know where to start. Pinstripe, probably."

She was on my mind more than I cared to admit even before her name came up on the PBG order. I don't know what it is about her that has me so wound up, trying to mentally redraw my never lines into a path that leads to Vance dead and her free. She has to want it. I know that. I've watched countless women turn away from the easy way out I've offered them time and again. Sometimes they come back, sometimes they get themselves out, and sometimes they don't. Either way, it's not my place to interfere on their behalf. The people who need my pies spend too much time having their choices stripped from them, their desires disregarded. Choosing men on my own crosses the serial killer line, but it also crosses the consent line. Not for the men, obviously—they lost that right the moment they put someone in need of my services—but for the women. If I act against their wishes or take matters into my own hands, then I'm no better than the scum who drove them to me in the first place.

And yet.

The temptation is real enough that I find myself wondering, not for the first time, if it's the magic that's broken, or me. I know the other Ellery women have seen women in horrible situations. They must've. Great Grammy Rose surely sold her share of magic bouquets to shitty men who thought some posies would make up for slapping their wives around. Those kind of men aren't unique to this decade, not by a long shot. Was she ever tempted to work something other than comfort and happiness into those arrangements? Something final?

I was only six when she died, but I still have the last daisy crown she ever made me, pressed between sheets of wax paper, and to this day it radiates pure joy. As much as I want to believe I'm not broken, I can't imagine Great Grammy ever using her power the way I do. Hers was too pure, too cheerful.

I wish there were a way to talk to her, to know more. I grew up with Nana and Mama, and even though I know their magic as well as the sound of their voices, I never bothered learning much about the ones who came before. I should've paid more attention to Nana's stories, asked more questions, but I was young and felt immortal, like the past didn't matter when I had so much future to look forward to.

What I wouldn't give for a pie that would let me talk to them, get to know just what type of women my great-great-grandmother helped with her embroidery or what kind of magic went into the meals her mother prepared. Were any of them like me, even a little bit?

I wonder if things would be different for me if they were still alive. Would I be more like them, quieter with my magic, more grounded? Or is this just how I was destined to turn out? It's possible the magic changed with me for a reason.

It's something I think about more than I'd like to admit—not just the nature of my magic, but the transmission of it. In every generation there's a single Ellery girl born with the gift. We're like vampire slayers that way. I inherited my magic from a long line of only daughters born to only daughters, but something changed when it got to me.

Is it meant to end with me?

That's a question that can keep me up at night if I let it, because the truth that I can barely utter aloud, even to Zoe, is that I think I want it to. The thought of procreating, even for the sake of the magic, fills me with such dread that I don't know what to do. I can't envision a world where I'm a mother, yet I feel a certain nagging obligation to someday pass the magic on. It's not a biological clock but a biological time bomb, because what if it changes again?

What if it gets worse?

Using the magic to rid the world of bad men is one thing. It has limits and rules and it's, well, kind of righteous, if I'm gonna be pompous about it. But what if version 2.0 lacks those boundaries? What if it's all murder, all the time? Even I can't condone that. So I certainly can't risk it.

I wish the elder Ellerys could give me answers, show me the right way forward, but I know they can't.

My mother always said the magic finds a way.

I just need to find mine.

Chapter Fourteen

I haven't been able to catch Pinstripe at any of the Saint Stan's meetings and decide if she doesn't turn up at today's farmers' market, I'm going to have to get proactive about finding her. It feels stalky, but I do have her home and work addresses at this point. It'd be stupid not to use them. Plus, every day that passes without seeing her makes me worry that whoever sent the PBG order has taken matters into their own hands. I haven't figured out what I'm going to say to her yet. It's not like I can just spring it on her that someone wants her dead and that I want her fiancé dead, but it feels reckless not to do anything.

I don't get to dwell on it, though, because we're slammed from opening. The late-May sun is hot, the sky cloudless, and it's the kind of day made for this kind of thing.

Noel has been sampling his sparkling nonalcoholic cider, and the line at his booth rivals mine. I'm happy for him. It's such an absurdly simple emotion, but there it is. It's a nice change from the weight of worries.

We fall into a pattern of sending people to each other's booths without even discussing it, and soon the common is filled with people who have a pie in one hand and a cider in the other. Zoe has even started going between my booth and Noel's to find the most people possible to pet her.

By the afternoon, both of our booths are in sorry states. The morning's bounty has been reduced to the batch of cutie pies I've just pulled out of the oven, and Noel is down to his last cooler, a few jars of honey, and a single bunch of wildflowers that he brings over with a slightly dazed smile.

"For you," he says. "I think half my customers bought things because you told them to."

"Same," I say, laughing. "You definitely beat the neighbor I had last year."

"Oh yeah?"

I shudder at the memory. "The meanest old lady you've ever seen. She made 'health bread,' but it's an insult to the carb community to even call it that. The loaves were like bricks. I don't know how she sold any. I can't tell you how many times I heard her carrying on about the evils of sugar."

Noel laughs. "Please tell me you gave her a pie."

"Oh, I offered all right. Sweet as can be. Hoped she'd choke on it."

Noel looks shocked for a second, but I flash him an exaggeratedly innocent look, and he grins. "Well, I'm glad she's gone. I rather like this spot."

Something about the words warms my cheeks, and I busy myself arranging the remaining few cutie pies. I sacrifice one for the cause, breaking it in half and handing him a piece. "I bet you do, Farmboy."

Now he's the one wearing a look of mock innocence.

I watch him as he eats the pie, eyes closed in appreciation, and say, "So I've been thinking about this pie contest of yours."

His whole face lights up. "Yeah? Do you know what you're making yet? Actually, doesn't matter. It's going to be amazing regardless. First-place amazing. I'm sure of it."

"Let's not get overconfident."

"Hell yeah let's!"

I laugh at his boyish enthusiasm. "I actually do have an idea." But before I can tell him what it is, I catch sight of a purple head of curls beelining toward us.

"Pie Girl!" Melly calls, waving a sheaf of neon papers above her head. "I didn't know you'd be here."

"Every week," I say.

"I thought you were just the school's pie wench. Cool." She comes around the table without waiting for an invitation, a camera swinging wildly from a pin-covered strap on her shoulder. Zoe gives a grumbling whine at the sudden flurry of activity, but Melly ignores it. She shoves a flyer into my hands before I can make introductions and says, "There's a big rally coming up, weekend after next. You want to come? It's in Boston. I'm friends with the organizer—well, exes, actually, but she's cool. I'm organizing buses from campus. Last hurrah before everyone leaves for the summer, you know? You should totally come."

"To sell pies? I don't think I can just set the van up in Boston without a permit."

"No, stupid, with me. I liked hanging out with you after the last one. I want to do it again."

For the second time today, my face gets hot from something that isn't the late-spring sun.

"That's the weekend of the contest," Noel says softly.

I look at the flyer for the first time, and my stomach plummets. The slogan across the top reads *A Woman's Place is NOT in the Kitchen!* A no-smoking symbol has been altered to show a slice of pie in the center where the cigarette should go. Underneath is an invitation to *Join Us in the Fight to Close the Wage Gap* with the details of the rally.

I look back and forth between Noel and Melly, and the shock must show on my face, because Noel asks, "What is it?"

I hand him the flyer, and as he reads it, something hardens on his normally gentle face.

"You're protesting at a pie contest?" he asks, not quite able to keep the edge out of his voice. "A pie contest that's not even remotely connected to your cause?"

"Our protest coincides with an event that reinforces archaic gender roles." She enunciates carefully, as if speaking to a child, but the rage is like fire in her eyes. "Besides, this Miss American Pie shit is straight 1950s propaganda. It's exclusionary and backwards and—"

"Not remotely political," Noel says. "It's a baking contest, that's it."

Before I can interject, we're set upon by a mother with two smalls boys. She looks apologetic and like she wants to be anywhere but at my booth. I give her a wide smile. "Can I get you something?"

"Two pies, pwease," says one of the boys. The other holds up a wad of crumpled dollar bills.

"Of course. Do you want them to eat now, or in a bag?"

"Now, pwease."

"Do you like apple or peach better?" They both opt for peach and I hand them over, accepting their money with as much seriousness as I can manage before sending them on their way.

When I turn back to Melly and Noel, they're both silent.

"So you in?" Melly asks.

"I kind of have something that weekend," I say.

She shrugs. "So skip it. Come on, we'll have fun."

I shake my head. "I can't."

"What is it, important pie business?" Her mouth quirks into a smile, the anger she directed at Noel falling away. It makes it somehow harder to admit the truth.

"Actually, yes. I'm sort of doing that pie contest. Hampshire County judges that weekend too."

I brace for an explosion, but instead she just studies me for one of the longest minutes of my life, then says, "Oh. Right. Well, maybe another time, yeah?"

She strides off without looking back, and it's like she takes all of the air with her. Part of me wants to race after her, explain the whole plan because it's not what she thinks. I could make her understand. I want her to understand. But I let her go because I know I can't, not really, not without putting myself in danger. It hurts, though, more than I want to admit.

"Friend of yours?" Noel asks after she's gone.

"Probably not anymore." I sit on Penny's steps and rub Zoe's head.

"She's wrong, you know." He says it without rancor, just quiet conviction. "About the contest. The contest isn't about politics or oppression or literally anything that isn't a pie. And pie is what you do. It's who you are. Even I know that, and I've known you for less than a month."

I don't answer him because I don't know if he's right or if Melly is. What she said about the contest is part of what almost stopped me from entering in the first place. Being crowned Miss American Pie Massachusetts does feel pretty archaic. And sexist.

A customer at the Hollow Hill booth forces Noel to leave me to my silence, and I roll his comment over in mind. Is pie really who I am?

Is that a good thing?

Or is Melly right? Does this all—the pies, Penny, the contest—make me a bad feminist?

I study the hem of my skirt as an empty ache grows in my chest. The floral fabric is silky soft with age, and it's one of the creations I actually remember Nana making.

The magic stitched into the seams is still there, buzzing with confidence and love, but it doesn't stop me from missing her. No magic can.

She made this dress for my mother, but it's the first one I learned to sew on. All the dresses I have from Nana are special: not only are the seams filled with magic, but they're padded with extra fabric at the sides and along the hems so the dress can always be altered to fit.

This is one of Nana's best designs, with self-tie shoulders, large pockets on the flouncy skirt, and ruffled white rickrack peeking out from the waist seam and hemline. Even now, all these years later, I can still see her working on it clear as day.

"It's in the details," she said, carefully lining up the wavy trim with the fabric. "That's true for dresses and it's true for magic. Everything has to have intention and add to the overall effect. It's no good to throw things in all willy-nilly. You have to have a plan." She plucked a pearl-headed pin from the strawberry cushion strapped to her wrist and stabbed it in my direction. "You must conduct yourself in a way that is true to yourself, that honors the Ellery power."

I was stretched on the fold-out ironing board, watching her work, and I squirmed, knowing exactly what she was referring to.

"I know it's new," she said, "and it's intoxicating. But you're ten, and that's old enough to know you should use your power for good. The Ellery magic lifts women; it doesn't trap them in the bathroom for entire days."

"They were being mean to me," I protested.

She leveled me with a stare as sharp as the pin she was using to secure the final bit of trim. "You have something they don't. Be a better person."

I huffed. "I shouldn't have to do ballet anyway. It's stupid and I hate it," I said, rolling onto my back and letting my head hang off the edge of the paisley-covered board.

Nana chuckled, running the pinned hem through her fingers, checking the rickrack for imperfections before she sewed everything in place. "If that's really how you feel, I'll talk to your mom. She just wants what's best for you. But it's still no excuse to poison the others during a bake sale."

"It wasn't poison," I protested. "It was destiny! They deserved it."

Nana raised an amused eyebrow. "Is that right?"

"It is!" I rolled over so I was sitting upright, and even though the blood rushing out of my head made me sway for a second, I carried on. "I swear, all I did was think about how much I hate them when I was making the pies, and then the mean ones got sick. It's not my fault. I ate the pies and I'm perfectly fine! Miss Darcy too, and Ellie."

"Sunshine, you can't work hate into the magic," Nana said, threading pale-blue thread into the sewing machine. "It doesn't work like that. You have to be generous and use it to bring out the good in people. Come down here so I can show you how to do the hem."

"But sometimes bad people deserve bad things," I argued, but I clamored off the ironing board anyway.

"That's not your place to judge," she said with a firmness that brooked no argument. I pulled up a stool beside her, studying the way she guided the fabric beneath the darting needle, keeping the extra fabric folded into a neat roll above the trim. She spoke over the hum of the machine, barely having to glance at her work. "The Ellery power is a gift, and a gift is something good, something positive. It's our legacy and our responsibility. Our honor. We use our power to make the world a better place. Now let me show you how to do the zipper."

In the aftermath of my very first murder pie, when I almost lost myself, those were the words that rang in my ears like a mantra: we use our power to make the world a better place.

So I did.

And I still do.

Even if it's not something I can explain to Melly, and even if my version of making the world a better place doesn't quite match up with Nana's, it doesn't mean I'm not trying.

Chapter Fifteen

I've come to realize that I completely suck at making friends. I can run my own business, avenge wronged women, and make kickass pies, but I apparently cannot function like an actual human in any other regard.

Take, for instance, Farmboy. I would consider us friends. Farmers' market friends for sure, with potential to be actual real-life friends. But I don't have his number or even a last name so I can stalk him online.

What I do have is the name of his orchard, which is why I find myself doing one of the things I hate most in the world: an unannounced drop-by.

Hollow Hill Orchard looks like something from a calendar. Rolling hills of fruit trees stretch far enough to form their own horizon. The wooden sign, hanging under its own little shelter, proclaims that the farm was established in 1922, and I wonder if it's been in Noel's family for all this time. I hope so. There's something to be said for passing down legacies.

I pull into a small parking lot in front of a weathered wooden farm stand. Out-of-season signs advertise apple picking and award-winning cider doughnuts. A white farmhouse with a wraparound porch that's seen better days looms over the stand from up the hill.

I let Zoe out of the truck and don't bother leashing her. I peek into the farm stand windows. Dusty shelves stand empty, awaiting a bounty that's months away. An old-fashioned cash register sits on the counter near the door.

I pat my leg to keep Zoe close, but I can tell she's itching to explore. We head toward a long, low-slung building with sliding doors along its side. The one at the end is open, and I take that as an invitation.

"Hello?" I call, stepping inside. The dirt floor makes me wish I had boots on instead of canvas sneakers, but oh well.

Further inside, a chestnut horse with a wide white blaze stands in the aisle with someone holding one of her feet up. I keep a hand on Zoe's collar. I don't think she's ever seen a horse before. "Noel?"

The guy lets the horse's hoof fall back to the ground and stands. "Daisy?"

I go over, still hanging on to Zoe, whose tail is whipping in happy arcs at the sight of her market friend. He crouches down with his arms out, and I drop her collar, letting her barrel into him. He laughs and gives her pets, looking up at me with a mix of confusion and delight.

"To what do I owe the pleasure?"

"I'm sorry to just drop by, but I realized I didn't have your number or anything, and well, after yesterday kind of blew up, we never got a chance to finish talking about the contest."

"So you're still doing it?"

"Of course I'm still doing it."

He stands, brushing his hands off on his jeans. "Good." There's relief in his voice that I didn't expect.

"So yeah, I thought maybe I could run some ideas by you." I feel awkward all of a sudden, unsure if the details I want to share with him are overstepping. I nod toward the horse, accepting her as a way out. "But you're busy. It can wait until the market."

"No, I'm glad you came."

He sounds so sincere that I believe him. I kick myself for almost running away. This contest is as important to him as it is to me; he just doesn't know it yet.

"Hey," he says, a twinkle in his dark eyes. "Have you ever ridden before?"

"Do carousel horses count?"

He laughs. "Not even a little bit." He looks at the horse, then at me. An impish grin pulls at the corners of his mouth. "Wanna? I was going to ride out and check the bees and the berry bushes. You could come."

"I'm one hundred percent not dressed for that," I say, holding out the edges of my full skirt for emphasis.

"Seems like a lot of fabric there. I bet you could manage. We can ride double. Sunny'll take good care of you, I promise."

I reach out and touch the horse's velvety muzzle, and she huffs a warm breath into my palm. She seems sweet, like Zoe, but bigger. I stroke the pale, almost-blond lock of hair that hangs between her eyes like bangs.

"Oh, what the hell," I say. It's a beautiful day, she's a beautiful horse, and I'm sick of everything being so serious lately. "Let's do it."

Noel grins and gently swings the saddle onto the horse's back. "You're gonna love it," he says, securing the girth around the horse's belly, moving with an ease that speaks to hundreds of hours of practice. As he does, Zoe tentatively reaches out to sniff the horse. Sunny stretches her long neck down until they're nose to nose. For a tense moment, I'm afraid one of them is going to freak out, but Zoe gives a happy yip and stretches her front legs out, bowing low with her butt in the air, tail wagging in an invitation to play. The horse looks at her like she's nuts but doesn't flinch. Noel pats the mare's neck affectionately. "You can set a bomb off from her back and she wouldn't care. Pups don't bother her."

He puts the bridle on, a complicated tangle of leather straps that the horse accepts with ease. I realize Noel moves around the barn the way I move around the kitchen, without having to think or concentrate, every movement automatic and ingrained on a molecular level. There's something impossibly sexy about it.

He leads the horse outside and I follow, Zoe running circles around the lot of us. Noel checks the girth, tightens it, and with seemingly no effort at all, swings himself into the saddle. He guides Sunny to the fence and asks her to stop. He's grinning like a kid in a candy store. "Climb up on the fence, then you're gonna throw your right leg over. I'll help you."

"I'm skeptical of any of this working the way you envision," I say, but I do as he says. My skirt is long, hitting a bit below my knees, with literal yards of fabric to maneuver as I climb the fence, but it means I should also have enough skirt to avoid flashing anyone. Noel reaches a hand down and I take it with mine. His strong grip is warm as sunshine.

He kicks his foot out of the stirrup. "Left foot in here," he says, and waits while I position my foot. "And on three, step in and swing your right leg over her butt. Try not to kick her, but if you do, she'll forgive you. Your goal is to land right behind the saddle. Ready?"

I nod, and he squeezes my fingers. "One—" I meet his eyes. "Two—" It's too late to back down. "Three—" He tightens his grip on my hand, pulls me up, and I swing my leg over the horse, skirt fanning out like a dancer's. I land with minimal commotion and am so pleased with myself I almost laugh.

"Nicely done," he says, looking over his shoulder. "Ready?"

"Hell yeah."

He grins. "Give me my stirrup back and hold on, then." I slide my leg back so the stirrup swings free and put my hands around his waist because it's the only logical place for them to go.

He makes a clucking noise, and as the horse walks away from the fence, I'm startled by how much movement I feel beneath me. I tighten my hold on Noel without meaning to, and he laughs. "You're okay. Just follow the motion."

The horse's muscles bunch and stretch beneath my legs, rocking me from side to side, but there's an easy rhythm to it, so I relax.

We walk through rows of trees, tiny buds showing where apples will be, and Zoe zigzags between them, trying to smell every single one.

"Think you can handle faster?" Noel asks. Like with the horse, I can feel all his muscles move as he turns to glance back at me. It's undeniably intimate.

"You tell me."

"Okay, so horses have four gaits: walk, which we're doing; trot, which is faster and bouncier; canter, which is faster still, but with more roll than bounce; and then gallop, which Sunny probably wouldn't have the energy for even if a bear was chasing us. Canter is the comfiest, especially from where you are. If you hold on and just stay in the middle of her back, you'll be fine, but if it's too much, I'll stop as soon as you say. She has good brakes."

Maybe it's the sun, or the abundance of fresh air, or the solidness of Noel in front of me, but I'm feeling a good kind of reckless. "Let's do it."

I wrap my arms tighter around his middle, and he makes the clucking noise again, shifting his legs in a signal I don't understand, and suddenly we're flying. It's the most exhilarating thing I've ever experienced, and I can't stop myself from laughing at the sheer joy of it. Zoe barks and races to join us, tongue flapping in the breeze.

My skirt streams around my legs, and I lift my face to the sun, wondering why I've never done this before. I find myself foolishly loosening my hold on Noel and throwing my arms out to the side like wings. He glances back and grins, dropping a hand back to hold my leg steady, just in case. But I don't need it.

We canter until we run out of trees, and Noel calls over his shoulder, "Slowing down; hold on."

I drop my hands back to his waist, and Sunny shifts from the rolling canter back to a walk with barely a bounce.

I hug Noel hard from behind before I can even think about it. "That was amazing!"

He laughs. It's a sound I'm coming to like quite a lot. "I thought you'd like it."

The apple trees give way to an open space with forest at the edges. A row of white wooden boxes stand like sentries along one side.

"Those are the beehives," Noel says, pointing at them. "They're kind of inconvenient all the way out here, but too many of the apple pickers were complaining about them, worried about their kids being stung, and that's money we can't just throw away."

It might be, if I have my way.

He guides Sunny past the hives and closer to the forest. "It's early for berries still, but I like to keep an eye on them."

He points out the bushes where the raspberries and blackberries will come in later in the summer, then asks Sunny to halt. He swings his right leg over the front of the saddle and slides down. "Stay there," he says to me. "There's no fence to help you get back on."

He loops the reins around the saddle horn, and Sunny stands stock-still while he inspects the bushes. He returns within minutes and holds up the tiniest, most perfect strawberry I've ever seen.

"First of the season," he says, handing it to me.

I bite into it, and it tastes exactly how the canter through the orchard felt.

"I want to buy all of them," I say. "When they come in. They're incredible."

"Another week or two," he says. He lifts the reins up, puts his left foot in the stirrups, and hops straight in the air. It's more awkward than the first time he did it, and I realize it's because I'm completely in the way of his right leg. I lean back to give him room, but he tucks his knee up to his chest and drops it over the other side of the saddle. Once he's settled, I return my hands to his waist, the fabric of his shirt warm against my fingers, and he asks, "We cantering back?"

"I'd love to," I say, and for a moment I contemplate forgetting why I came here and just enjoying another race through the orchards, but I don't. "I'm not sure I can talk and canter at the same time, though."

"Fair enough," he says, clucking Sunny into an easy walk. Zoe follows in our wake. "Pie talk time?"

"Pie talk time," I confirm. "So it looks like each state is supposed to enter a pie that actually represents their state so that the cookbook is like an overview of American pies."

"Them's the rules," he agrees.

"So I was thinking . . ." I draw the word out because I'm not sure which part to start with. I'm glad he's not looking straight at me for this. It's easier to be honest that way. Mostly honest, at least. "Okay, before I say anything, I want you to know you can veto it at any time. Seriously, I won't be offended; we can keep being market neighbors, no harm, no foul. But since the emphasis is on state-specific pies, I was thinking about doing something hyperlocal. Using local fruit and local honey."

"I like it," he says.

"From you," I clarify. "I want to use Hollow Hill apples, Hollow Hill honey, and Hollow Hill cider. All of it. I'm not sure exactly how yet, but I want to incorporate everything you offer, and I want to be really vocal about it. This isn't going to just be a Pie Girl pie, it's going to be a Pie Girl and Hollow Hill collaboration. I know teams can't enter, but I want to make sure the orchard is named at every opportunity, including in the baker profile in the cookbook write-up."

He doesn't say anything, and without seeing his face, I can't tell if that's a good thing or a bad thing. His body has stiffened, just slightly, but it could be with attention as much as with offense.

"I'm not trying to be patronizing or anything," I assure him. "But I've been thinking about what you told me, about your uncle and the fate of the farm, and I want to help. I know it's going to sound pompous, but I know I make good pies. I have a real chance to make it to the finals, and if I can use that to spread the word about who you are and what you do, I want to do that. Your ciders are incredible. If you want to keep this orchard, I think that's going to be your ticket, but you need people to buy them. More people than there are at our market. If I can make it into the cookbook, it could potentially get you national name recognition."

I stop because I'm out of air. It's a good thing, because my brain is all set to keep rambling. I bite my tongue and wait for a response.

Nothing comes, apart from a further stiffening of his spine. I drop my hands to the back of the saddle, because that's as much space as I can give him from the back of a horse, and curse myself. I should've waited.

The house and barn come into sight before he says anything. His voice is level but succinct. "I don't need charity."

I didn't think it was possible to feel so isolated from someone who's mere inches away, but it's like a chasm has opened between us, and I wish I could take it all back.

He guides Sunny back to the barn and halts her, sliding down with the same ease he had in the field. He looks up at me, searching my face, and holds out a hand.

Instead of taking it, I put both hands on the back of the saddle, lean forward, and swing my right leg over Sunny's butt, folding over her back and sliding down in a puff of fabric. I land facing away from Noel, and part of me, the embarrassed part, wants to just keep walking and not turn back.

Zoe nudges my leg, and I reach down to rub her ears. "It's not charity," I say. I turn and face him, suddenly pissed. "And even if it was, so what. Friends help friends; it's literally their raison d'être."

He looks like he's about to argue, but instead he just deflates, like all the fight goes out of him. "You're right. It was shitty of me to say." He leads Sunny back into the barn, and I follow, Zoe at my heels, because we're obviously not done yet.

"Noel," I say softly, and his head snaps around as if I'd shouted. "You brought the contest to me. All I'm doing is bringing you to the contest."

His lips twitch into an almost-grin. "What happened to Farmboy?"

I raise an eyebrow. "Farmboy has more sense than Noel."

He takes Sunny's bridle off and replaces it with the simpler halter before he speaks. "You're right," he says, tying the horse up and going to remove the saddle.

"You can tell me to piss off," I remind him gently.

"I can't." He sets the saddle on its rack and starts to brush the horse's coat. "It's just hard. I feel like I should have this figured out already, that my uncle should be on board. This is my grandfather's property, it's been in our family for generations, and I'm tired of worrying about losing it. I don't know anything about running an orchard. I know about growing things and making cider, sure, but my uncle's the one who knows about money. And maybe he's right. I don't want to drag you into this mess."

"It's not dragging if I'm the one offering," I say.

He finishes brushing the horse, and I don't badger him. There's something to be said for having time to think. He puts Sunny back in her stall and throws her a pile of hay. He leans against the half door, watching her eat. Zoe is lying contentedly in a patch of sun, so I join him, resting my arms on the rough wood by his side.

"The male ego is a bitch," he says after a while. "I apologize."

"I accept."

"Tell me what you have in mind."

Chapter Sixteen

I wish I could take care of the Pinstripe problem as easily as Noel's orchard, but I haven't seen a trace of her since that first farmers' market, and the cheery *Just checking in re: wedding!* email I sent to the address Vance left goes unanswered.

Which is how I find myself sticking a toe over one of my never lines.

I pull up the Galen and Harris Law site and find Pinstripe—Emma Rogers—listed under their support staff page. She doesn't have an email address listed, but the law partners do, and they're consistently last name plus first two letters of the first name. Ergo, rogersem@galenharris.com should be my girl.

It's not lost on me that I'm sending a murdery email to a law firm's email address, but it feels like my only choice. If I show up on her doorstep and Vance answers, then what?

The email takes ages to compose, despite being short. After all, it's not like I can just come out and say, *Hey, someone wants you dead and I want your fiancé dead; let's chat.* I have zero doubt that the law firm monitors its employees' emails.

I consider making a throwaway email account, but in the end I stick to ThePieMaker@piesbeforeguys.com. I hope it will be enough to get to her attention.

Emma,

Congratulations! Someone has selected you for a free Pies Before Guys pie! Find out who your secret pie-admirer is when you pick it up. Does St. Stan's on Wednesday work for you? Remember, it's not too late to send a pie of your own!

–The Pie Maker

'Our pies are to die for!'

I go back on forth on whether it's too obvious or not obvious enough. I'm counting on the tag line, admittedly a little on the nose, combined with the email address to be enough to catch her attention, but who knows.

I click send and promptly start second-guessing the shit out of myself while I wait for a reply. Maybe I should've sent it as the Pie Girl, under the auspices of needing to discuss the wedding, or maybe the burner email was the way to go.

I hit refresh so many times on my email that my phone freezes and I have to restart it. Damn it. All I want to do is save this damn girl's life, and she's making it incredibly difficult.

I distract myself by testing contest pies.

I know a classic apple pie isn't going to cut it, no matter how tasty it is, and besides, I want to put as many Hollow Hill products in as possible. Noel has agreed to hook me up with whatever I want, including any of the apples he has in cold storage. I'm going to Instagram this contest to death, and regardless of the outcome, Hollow Hill is going to get plenty of credit.

The crust is simple. It's going to be my regular all-butter, easy-to-magic flaky beauty. It's reliable and perfectly textured. There's no need to mess with something that works.

The question is, what to put inside it?

* * *

Tonight I bring a trio of pies into the diner's kitchen. "I need guinea pigs," I announce.

"Don't have to ask me twice," Juan says. "What do we got?"

I give him the rundown on the contest, and by the time I'm done, I've got him, his line cook, the dish boy, and two of the servers attacking the pies with forks. It's a small test group, but enough. I already have one option I'm leaning toward, and I mostly want to make sure no one hates it.

Option one is apple crumb, full of honey-sweetened apples and topped with a brown sugar and cinnamon streusel. It's the homiest pie of the bunch and would be right at home in Frank's rotation.

Option two is apple cranberry. Yes, I need to use frozen cranberries, but they're from Massachusetts bogs, so that gets me double state points. The whole thing is sweetened with honey and topped with a rustic lattice crust and lots of crunchy sugar.

Option three is apple cream and starts with a thick layer of firm, honey-flavored custard that's topped with a mile-high pile of apples soaked in a hard-cider caramel. The alcohol in the cider makes the caramel almost butterscotchy, and the honey custard is completely unexpected.

"Votes for one?" I ask. The dish boy and one of the servers raise their forks.

"Two?" This gets the line cook and server number two's vote.

"Three?" Juan.

And me.

Even fucking split.

"Well, that wasn't helpful," I say with a laugh.

"They're all good," one of the servers says.

"Yeah, I think any of them could win," the dish boy says.

The first server disappears back into the dining room, and her sidekick says, "We could cut them up into small pieces and sample them to the customers? No one double dipped."

"Oh, that's perfect," I say. We set about cutting tiny slices of each pie and arranging them into sets while the guys get back to work.

She loads them onto a tray that she deftly raises to her shoulder. "Final verdict coming up."

I get the diner pies going while she circulates among the customers, letting Juan fill me in on the adoption progress. He's equal parts excited and panicked at the thought of the little girl they're meeting next week, a five-year-old who has been in the system since she was two.

"There's just something about her," he says. "I can't describe it. I saw her picture and I just knew. I can see that picture being on our fridge. I can see her at our kitchen table. We started off wanting a baby, but I think this is our kid."

"Oh, Juan, that's so exciting." Impulsively I run around the prep table and give him a fast, hard hug. "I promise I'll make her birthday pies every year."

"I'm-a hold you to that," he says, pointing a pair of tongs at me.

I go back to my pie station and start rolling love and good wishes into my next crust. It's already infused with a minor dose of happiness, since it's a diner pie, and it's relatively easy to layer on a few more positive elements. After it bakes, I load it with coconut custard, the week's special, and whip up a separate batch of rum-spiked whipped cream for the top. There is no occasion a pie will not improve.

I box it and write *Juan* across the top in a Sharpie I steal from the arm pocket of his chef coat.

"A happy-thoughts pie," I say, presenting it to him. "Share it with Eric. And bring me back the pan."

He holds out a fist, and I bump mine to it. "Pies for your favorite guys," he says.

I laugh. "Something like that."

Our server returns and drops her empty tray on the prep table. "I have results!"

"What do you got?" I ask.

"Cranberry is in a solid third. Consensus says if it was fall, it could be in first, but not now. Seasonally inappropriate."

"Fair enough," I agree.

"The crumbly one and the cream one are pretty much tied, slight edge to cream, but even the people who voted crumb still ate every last bite of the cream. A couple of them, two old guys especially, said it was weird, but in a good way. I don't know if that helps?"

"It does," I say. "Thanks."

"So which one are you going with?" she asks.

"The honey cream. I think weird-in-a-good-way is exactly what I need."

I also need to work out the magic that's going into it, but that's obviously not something I'm going to be polling the dining room on.

It may seem like cheating to magic my contest pie, but there's nothing I can do. If I make it, it's getting magic, one way or another. I don't know any other way to bake.

I never knew a time without magic. I grew up surrounded by it, immersed in it. It wasn't something that had to be earned with time, like first periods or freedom from braces, but something that was part of who I was from the moment I knew my name. Earlier, perhaps. I did, after all, leave the hospital in a gown my Nana made, magic seams sewn full of love and hope for the future.

So the question is only what to add. Making it like a diner pie is the most obvious answer, with just a light sprinkle of homey happiness. But I feel like I want a little something more, something personal.

When I was first learning to bake, Mom and Nana used to tell me that the secret ingredient should always be love. Looking back I realize it was probably their way of directing my power, making sure I wasn't infusing my pies with anything dangerous. Given the seriousness of my dinosaur and monkey phases, that was probably smart. I'm sure the last thing we needed was to have a street full of sugared-up kids climbing everything and trying to eat each other.

But they were also right. Love, even if it's not the magically imbued kind, is an excellent secret ingredient.

I'll add just a pinch to give a hint of the feeling I had in those early days, when I had to stand on a stool to reach the counter and I could feel Mom or Nana hovering behind me, just in case I lost my balance when the whisking got too crazy. That happened more than once while I was learning to make whipped cream by hand, but I never had to worry that they would be upset or try to stop me. Even when an entire bowl of half-whipped cream went flying, sending white flecks up to the ceiling and down to the cupboards, they just laughed and we dabbed the sweetened cream on each other's faces until we were as messy as the kitchen.

It's the kind of fun, raucous love everyone deserves to experience when they're little, and it's that feeling I'm going to add to this pie. In a way, it'll be like taking the rest of the Ellery women along for the ride.

Chapter Seventeen

On Wednesday I feel like I'm getting ready for a date. Almost every dress I own is heaped on my bed, and I can't make up my mind.

The magazines don't really offer tips on the perfect outfit to save a girl and plan a murder in.

I'm torn between going in my regular meeting disguise and wearing my normal clothes. I check the time on my phone and realize I needed to make a decision like five minutes ago if I want to stay on schedule.

I consider what I have on: a navy-blue shirtwaist with ruffled white piping down the front placket. By my normal standards, subdued. It'll have to do.

I make sure I have everything I need, which isn't much, and kiss Zoe on the head. "Be a good girl." She looks so dejected that I say, "Okay, ride in the car."

She scampers happily to the truck and waits while I arrange the pie boxes on the floor: a box of strength cuties for the meeting and one for Pinstripe.

If she shows.

I get there early, not wanting to risk missing her, and end up having to wait for the Narcotics Anonymous meeting to clear out before I can even bring the pies in. I find a parking spot with a good view of the side entrance and wait. Before long people start swarming up the stairs. Unlike the domestic violence group, the NA group is massive. It's a mixed-gender group, although it tends to be male dominated. I try not to watch the faces too closely, anonymity being a pillar of these groups and all, but suddenly Zoe's tail starts whipping back and forth and she's making excited little sounds as she tries to jam her head through the gap of the open window. I follow her gaze, expecting a squirrel, but no. Not a squirrel. Not even close.

I'm like a moth drawn to the light of his face.

Noel.

His gangly height makes him hard to miss and that floppy hair hard to mistake, but I still close my eyes and try to shake the image from my head. I must've imagined it. When I look again, I'll see I was wrong. Of course I am. There's no way it's him. Not my Noel.

But it is.

I watch him as he shakes hands with one of the guys, departs from another with that back-pounding bro-hug thing straight guys do, and climbs in his truck like this is all an ordinary thing for him.

I'm so dumbfounded that I just sit there, staring at the empty parking spot he leaves behind, forgetting completely that I'm supposed to be delivering pies and watching for Pinstripe.

I force myself to dam the torrent of emotions coursing through me. I can deal with them later. Or not.

Right now I have more important things to do.

Women are starting to trickle in for the domestic violence meeting, and I grab my box of pies. "Be right back," I tell Zoe, and dart inside. I have the uncomfortable feeling of being watched as I go, probably an aftereffect of the inadvertent spying on Noel.

I scan faces for Pinstripe, but she isn't in the hall or the meeting room. I attach myself to the fringes of a small group of women lingering near the refreshments table and slide the box in next to the coffee urn before ducking back out, making a show of being distracted by something on my phone.

I stand at the top of the church steps, where I can watch the parking lot and the surrounding bits of street.

I see her coming well before she sees me.

I fetch the pie I've brought for her—peach, with a heaping dose of clear thinking—and meet her on the sidewalk.

"Emma," I say. It's weird to use her name out loud when she's still Pinstripe in my head.

She's dressed for work in a charcoal-gray skirt suit. No scarf anymore.

She cocks her head, clearly trying to place me. "Can I help you?"

"I'm hoping I can help you," I say. I raise the pie box like an offering. "You've won a pie."

"Oh," she says, relieved laughter bubbling out of her. She touches a hand to her chest, the very picture of embarrassment. "This isn't at all what I was expecting. You're the Pie Girl, for our wedding. I thought this was something else."

Here goes nothing. Or everything. "Can we talk for a minute?"

"Of course," she says. "What did I do to win a pie? And why did you want to deliver it here?"

"Let's sit," I say. "Do you mind dogs?"

"I love them," she says wistfully. "I wish Jackson wasn't allergic."

I let Zoe out of the truck, and she follows us to a bench beneath a tree. I set the pie box between us.

I've practiced a hundred variations of this scenario in my head, trying to find the best way to approach this, but I figured when she was in front of me, it would come naturally.

I was wrong.

"There's no good way to say this," I admit, "but I think you might be in danger. A lot of it."

Her hand goes to her throat in an unconscious gesture that confirms that she understands this. The bruises may have faded from her flesh, but they're fresh in her mind.

Zoe plunks her head on Emma's lap like she knows the woman is going to need a distraction. Emma lets her hand fall to the dog's fur and asks in a guarded voice, "How do you know about that?"

"That's actually not what I mean," I say. "Not completely."

I decide on the spot how to spin this. "But that's part of it. I understand you were approached by a member of Pies Before Guys a few weeks ago. They're familiar with your situation, and now I am as well. Pies Before Guys is a network of wronged women who look out for those like them. Membership is completely voluntary, but it is for life. We are a sisterhood in the truest sense of the word."

"The girl I talked to," she says warily, "she made it sound like the Mafia. Like she could arrange a pie that would kill Jackson."

I don't answer because I know she's not done.

When she speaks, it's to Zoe more than me. "It's you, isn't it? You're the one who makes the pies."

"I'm affiliated with them, yes," I say. "And that is something that is still one hundred percent on the table, but it's not the only reason I wanted to meet. Can you think of anyone besides your fiancé who might wish you harm?"

"No," she answers without hesitation. "And Jackson doesn't really mean me harm either, not really. It's just—"

I raise a hand, cutting her off. "Don't. I have no interest in your justifications for his assholery. No one chokes someone hard enough to leave a collar of bruises because they don't mean harm. In my book, that is unforgivable." My tone is sharp, and I pause, having to force the next sentence out. "But how you want to handle that is your decision, and we respect that. Consent matters, and Pies Before Guys will not act on your behalf without it. You have my word."

She nods without looking at me, but her eyes are shining with unshed tears, and I wish she could be as angry on her behalf as I am. She strokes Zoe's head like it's a crystal ball that will give her all the answers.

"He doesn't want to hurt me," she says, "but he does."

"I know," I say, my heart breaking for her, for the fact that I'm about to make her life harder before I have any chance of making it better. "Your name has been brought to my attention via the Pies Before Guys network along with two others. Do you know a Brittany Cline or a Kerenza Vallery?"

She shakes her head. "Should I?"

"I don't know. I was hoping you could tell me what links you together. Or who. From what I can gather, you have all crossed paths with the same person, and that person wants you dead."

Her hands fly to her mouth. Some people give away their feelings through their eyes or their expressions, but for Emma, it's her hands. "You can't be serious," she says.

"I am." I give her the details I know about her—her address, place of employment, and pie preferences. Her eyes widen above her fingers. She's shaking her head back and forth, wrapping denial around herself like a comforting blanket.

"There must be some mistake," she says. Her eyes widen in sudden fear, and she shoves the pie box toward me. "Is this it? The pie they ordered for me? Are you working for them?"

I reach out, take one of her trembling hands in mind. I need her to understand this. "I'm not," I say. "I'm on your side. This pie is completely safe. Pies Before Guys doesn't even have a pie that could hurt marginalized genders."

"You promise?" she asks, voice desperate. "You won't make their pies?"

"I promise. I just need you to help me figure out who's behind it. The order came anonymously, with no referral, and the only clues I have are the names of the targets. You're sure you don't know them?"

"I'd remember a name like Kerenza," she says. "And the only Brittany I know is from elementary school, and she moved to Ireland when we were eleven."

There's no delicate way to ask this next part. "Does Jackson know any Kerenzas or Brittanys?"

"Not that I know of," she says. "Maybe from college? He was at Amherst while I was at UMass, and we didn't really mix friend groups." Her voice has lost its wobble. She's made of sterner stuff than I thought.

Which is good, because I have to turn the screw. "Do you know if your fiancé is having an affair?"

She deflates completely at that, dropping her forehead to Zoe's. "I've suspected," she says.

“I have confirmation,” I say, as gently as I possibly can. I take out my phone and pull up one of the photos from the restaurant. I zoom in until it’s just the girl filling the screen. “Do you know her?”

Emma takes the phone, studies it. She pinches in, zooming the picture back out, and when she sees the girl sharing a table with her fiancé, the phone starts to shake in her hand. “Is she one of the ones you mentioned?”

“I don’t know. I was hoping you would.”

She hands the phone back. “I don’t. But thank you for asking. For showing me that. I’m sure it has nothing to do with whoever has given you my name, but I suppose I should be glad to be seeing this before the wedding.”

“I know how terrible this must be for you,” I say.

She snorts. “You really don’t,” she says. “But there is a part of me that’s going to be grateful we had this conversation, I think.”

* * *

My brain is so full of thoughts about Noel and Emma that I don’t even notice that Penny’s door isn’t quite closed until I’m putting the key in the lock.

I hesitate, trying to remember closing the door and locking it before leaving for Saint Stan’s. I assume I did, but I can’t picture it, not with all the problems I have buzzing around.

I put a hand on Zoe’s collar, lead her back to the truck, and open the door for her. She jumps up obediently, and I close her in.

I turn my phone’s flashlight on and return to the van, examining the door. The lock looks unmarred, but there’s a slight warping at the frame that could be new or could just be something I’m noticing because I'm looking for it. I picture the layout of the tiny entryway and the kitchen. Knife rack on the far side, rolling pins in the drawer, but I'm ninety percent certain I left a pair of Nana's heavy dressmaking shears on the serving counter where I was cutting twine for the pie boxes before I left. Those would do.

I pocket my phone, ease the door open, and wait. Silence greets me, and I creep up the metal steps, knowing every creak by heart. I grope blindly at the counter, and my fingers find cool steel. The scissors have a reassuring heft to them. I flick the light switch, trying to see everywhere at once. No movement, nothing immediately out of place. Part of me expected to find the place ransacked, but who robs a pie van? The only things I have of value are the KitchenAid and the van itself, neither of which are easy to pocket.

I do a sweep of the RV and find everything else exactly as I left it, including the heap of dresses on the bed that I definitely don't have the energy to deal with right now.

I'm about to go get Zoe when I almost step on it: an index card. I know what it is before I pick it up, and when I turn it over, I am indeed confronted with my own handwriting, detailing the ingredients for mango mint mojito pie.

My stomach plummets. I go to the drawer the box of cards usually lives in and pull it open, throwing the pile of spare potholders on the floor in my haste.

The box is gone.

I rush out of the van and straight through the diner's back door, praying that I'm right. "Did anyone borrow my recipe cards?"

"Hello to you too," Juan says. One of the servers, a high school girl, is in there with him, filling sugar canisters in the corner. She looks up at the commotion and immediately away when she sees my face.

"You," I say, pointing at her. "Did you go in my van to get my recipes?"

The girl shakes her head, scarlet splotches blooming on her cheeks under my scrutiny.

"Yo," Juan says, moving in front of the girl so I can't ignore him. "What's got you so heated?"

I suck in a breath, channeling all the self-control I can muster. I glance back at the girl and realize it's not guilt on her face, but fear. It's enough to make me check myself.

"Shit, I'm sorry," I say, rubbing at the tension in my neck. "You didn't happen to see anyone nosing around Penny while I was gone, did you?"

Juan shakes his head. "No, but I'm the only cook on, so I haven't had a break. Why, what's going on?"

"Did you go out back at all?" I ask the server as gently as possible.

"For like ten minutes? Amanda did too. I didn't see anyone, but I can ask Amanda?"

"Please," I say. She scurries out into the dining room. I don't wait for her to return before telling Juan what happened.

"You think someone broke in just to steal your recipes? Man, that's cold. Who knew the pie world was so cutthroat."

"It's not funny," I snap. "Someone was in my van. My van, Juan. That's like someone breaking into your house."

"I know, I know, I'm sorry. Bad attempt to lighten the mood," he says, and I can see he means it. "You gonna call the cops?"

I snort. "And what, get the same reaction I just got from you? I don't think so."

"I really think you should reconsider staying at my place," he says. "It's one thing to have someone hanging around, but breaking in is crossing a line."

"So is stealing my shit." There's nothing inherently incriminating about the recipe box. There isn't a card in there listing the steps to make a murder pie, but knowing that doesn't make the violation less significant. Those are *my* recipes, as in originals. Yes, the index card thing is old-fashioned and I could just as easily keep a digital copy, but I like the tangibility of the cards. They're real. I can hold them, read them like a memoir of the pies I've created. I can spread them out like tarot cards and see the future. My future, but also the future of whoever gets my pies. It's alchemy, in its way. The alchemy of apple pie.

And now it's all in the hands of some piss-gibbon who felt they had the right to violate my home. My privacy.

My never lines collapse like dominoes as I think about someone rooting around inside the van, inside my space, my life. I want to start baking immediately, pouring all the hate and rage into a crust that will kill at first bite, with a filling that will draw it out for agonizing eternities.

I let none of this show on my face.

"I'd feel better if you moved, at least for a while," Juan says.

I'm saved from answering when the flushed server bursts into the kitchen, dragging her friend by the arm. "Tell her," she says to the girl.

"It might be nothing," Amanda says, "but there was a motorcycle leaving when I went on break. That was the only weird thing. Usually the motorcycle guys come Sunday morning and park together out front. I don't think I've ever seen one by himself."

I fight the urge to curse. "Thanks. That's actually not nothing. If you see him again, can you try to take a picture? Maybe a license plate?"

Both girls nod. I have no idea what I would actually do with a license plate number, but it would probably involve a very manipulative pie and a particularly gullible cop.

Chapter Eighteen

The college is starting to wind down now that finals are mostly over and I'll get only a trickle of customers at my library spot, so I don't feel bad for taking a detour on the way over this morning.

I convinced Juan to let me stay where I was, but that didn't mean I slept well. I'm starting to think the only way I'm ever going to get another decent night's sleep is to uncover who my mystery stalker is and do something very final about it.

Hence the detour, where ten minutes and two hundred dollars at the big-box store gets me a little piece of mind in the form of an outdoor security camera. The box promises easy installation and real-time monitoring. Just what I need.

I'm tempted to head straight back to the diner and get it set up, but there's no rush if I'll be in Penny all day anyway. Still, just having the camera in my possession feels like a step in the right direction.

I spend the rest of the morning outside the library, selling pies and making lists. Lists of all the people who could possibly be blackmailing me.

I try to list people I know personally that could be behind this and come up empty. It's not Frank or Juan, and Noel is just too nice. I don't have a string of salty exes out there, and it's probably not my middle school bully.

I shift to what I know about him: He rides a motorcycle. He knows where I live. He knows magic is real.

As far as who he *is*, I know nothing. At least with the camera, maybe I can finally get a look at him.

* * *

After a small lunchtime rush, I switch gears to finalizing the plans for the pie contest. I don't think about whether Noel will be with me or about what it means that I saw him at that meeting. I can't.

I submit the recipe through the website, pay my entry fee, and start working on a timeline. I'll be bringing fully baked pies with me, so it's just a matter of getting myself and them to the judging in time. Easy peasy.

My thoughts are interrupted by a sharp knocking on the side of the van. Zoe barks in surprise, and I don't blame her. I've been so caught up in my planning that I completely missed Melly's purple-headed approach.

"What's a girl gotta do to get a pie around here?" she says with a coy grin.

"Sorry," I say, surprised to see her here after our farmers' market encounter. "What can I get you?"

"Whatever's best," she says. "You know I still haven't tried one of these things yet?"

"You haven't?" I ask incredulously. "But you had me come to your rally."

She shrugs. "People need to eat. You provide food. Seemed logical."

"And you don't need food?"

"God, I wish I didn't," she says. "It's such an inconvenience. If I could just inject the nutrients I need, I'd be all over that."

I shake my head in astonishment. "You mean you don't enjoy food at all?"

"Waste of time," she says. "But I figure I should see what all the fuss is about, right?"

"I have banana fosters and hazelnut left," I say, but I'm already getting a hazelnut out. The banana is straight study-buddy, but the hazelnut is still getting the extra dose of calming. "Let me heat it up for you."

"Cool." She opens Penny's door and marches up the steps without waiting for an invitation. She slings her bag onto the counter and hops up on a stool, pretzeling one long leg up beneath her. "So, Pie Girl, what makes these pies of yours so damn magic?"

I freeze with my back to her as panic floods my core, but I realize she's just being hyperbolic. "Made with love," I quip, popping the cutie pie under a low broiler to warm.

"I've been trying to understand," she says, looking around the van like she's trying to decipher a secret code, "just why it is you're doing this."

Given our last interaction, I don't know if she means the contest or baking in general. There's no way I trust her enough to fully answer the first part of that, but I can answer the second. "Because it makes people happy. It's the one thing in the world I can do that makes a tangible difference in people's lives." I hold up a hand to forestall her protest. "It may not be a global revolution, but a single pie can make a single person's day better, even if only for a few minutes. And I have to think that counts for something."

I pull the cutie pie from the oven and slide it onto a red melamine plate. I pass it to her along with a fork from one of the drawers.

She doesn't even glance at it. Instead she keeps those sharp blue eyes fixed on mine as she spears the pie, breaking off a piece and popping it into her mouth. She leaves the tines of the fork resting against her lips as she chews. She swallows audibly, taps the fork on her lips a few times, and finally nods.

"Okay, yeah," she says. "Magic is not an exaggeration."

I grin, perversely pleased with the compliment, but a pair of students are heading toward the van, and I turn to greet them. After I serve them, I turn to find Melly going through my drawers with a freshly washed fork in hand.

She catches me staring and flushes. "I'm a neat freak."

"There are worse traits to have," I say, showing her where the silverware lives.

Now that she's had pie, I expect her to go, but she doesn't. She reclaims her spot at the counter, and I find I don't mind.

She stays for a while longer and it's nice, talking between customers. The calming element of the pie has a subtle but noticeable effect, easing the frantic pace of her speech and, presumably, her thoughts.

"So make me understand," she says at last, "about the contest. You know it's archaic. You're not stupid. Is it the money?"

"Partly," I say. "But not only."

She waits instead of badgering me with questions, and that's all the proof I need that the pie is working.

In the silence, I find myself tempted to tell her the truth of what I have planned, but I can't. I know that. But it doesn't stop me from wanting to. She would appreciate it, perhaps more than anyone else, and she would understand. But it's too risky.

"I just think I can use the contest to make a difference," I say. I start to tell her about my plan for highlighting Hollow Hill Orchard, but the memory of Noel walking out of Saint Stan's last night freezes the words in my throat and I let the statement hang, unfinished.

"So," she says, drawing the word out. "About that. I think I need to apologize."

"You think?"

"I was a bitch to your friend. To you. It was shitty of me."

"It wasn't great," I admit.

"I can be abrasive. It's a flaw." She shrugs like she's accepted this part of herself as immutable, and I suppose there's something to be said for that kind of self-awareness. "Truth is, this contest has been on my nerves since before you even entered it. My sister is one of the final judges—her husband's company is one of the local sponsors, so he pretty much bought her the position—and it just feels like more of her barefoot-and-pregnant-in-the-kitchen nonsense. She's a Wife with a capital W, like it's her primary identity. I swear, that pledge to love, honor, and obey scrambled her brain. Obey. Can you imagine, in this day and age?" She shakes her head. "So yeah, even though I know at the end of the day that the contest isn't about politics, it still feels like it's about personal ones because of Aria. And it's hard for me to think straight sometimes where this stuff is concerned."

I nod, watching her. There's a seriousness to her expression that I can't blame on the pie. I switch the kettle on and drop two ginger lime tea bags into mugs. "What got you into the activism?"

She toys with one of the pins on her bag, the *Grow a Pair* ovaries. "Pure self-righteous indignation," she says with a wry smile.

I laugh and add sugar to each mug. "Why does that not surprise me?"

"I still don't know how we got ourselves into the dystopian nightmare that was the Donnelly administration. Think about it. If someone wrote a novel with a billionaire televangelist using the White House as his own personal pulpit to promote making women subservient little house pets and demonizing anyone who is somehow 'other,' it would've been a farce. But then it was real, and I thought hell, if this was a dystopian novel, the only person who could save the day would be some hot chick with superpowers. So there I was, ready to go." She spreads her arms as if the answer is obvious.

"Well, at least we know you don't have a messiah complex or anything," I say with a grin, sliding her a mug.

"I don't see you arguing," she says, with a spark back in her eyes that makes it impossible to look away.

"That we lived through an actual dystopian hell or that you're a hot chick with superpowers?"

She holds my gaze, a smirk playing on her full lips. "Either."

The bees that are usually in my brain dive for my stomach, but they're not hornets anymore. No, they're fat, fluffy bumblebees bumping around in there and making me go all fluttery. "Well, I haven't seen any evidence of superpowers yet," I say.

She bursts out laughing. "Touché, Pie Girl, touché."

"So, are they working, these superpowers of yours?" I ask.

Melly's face shuts down so quickly I wish I could snatch the question back. "Sorry, I was just teasing. I get that it's a long-haul kind of fight. I wasn't trying to be flip."

She wraps her hands around her mug and gives a small shake of her head. "No, you don't get it. Like I said, that's what it was like at this beginning, an abstract save-the-world kind of thing. It's different now."

"How so?"

"It got personal." She looks up from her tea, and her eyes are hard with anger and something else. Pain. A lot of it.

I steal a glance at the clock on the stove and make a split-second decision. I slide the serving window closed and draw the eyelet curtains across it. Any straggling customers can wait.

I sit beside Melly at the counter and ask gently, "In what way?"

Her foot starts bouncing on the stool's rail, but the rest of her is very still. The controlled, careful kind of stillness that comes from too much practice keeping yourself glued together. It's a stillness I know well, and I want to reach out, take her hand to let her know that, but I don't. Not yet. Instead I just wait, sit with the thrumming tension and let it be okay.

After a moment, her knee stops pistoning and she says, with a quiet deliberation, "He killed my aunt."

For a moment I'm confused, and it must show, because she says, "Donnelly. He killed my aunt. Three years ago." Her knuckles are white around the mug.

"I don't understand." I say it softly and without judgment, but I still worry it will set her off. The air in the trailer feels electric, like the slightest spark could set us ablaze.

She doesn't answer right away. One finger starts to move, tapping a hard staccato beat against the side of the mug that sends ripples across her tea, but then it's like the words are stuck. I don't rush her.

"Her name was Faith," she says. "She was the only one in the family who got me, who liked me for exactly who I was, who accepted me without question. I used to wish she was my mother, because she would've been great at it. She wasn't anybody's mother, though, even though she and my uncle tried. For years they tried, with no luck. And then one day there was, and the test was positive. She was thirty-eight. I've never seen anybody so happy."

Melly stops, takes a long sip of tea with her eyes closed. When she sets the mug down, she continues, speaking to the cup as much as me.

"It was ectopic. We were at the movies, just the two of us, and she doubled over in pain. She thought it was her appendix. It wasn't. We went to the emergency room and they diagnosed the ectopic pregnancy, but they wouldn't do anything. This was when we were knee-deep in Donnelly's dark-age policies. If they removed it, both her and the doctors would've been charged with feticide. It didn't matter that it was already ruptured and completely unviable. It didn't matter what she wanted. They gave her painkillers and a bed, because that was all they could do. They just let her die."

Her voice cracks then, and with it, something inside me. In that moment I understand that *gut-wrenching* isn't just an adjective, it's a physical reaction to someone else's pain. It's the feeling of your heart trying to break. I reach out then, because it is impossible not to. I want to take her in my arms and tell her it's okay, but it's not, and I can't, so I just take her hand and let her finish. It isn't enough, but it isn't nothing either.

She squeezes my hand to the point of pain, but I don't flinch. She could break my bones and I would keep holding on.

Before she continues, her eyes find mine, and they're bright with tears and conviction. "They let her die with a bellyful of blood because Donnelly made it criminal to save a woman's life. So yeah, it's personal now, because politics are personal. If it's not my aunt, it's someone else's. And even though Donnelly's gone, there are still fights to fight. Always will be."

I want more than anything to make her a pie, right now, to deliver to the bastard ex-president who robbed her of her aunt and her aunt of her life. My never lines scroll through my head like a marquee, and I try to twist them into a shape that has room for revenge. For vengeance. For cold-blooded murder. But the anger is overcome by something else. Empathy.

"My mother died too," I say. Her hand is still in mine, and I trace small circles on the back of it with my thumb. "I was fifteen. I know it's not the same, but I understand. I get it, the hole that's left behind, the rage."

She shakes her head but doesn't pull her hand away. "Does it get better?"

"Sometimes. And not really," I say honestly. "It's complicated."

"Isn't it always?"

Chapter Nineteen

For the first time since I've been in Turnbridge, the thought of the farmers' market fills me with dread. Noel, of course, is the reason I want to skip, but also the reason I know I can't.

If I hadn't had so many pies to make, I would've ambushed him at the orchard yesterday, but it was after ten by the time I finished and I remembered most normal people go out Friday nights. It made me realize how little I really know about him, whether he has friends to go out with, a girlfriend, a boyfriend, any interests outside the orchard.

Our relationship is confined to who we are at the market, Pie Girl and Farmboy, and it's not like he knows any more about me than I do about him. If I'm honest, that's been part of his appeal. He's let me be a lighter, simpler version of myself, and I hadn't realized how nice that could be. How fun. And then that ride through the orchard made me think I could even get used to it, maybe even wanted to get used to it.

Relationships haven't been on my radar since boys still had cooties. I wish that was an exaggeration, but it's not. Sure, I had some school crushes, a few lunchroom dates, but nothing serious. I missed that phase when Mom got sick because I didn't want to leave her alone, and after she was gone and things got bad with Dad and the pills, well, dating pretty much fell straight to the bottom of the priority pile.

Besides, being on the run doesn't exactly leave a lot of time for romance. Especially at the beginning, when Zoe and I were constantly on the move. I knew it was only a matter of time before school or social services caught up to me, so it was all about getting as far away as fast as possible. Even when I slowed down, it wasn't something I cared about. I met people on my travels, sure, and had just enough sex to realize it wasn't something I cared all that much about. Like with the magic, I'm not sure if it's my sex drive that's broken or if it's just me in general, but it made it easier, in a way, knowing I wouldn't be stopping to fall in love anywhere.

Not that I'm doing that now. Falling in love. But I'm doing something, even if it's something I can't define. I've been playing at being a normal girl with Noel and Melly both, acting like I don't have an entire secret life to worry about. I've let myself start getting close to not just one person, but two, and that way can only lead to badness. There's only so far into my world I can bring someone, so much I can show of myself before I have to shut things down. I should know better than to even mess with this fire, but the truth is, I like it too much. It surprises me how much. I like Noel's earnest charm and Melly's passion; I like the happy bees that buzz in my belly when I'm with them. I may be grown now, but I still like playing pretend.

And that's why seeing Noel walk out of that meeting was like taking a rolling pin to the gut. There's nothing pretend about that kind of thing. I know the damage an addict can do, and I know the damage I can do.

It's an impossible mix.

So I do the only thing I can think of.

I avoid him.

I arrive as close to opening as I can in an effort to sidestep the prolonged small talk that has become our morning routine.

The Hollow Hill booth is already set up, and Noel sits on the open tailgate of his truck, long legs dangling. He leaps down when he sees the van pull in and grabs a white paper sack from the bed of the truck.

He doesn't even wait until I have my awning up before he's at my side.

"I come bearing gifts," he says. Zoe, the traitor, rockets out of the van and crashes into his legs.

It's hard to be upset with someone your dog is so fond of, and a tiny part of my brain realizes it's not anger I'm feeling but apprehension. I don't want whatever we might be to implode just yet. So I bury the emotions with busyness, planting the awning poles and setting up my table while Noel plays with Zoe, the white bag at his feet.

I grudgingly appreciate the fact that he doesn't interrupt my setup by offering to help. I have a system, and explaining what I need done would only slow it down. He gets that.

Only once I have pies out does he gather up his bag and give Zoe a final belly rub.

"One week to go," he says, grinning like a kid counting down to Christmas. "I brought you apples." He starts pulling them out of the sack, placing them on my table. Five total, each with a white sticker stuck to it, the apple's variety handwritten across it in scratchy block capitals. "These are what I have the most of in storage. I washed these already in case you wanted to try them now, but the ones still in storage are all waxed, so they'll just need a good scrub before you use them. Or a peel. Either way. I can help. If you want."

He's rambling. It'd be cute if I thought I could still trust him. Staring at his open, excited face and the obvious enthusiasm he has for these apples and this contest, I find myself wondering if maybe I didn't really see him that night. I must've been wrong. There's no way this guy is an addict.

I put the apples back in the bag and tuck them under the table. "I'm going to save them for later." His face falls, and I hurry to say, "So I can give them the attention they deserve. I don't want to get interrupted by customers and forget what I'm tasting."

I luck out with another packed market, and the stream of customers is steady enough to keep Noel in his own booth and me in mine. The hours slip by with barely a break.

But when the vendors start breaking down their booths, everything comes rushing back, including Noel's presence. I remind myself that no matter why he was at that meeting, he's not my father, and just because that ended badly doesn't mean this has to.

"Are you nervous?" he asks as we pack up.

For a second I stare stupidly, thinking he's referring to this thing going on between us that he has no knowledge of.

"Next weekend," he clarifies. "Are you nervous?"

I shake my head, both to clear it and to signal the negative. "Not really. I know my pie is good." An idea hits me like a falling apple. This thing with Noel, I can fix it. Or at least get a handle on it. "Are you busy later?"

"Today? No," he says. "Why?"

"I just realized you don't know what pie I'm entering. I can make up a sample, bring it by tonight?"

"I'd never say no to a special pie delivery," he says. His face takes on a sudden awkwardness, then his lips twitch into an excited smile. "I could make something for dinner? If you want? And we can have pie for dessert?"

His earnestness makes me feel like a complete shit.

"That'd be great," I say. "Seven?"

* * *

I get to the orchard exactly at seven. The miniature honey-cream apple pie feels like a bomb tucked in its wooden Pie Girl box.

I let Zoe out of the truck and take the pie.

Noel pops around from behind the house to call a greeting. Zoe bounds up the hill toward his voice, and I follow.

Here goes everything.

The first thing I notice is that he's changed since the market. Instead of his usual plaid, he has on a smart blue button-down, the sleeves rolled up to his elbows, and his hair is still slightly damp from the shower.

By contrast, I'm still in the same fox-print dress I've had on all day, complete with a dusting of flour where I brushed my hands off, and I can feel frizzy tendrils of hair escaping my braid. I must look l like a slob, but I remind myself this isn't a date.

Far from it.

The second thing I notice is the scent. "What smells amazing?" I ask.

Noel grins and opens the grill with a flourish to reveal a long flatbread, its thin crust charred black along the edges. "Grilled peaches with local goat cheese and red onion. I didn't know if you were vegetarian, so I thought I'd play it safe. The peaches are ours, the last few I had in the freezer."

He deftly slides the pizza onto a cutting board and nods to a picnic table already set up with plates, cups, and condiments. "I figured we could eat outside."

"Works for me." I follow him over and put the pie on the far end of the table. It practically vibrates with possibility inside its box.

Noel pushes aside the wooden bowl of salad to make room for the cutting board and whips out a pizza cutter that he rolls through the flatbread in quick, self-assured passes.

As he serves me, I get the uncomfortable feeling that, to him, maybe this is a date.

Worse, there's a part of me that wants it to be. A big part.

If it were a date, he'd absolutely be winning. The food is incredible. He's even made a honey balsamic dressing for the salad from the orchard honey, and the whole thing is just amazing.

"You could be a chef," I say. "Seriously."

He shrugs modestly. "It's more that I fake it well. I have a few recipes I can really bang out, but I could never work in a professional kitchen. Too much pressure." He gestures at the spread with his salad fork. "This is relaxing to me. If I had to do it for money, I think it'd take the fun out of it."

"That's fair," I say. "But still. It's great."

"Coming from the famous Pie Girl, I'll take that as high praise."

I raise my cider bottle to him in a toast. "As you should."

It's so peaceful here, with the crickets beginning to chirp and Zoe stretched out on the grass, that part of me is tempted to just chuck the pie and forget I ever saw him at that meeting. Would it be so bad to just pretend?

But I know I can't. Not again.

"So who lives here with you?" I ask.

"Just me," he says. "My uncle's pissed about it, but I'm not above claiming squatter's rights."

"Seems like a lot of house for one person."

He laughs. "There's a reason we aren't eating inside. My grandfather was a bit of a hoarder. It's going to take ages to get things back to being presentable."

"And you really want to stay?" I glance at the pie box and decide to be honest with him. I might as well, at least about this. "I've gotten so used to Penny that it'd scare me now, being tied to a place like this. I might not have a lot of living space, but I can take that space anywhere I want. I like that freedom."

"I love it here. I did when I was a kid, and I do now. If I can get the house fixed up and the orchard supporting itself, I could stay here forever." He shrugs that sheepish shrug again. "Who knows, maybe get married someday, have a yard full of dogs, grow old among the apples. There are worse lives to have."

The way he says it makes me almost believe it.

He nudges my foot under the table with his. "So that's the dream you have riding on this whole 'make Hollow Hill famous' campaign. No pressure or anything."

"Lovely."

He pushes his plate aside and reaches for the pie box. "I'm ready to taste the creation that's going to save the orchard."

He slides the lid off and gives an excited little *ooh* sound.

The pie is exactly as I served it at the diner: a thick layer of honey cream topped with a mountain of cider-caramel apples, but this time I've added a sprinkling of honey pecan streusel for crunch.

And magic.

A whole helluva lot of magic.

Chapter Twenty

I snatch the box from him with enough force to rattle the plates on the table. "Don't eat it."

He looks at me like I've gone mad.

I feel like I have.

I slide the lid closed and cradle the box in my lap.

"But I thought that's why you were here," he says, bewildered. "So I could try it?"

I stare at the logo burned into the box top and realize I can't go through with it. "I need to ask you about something."

"Can you ask me over pie?"

"No," I say. The setting sun is painting pink-and-red swaths over the fields of fruit trees, but the knot in my stomach makes it impossible to appreciate it.

"You're kinda scaring me," he says, coming around to sit next to me on the bench.

I nod, more to myself than to him. I trace the Pie Girl logo with the tip of my finger. "On Wednesdays, I donate pies to a domestic violence group at Saint Stan's."

He stiffens beside me, just a fraction, but I feel it, that shifting away. He knows that I know.

"Okay," he says slowly. It sounds like he's on the other side of the orchard, or like I'm underwater.

"And I saw you."

He inhales a long breath and rubs his hands over his face. "Fuck," he mutters. He drops his head into his hands, long fingers grasping at his hair. "It's not what you think."

Blood thunders in my ears. Those same words, echoing in memories that have nothing to do with him, make it hard to think. Zoe, sensing something, comes over and lies across my feet. The solid weight of her keeps me anchored.

"I'm not an addict, I swear." He rakes a hand through his hair and groans. "Shit. The truth isn't going to sound any better."

"I need to hear it," I say.

"It doesn't matter, though."

"It does to me."

Something in my voice must convince him, because he sighs. He leans forward and props his elbows on his knees and doesn't look at me as he speaks. "It's a condition of my probation."

"Explain."

"I used to go to college," he said. "I was studying agribusiness and botany."

Something occurs to me, and I groan. "Please tell me you weren't running the campus pot farm."

He chuckles wryly. "Worse, actually. I had developed my own strain of magic mushrooms. It was part of my research, I swear. There's a theory that micro doses of psilocybin, the stuff that makes mushrooms magic, can practically cure depression and anxiety without the side effects of chemical medication. I'm not smart enough to be a doctor or a therapist, but I can grow things better than most people. I was working on a strain that had a predictable half-life without anything that would trigger the nausea that some people get when they ingest it. Medical marijuana is already an accepted thing, with real research backing it. Mushrooms are going to be the next thing, and I wanted to be ready for it. Beyond the good it could've done, the profits would've kept this place going without question."

It made sense, in a slightly off-kilter kind of way. "So what happened?"

"I needed test subjects. I got caught. Distribution of a class A drug." He shakes his head ruefully. "Should've just stuck to apples."

"You were arrested?"

"It was awful. I've never been so scared in my life."

I find myself softening, believing him.

"In the end, I walked away with probation and an expulsion. It's a good thing I was a white kid at a hippie college. It could've been a lot worse."

"Indeed." The pie is leaden in my lap.

"And really, it all kind of worked out. My grandfather got sick right after that, and I was able to help out. It's not like I was busy with school or anything. I'm glad I had that time with him."

We sit in silence for several minutes.

"Thank you," I say finally. "For telling me."

He shrugs. "I probably would've told you at some point anyway."

"Yeah?"

"Yeah. Eventually. Friends always tell each other their dirt, right?" He nudges his shoulder into mine. "So has my confession earned me pie?"

I don't know if it's the magic of this place, with its purpling sky and rolling hills, or the naked honesty in Noel's face, or maybe just the heady effects of the cider, but I shake my head. "No."

"Seriously?"

"You said we're friends?"

"Well, yeah," he says, like it's the most obvious thing in the world. "At least I hope we are."

"Me too." And then, before I can change my mind, I say, "So friends tell friends dirt, right?"

He cocks his head at me. "Then I get pie?"

"If you still want to eat it, yes."

* * *

I tell him everything, starting with how we've always kept the Ellery name as an homage to the magic, even when it wasn't acceptable for women to use their own names after marriage. I tell him about the magic, the women who bore it, and about Penny.

"Penny started as my grandmother's, a gift from her own mother around the time mine was born. My grandfather thought the RV would be perfect for family getaways, but Nana had other ideas. She made Grandpa strip everything out of the kitchen and living space and turned the RV into her personal sewing studio. Women would come to see her for all sorts of party dresses, and she'd stitch hope and happiness into each one. She did more christening gowns than she could count, with wishes of long and healthy lives sewn into the soft linings. She even did wedding dresses with love and patience embroidered around each bead and bit of lace."

"That sounds like a Disney movie, not real life."

"It practically was. The magic tailored into Nana's dresses was an open secret and a skill that was not passed on, much to the community's disappointment, to my mother."

"So everyone knew? And just accepted it?"

"In small towns, everyone knows everything, and word spread from there. I'm sure there was a time further back where it had to be kept secret, but Nana never hid it. Neither did Mom. It's not like they advertised it, really, but it wasn't a secret. I'm sure if I stayed, someday I would've been called the magic pie lady."

Even in the growing dusk, I can see the deep furrow that creases his brow and worry that he's trying to decide how to tell me I've lost my mind. I sit very still, although my heart is dancing like water on a hot skillet.

"I have a cousin," he says, and I'm thrown by the non-sequitur. "Well, step-cousin, technically, but we grew up together. She talks to animals. Or I guess *with* them is more accurate. Like everyone talks to their pets, but with Ivy it's different. It's silent, and when she's done she can tell you everything about that animal—what he feels, what he likes, what he knows. It used to freak me out when we were little because she'd say she could see their mind pictures. My uncle acted like she was just making it up, but Auntie Cora said it was her magic talent. And it did seem like magic. Real magic."

I grin. "Like a Disney movie."

"If Disney wrote about animal communicators who talk to the pets of murder victims to find out if they saw the killer, then yes, exactly like a Disney movie."

"Get out. That's what she does?"

"Gets paid for it and everything," he says. "And she does pet therapy too, mostly for cats who are unhappy with their human servants."

"I have to meet your cousin," I say, imagining the tales Zoe could tell.

"Oh no," he says. "I don't think we're quite at the meeting-my-crazy-family stage of things yet. I'd rather you not run screaming for the hills. Besides, we're still talking about your family. Tell me more about your mom. She couldn't sew?" Noel asks.

"Not to save her life," I say with a laugh. "But Nana didn't care. Her own mother's magic had been entwined with gardens and flower arranging, and Nana knew Mom's would manifest in its own way, and eventually it showed up in the braids and curls she styled in her friends' hair. She studied cosmetology in high school and then spent years styling confidence and self-love into the hair of the women in her chairs. She used to say people came to her to talk as much as to get their hair done, and I think if she didn't have the magic, she might've been a therapist. She would tailor the magic to what they talked about. She always said a good haircut might not change your whole life, but it might change the part that needs it most."

"Did she have Penny too?"

I nod. "When I was little, she turned it into a mobile salon so she didn't have to put me in day care. Every day we'd go to a different nursing home or hospice and she'd offer her services to the women who couldn't make it to a regular salon. I practically grew up in the bedroom, watching her talk and take care of all these doddery old ladies." I laugh. "Even now, I can still smell the perm solution. So. Many. Perms."

"It's the official hairstyle of little old ladies everywhere," Noel says.

Sharp on the heels of the scent memory is what comes next, and it's harder to talk about, but I do. "The magic for these women was full of comfort and compassion, and when Mom got sick and started to look like her dying clients, I tried to remember that. I tried to bake it into pies, along with love and a cure, but no matter what I did, the pies soured with sadness. Mom ate them anyway."

A lump like a peach pit lodges in my throat, and I have to stop to swallow it. Noel leans into me, just slightly, so his upper arm and thigh are pressed into mine, a reassuring sense of solidity in the darkening night.

"Cancer?" he asks.

"Ovarian, but that's not what killed her. It didn't have a chance to. My dad, he couldn't cope with her diagnosis," I say, keeping my voice level, recalling only the events and not the emotions. "He always liked to drink, but it got worse after she got sick. He was like a whole different person. He'd disappear for whole nights and come stumbling home the next afternoon without even an apology. He was driving the night she died. They hit a tree. He broke both of his legs, but she was killed. The police said it was instant, but who knows. Things got worse after that. The doctors gave him Percocet like they were Skittles. He became a zombie."

"That's why seeing me at the meeting freaked you out," Noel says.

"Right. I get that it's a disease, addiction, but that doesn't mean it's not traumatic. There's collateral damage. I've been that damage and once was enough, so when I thought I might be facing that again with you, I wigged. Which was completely unfair when you've given me zero reason to think that, even with an addiction, you'd be anything like my dad. I mean, for one thing, you were at a meeting, which is more than he ever tried." I stop because the peach pit is back in my throat. I've never told this story to anyone, and I'm not sure I can finish it. I want to, though, because it's Noel. "It was the worst when I was in high school. Social services were sniffing around, so I did everything I could to cover for him. I went to school and got good grades; I made sure we had enough money to keep the lights on and took care of the house. I tried fixing it with pie. I just wanted to get my old dad back, but no matter how much happiness and love I worked into the crusts, he barely ate a bite. The last one was different."

It's dark now, the bright glow of a nearly full moon providing the only illumination, and I'm glad. It makes it easier to finish telling the story.

"Two days before my seventeenth birthday, I found a letter from social services confirming that they'd found a group home that could take me. I would've lost Zoe. I would've lost everything. I tried to talk to him about it, get him to act, but he said it was for the best." The memory of that conversation is like a fist around my throat. "So I made a pie, because that's what I do when the world is ending. I put everything I had into it, every desperate hope, every ounce of begging. It was an edible plea to make it stop."

I'm silent for a moment, and Noel asks quietly, "But it didn't?"

"Oh, it did all right. He died that night."

Noel's intake of breath is sharp in the still night, but his voice is nothing but gentle. "Daisy, you can't possibly blame yourself for that."

His sympathy could break me if I let it, so I plow forward. "I blamed the drugs." Not quite true, but not quite a lie either. "I left the next day. Took Zoe and the van and just left." I sit back until the picnic table presses into my spine. "And here we are."

Now it's Noel's turn to sit in silence, reflecting on what he's just heard. He takes his time, and I don't rush him. It's a lot to process.

Finally, he turns to me, profile silhouetted in the moonlight and asks, "So what's in this pie?"

"Honesty and candor," I say. He laughs. "And honey cream, cider-caramel apples, and crunchy-munchy honey pecan topping."

"Well, I'll still eat it if you will," he says.

Chapter Twenty-One

The messages start in the middle of the night, the incessant pinging of my phone sounding like an alarm in the dark.

First, it's just photos, shots of Penny parked outside the library, a rain-streaked image from the rally, several from the farmers' market, including one of Noel and me on Penny's steps and one that zooms in tight on Zoe. Marissa06906's looping driveway with my truck parked near the fountain. A shot of my bedroom. Taken from inside it.

They're professional, high-resolution zooms, and they're the visual equivalent of being woken up by having a bucket of ice water dumped on me.

I keep scrolling. Shots of Penny parked behind the diner, me walking to the kitchen, and one of me and Juan sitting on milk crates at the back door during a break, bathed in the warm glow of the light above the door. It would've been a nice shot in any context except this.

My phone chirps faster than I can scroll, messages stacking up below the ones I'm looking at.

Fear forces me up into a sitting position, and Zoe stretches into my warm spot, oblivious to this unseen threat.

The messages turn to texts.

Time is running out.

Destroy them before I destroy you.

Your family ruined mine. This is how you repay me.

That stops me. Shit. Is it someone connected to a murder pie? Someone other than the woman who ordered it? A brother, maybe, or a friend?

But no, it says "your family," not me specifically.

More messages come before I can work it out.

You stole my childhood, I will not lose my future.

They must be silenced.

I will expose you.

A perverse laugh bubbles in my chest. Expose me as what exactly? The magic murder-pie girl? That'll go over well.

I have evidence.

Another photo, this time of my recipe box, the cards spread out like a winning poker hand.

Another photo, an obituary for one Victor Layton, of Stamford, Connecticut, who left behind his loving wife Marissa.

I can make her talk.

I have connections.

Do not disobey me.

I will ruin you.

You owe me.

I know about November 5.

Another photo, grainier than the rest, as if taken with a different camera, maybe in a different time.

It's the house I grew up in.

Another photo arrives, a blurred crop from the previous one, framing only the back porch.

There are parts I didn't tell Noel about that night, that I've never told anyone. Parts no one could possibly know about unless they were there.

Flashes of memory sear like flashbulbs behind my closed eyes.

Remember, remember the fifth of November.

As if I could ever forget.

The phone shakes in my trembling hand. Another ping, then another. Two more texts.

I know the truth.

Deliver the pies.

* * *

I'm at Kerenza's door before seven. According to her company's website, their offices open at eight, so if I want to catch her, it has to be early.

The lemon raspberry pie, with its pillowy cloud of meringue, is heavy in my hands.

I ring the doorbell and set off a cacophony of excited barking. I glance back at the truck, hoping Zoe won't join in the chorus.

The door opens to reveal a confused-looking blond girl. I recognize her from the website's photo. "Yes?"

I put on my best pie smile, start my pitch. "Hi, I'm sorry to show up so early, but I wanted to catch you before work. You're the recipient of one of our free pies."

Two small poodle mixes try to sneak past her legs, and she blocks them with a foot. "I didn't order a pie."

"I know. It's a gift," I say. "May I bring it in?"

Another dog joins the fray at the door, and flustered, she says, "Yes, sure. I have to be getting to work, though."

I slip in and shut the door behind me. "I know."

Her little dogs sniff my legs excitedly, unaware that I'm about to turn their owner's life completely upside down.

"Should it go in the fridge?" Kerenza asks.

"Unless you want to eat it for breakfast," I say, sliding the top off the box and setting the pie on her kitchen counter. I baked it in the small hours of the morning, working calming magic into the crust, not murder.

I will not kill these women, no matter what he thinks he can blackmail me with. I may not be an angel, but I don't work for devils.

She giggles, like having pie before work would be the most scandalous thing ever, and I hate what I'm about to do.

"Actually, the pie isn't the only reason I'm here," I say. She looks at me curiously but without fear. It's a look that won't last. There's no tactful way to phrase the next question, so I just ask, "Can you think of anyone who might want you dead?"

She gives a surprised little chuckle. "What? No, of course not." She looks around like I'm setting her up for some kind of prank. "Who are you?"

"The person trying to help you. Do you happen to know an Emma Rogers or Brittany Cline?"

She mulls it over. "Emma Rogers, no, I don't think so, but I was at school with a Brittany Cline. Why?"

"High school or college?"

"College. UMass. We were in the same dorm. Friendly but not really friends, if that makes sense. Why?"

My brain fizzes with this, the first real link between the women. This has to be it. They work in different fields, live in different towns, but they were all at UMass. He knows them from school.

"Because someone wants her dead too. And Emma Rogers, who was also at UMass." I pull up Galen and Harris on my phone and show her Emma's staff photo. "You're sure you don't know her?"

She studies the picture and shakes her head. "It was a big school, though."

"Do you have any idea where Brittany lives now?"

"No. I don't even know if she graduated, to be honest. I didn't see her after junior year, but she might've got off-campus housing or something."

This is interesting. "Did either of you have any conflicts with anyone while you were students?"

Something about the question is like throwing a switch, and her bemusement morphs into a shuttered hostility. Everything about her face closes in, becomes a mask.

"I think you need to leave," she says crisply.

"Who was it?" I ask. She knows. She has a name. "Please. There are women in danger. You can help protect them." It's a slimy guilt trip of a thing to say, but I'm desperate.

"I would like you to go." Her mouth sets into a rigid line that makes her look older than she is, harder.

"Please. I'm on his list too, only I don't know why. I don't know who he is," I say.

"Then it's not the same person." She folds her arm across her chest, but it's as much a gesture of comfort as defiance. "I really have to get to work. Please don't come back here again."

I leave because it's obvious I won't get any more from her and I've already gotten more than I had. At the door, I say, "If you change your mind about that name—"

"I won't."

"I'm online as the Pie Girl," I continue, as if she hadn't interrupted. "It's easy to find. Either way, be careful."

I email Emma from the truck, asking if we can meet. I get an immediate out-of-office reply saying she won't be back until Monday. I curse myself for not getting her phone number when we met at Saint Stan's the other night.

It's okay, though. I have a lead. It's more than I had when I woke up.

My phone dings moments later, and I think maybe Emma saw the email anyway, but no, it's a text from Melly.

> *Finals finally done! Let's do something fun since you're ditching me this weekend.*

The next comes almost immediately: *And don't say you have pies to make. You're your own boss. You can give yourself a day off.*

I shake my head. The truth is, I do have pies to make; I always have pies to make. But a few hours away won't kill me.

Ok, I text back. *But I make the plans.*

She writes back at once. *Intriguing. I'll wait at the library.*

I'm not sure why I decided to be in charge of this little outing, except that it's novel. Or maybe I just wanted a little control over something somewhere in my life that isn't pies. Everything lately, from my mystery man to the contest to whatever has been brewing—if there really is anything brewing at all—with Noel and Melly all seems to be whirling around me. I want to do some whirling of my own.

As promised, Melly is waiting on the front steps of the campus library when I get there. I've swung back to the diner to drop Zoe off and to promise Frank I'll be back in plenty of time to get his pies done. It's given me just enough time to figure out where we're going.

"So what's the plan, Pie Girl?" Melly asks, after she hops in the truck. She's dressed in black skinny jeans and a tight purple T-shirt that matches her hair. She stretches one combat-boot-clad foot up onto the dashboard, folds the other under her, and leans against the door so she can watch me.

Something about the casual confidence and the unapologetic way she sprawls out makes me smile. "You'll see."

The drive into Springfield is easy at this time of day, with the commuter traffic cleared and the casino crowd not yet awake. While the colleges are mostly finished with classes, the elementary and high schools are still in session, so I'm expecting we'll have the place mostly to ourselves.

I take the side streets and can't help noticing how much easier it is without pulling Penny behind. Melly's alternating between watching me and gazing at the passing houses with a slight quirk to her eyebrow.

"Any guesses?" I ask.

"I have literally no idea where we are," she says with a laugh. "All I know about Springfield is that there's a casino and a crime problem, and I'm guessing it has nothing to do with either of those."

"You would be correct."

For a slapdash plan, I think I've picked a pretty good spot. I pull into a mostly empty parking lot, and we get out, crossing a quiet street to our destination. "The Quadrangle," I announce, knowing it doesn't answer the question. Springfield may not be the nicest city, but this part is like its own little world. A grassy center square, filled with huge bronze sculptures of Dr. Seuss characters, is closed in by five art and history museums, a massive library, and an old stone cathedral. I point to the library at the far end. "They invited me to park here for their summer reading party last year, and I just thought it was a cool place."

Aside from us, the only other people here are an old couple sitting on a bench and a young guy heading toward the library. The sun is shining, the air is warm, and I have to admit it's nice, being out in the world like this.

Melly approaches one of the statues, a life-sized Seuss sitting in a chair beside a person-sized Cat in the Hat, and considers its little plaque. She gestures at the bronze author. "You know he was a flaming racist, right?"

"Yes," I say, because I already knew those statues would be the one thing that might throw this off. "But we're not here for Seuss."

"No?"

"You have two choices," I say, hooking my arm through hers the way she did that first day when she ambushed me at the college. I spin her toward one of the museums. "The science museum has dinosaurs. It's really for kids, but I consider dinosaurs to be equal opportunity."

"I concur," she says. "Second choice?"

I pull her in a one-eighty so we're facing the opposite way. "Or we have a traveling exhibit from the Museum of Bad Art."

She bursts out laughing. "That. Definitely that. And then dinosaurs."

I feel a glow of pride for having landed on something that pleases her. Inside the museum, the docent directs us to the second floor, where the Bad Art exhibit is housed, and even though the museum seems empty aside from us, we both find ourselves whispering and stifling giggles as we try to find the absolute worst piece of art. We decide on a pair of alien-looking blue bunnies with frazzled expressions on their cartoonish faces and naked human nipples on their little bunny chests.

"I bet we can find other things here that belong in this collection," Melly says in a low voice, close to my ear. Her breath is warm on my skin, and unexpected goose bumps erupt at the nearness of her. A little snort tells me she's noticed, but she doesn't comment. Instead, she just takes my hand in hers, easy as can be. "Come on, Pie Girl, let's go find them."

In that instant, with her palm warm against my own, I'm hit with an urge to tell her everything, the same story I told Noel. It would be easy, almost, to whisper it in these hushed rooms, but something stops me. I'm enjoying this moment too much for exactly what is: a desperately needed break from the pie-related stress in my life. There will be plenty of time for pie. Today is about bad art and dinosaurs and the electric feel of her fingers in mine.

We spend a pleasant hour roaming the museum and find at least three paintings that we decide are contenders for the visiting exhibit and another two we don't agree on.

"That dog looks like a baby," I insist. "It's horrible. Like the artist never saw a real dog in his life and just figured slapping fur on an infant would do the trick."

"Nope, it's disturbing and I like it," Melly says. She drags me back to her choice. "This one is literally of a dead duck hanging above someone's dinner. It has to go."

"The content is gross, but the painting itself is really well done. Look at the colors," I say, like I have half a clue what I'm talking about.

"Look at the duck," she says. "It's dead."

"You're not wrong," I say, but I draw it out like she might be.

"Ha! I win," she says. "Mine is worse than yours."

"Fine, you win," I concede. "I still think the dog-child is worse, but I'll allow you your victory."

"Hey, I earned it fair and square."

"Does that mean you don't want to go to the science museum and look at actual dead things?" I ask.

"I was promised dinosaurs," she says. "I expect dinosaurs. And then lunch?"

"Lunch?" I ask as we stroll through the Seuss sculpture garden to the science museum. "What happened to food is a waste of time?"

She bumps me with her shoulder, then stays there, snugged close to my arm. "I didn't say I didn't need it, just that it bores me. But you don't, and it is kind of tradition to partake of food while on a date, isn't it?"

"I wouldn't know," I say with a laugh.

"Well, I do, and it is."

"Dinos and lunch it is, then."

One thing I hadn't counted on was the science museum being packed with a horde of third graders on a field trip. A pair of harried-looking teachers are attempting to herd them into a single group, but kids shoot off in all directions, and in the end, we do little more than say hi to the dinosaurs. Before we leave, we ask the lady at the desk for restaurant recommendations, and she points us to an Italian place a short walk away and tells us we absolutely must order a house salad to share because the dressing is to die for. We assure her we will.

The sidewalks are crowded with people happy to be out in the sun, and I'm hit with a wave of nostalgia for something I've never really had: a normal life.

I don't know what I'm doing with Melly any more than I know what I'm doing with Noel, but I know it's nice, this thing I've never let myself do. Socializing. Having friends. Having more, maybe.

Since I left home, not getting close to people has been vital in keeping myself safe—safe as in not compromising the Pies Before Guys mission, safe as in staying out of the system, but also safe as in not getting hurt. I've already lost everyone in my life once, and I don't want to do it again. The easiest way to ensure that has always been to make sure there's no one there to lose.

But now I don't know. Maybe the risk is worth it to be able to have days like this, horseback rides through orchards. It's addicting, in its way, the intimate talks and silly conversations, even the casual physical contact. I forgot how nice it can be just to be near someone.

With Noel, I'm in my element; he's comfortable and homey. Melly is intense, a force of nature I don't always understand but I like. It's self-indulgent and more than a little bit dangerous to be letting my guard down so much around either of them, never mind both, but for right now, I'm enjoying it too much to stop.

Chapter Twenty-Two

Even though we leave with plenty of time, I'm irrationally worried we're going to miss judging.

"I'm not sure scheduling deliveries for the day of the contest was your best idea," Noel says from the passenger seat. We dropped Zoe off at Juan's before we left because, after receiving those photos, I wasn't comfortable leaving her alone in the van. Juan's dogs happily swept her into the pack, and I'm sure I'll have a tired pup when I get back.

"It's on the way." In addition to the wooden box I have containing my contest pie, there are two white boxes tied with pink twine on the floor between Noel's feet. The contest pie has the same low-dose farmer's market magic that's become my default, but the variety of cutie pies filling the white boxes are packed to the brim with a disregard for rules and a desire to be helpful.

GPS tells me to turn left onto a one-way street full of oncoming traffic, and I switch it off. Sometimes technology is more trouble than it's worth. I have a good enough idea of where we need to be.

The registrar's office is housed in the Whitmore Administration Building, smack in the heart of the sprawling campus.

Deciding to act like a proper Masshole, I throw my hazards on and double park next to a Jeep. "Be fast," I tell Noel. "I can't afford a ticket."

He takes the white boxes, unfolds himself from the passenger seat, and disappears inside. It takes him a full ten minutes to make the delivery, during which I do my best impression of a traffic cone and thank the stars it's not term time, or else I definitely would've been ticketed.

Noel returns, looking flustered, and I pull into traffic before he even has his door shut. According to my errant GPS, it should take us only twelve minutes to get to Hotel Northampton for judging, but I'll believe that only if we get there.

"No one in the office seemed to know they ordered pie," Noel says, "but they were damn happy to take them anyway."

"Good."

The trip ends up taking twenty-seven minutes. We're greeted at the lobby by an older woman at a desk who is handling check-ins.

"Name?" she asks.

"Daisy Ellery."

She scrolls through her iPad with studied concentration. "Ah, yes, here we are. Pie?"

"Hollow Hill Honey Apple."

"Lovely," she says, tapping something and spinning the iPad to face me. "Just give me a squiggle here, and you'll be all set." I sign my name with my finger where she indicates, and she hands me a folder. "You'll be entry number sixty-six. Take this hall here, then you'll see signs. Good luck, dear."

"If I'm sixty-six, how many more do you think there are?" I ask Noel, flipping through the folder. There's a name badge, a page of rules, a list of local restaurants and attractions, and a copy of the scorecard the judges will be using.

"Apparently a *lot*," Noel says, stopping in the doorway.

He's right. The long tables lining the room are absolutely filled with pies. The smell is incredible, fruit and spice and sugar blending into a heady perfume. There are people milling around, admiring the entries, but the stern-faced men and women behind the tables keep them from getting too close. The judges? Pie police?

We find spot sixty-six, and I have a moment of panic when I take the box from Noel. What if the apples have slid off or the custard has collapsed?

I slip the lid off and exhale. Perfect.

I place the pie on the table along with the recipe card.

"Shall we check out the competition?" Noel asks.

"Let's."

The array and quality are vast. Everything from humble cherry to exotic dragon fruit, artfully woven lattices to burnt edges.

"Can you imagine trying all these?" Noel asks. He looks equal parts excited and horrified by the prospect, and I laugh.

"That's what these are for," I say, fishing the scorecard out the folder. "It would take forever if one person was judging all of this." The pies will be judged on a number of objective criteria by a panel of judges, with each factor being worth one to ten points. Those totals will determine the placings. In the event of a tie for first, the dueling pies will be sampled by the entire panel and the new scorecards will determine the winner.

The list of criteria is exhaustive, including visual appeal, mouthfeel, structure, flavor profile, crust, filling, interplay of elements, and state representativeness, plus a ton of subheadings.

Pies are due in the judging room by noon, but the winners won't be announced until three in the ballroom, leaving entrants with a good chunk of time to kill. Many will be swarming the local restaurants and shops, but Noel and I are going back to school.

* * *

This time I do take the time to find an actual parking spot, since this part of the mission is my responsibility.

"Why are we doing this again?" Noel asks.

"Because I need them to help me with something." I don't want to tell Noel the full story. I can't, not without revealing what Pies Before Guys is, and that's something I have no intention of doing. I give him a half-truth instead. "Someone's been nosing around Penny and bothering some of my customers. I'm trying to find out who it is."

Noel looks aghast. "Shouldn't you tell the police about it at home?"

I shake my head. "It's not that serious. Really."

"It is if there's a guy hanging around the van you live in," he insists. "What if he tries to get in? Attack you?"

"Thanks for the reassurance, Knight in Shining Armor," I say with a wry smile.

"I'm serious. You could get hurt."

Or someone could.

"You put something in their pies, didn't you?" he asks.

"Just a little extra motivation to be helpful," I say innocently.

"And you made me your accomplice."

"Yup."

I leave him in the lobby so as not to risk him giving me away and go inside. The girl at the information desk has a half-eaten cutie pie on a napkin and a pile of crumbs that says it isn't her first. Perfect.

"I was wondering if you could help me with something," I say.

"Of course," she says cheerfully. "What can I do for you?"

"I'm hoping to get a list of all the male students who graduated within the last ten years," I say, as if it's the most normal request in the world.

"I'm not sure I can do that," she says, still smiling.

"Can't as in don't have access or not allowed?"

"I think not allowed," she says.

"I'm not looking for grades or any private information like that, just names. If you can filter it by Massachusetts residents, that would be even better. It would be a huge help." I lean into the last sentence, hoping the pies have her primed to be on my side.

"Just names?"

I give her my best smile. "Just names."

"Let me see what I can do."

She types something into her computer and clicks around with the mouse, and within minutes the printer beneath her desk whirs to life.

* * *

We get back to Northampton with an hour to spare and take full advantage of the taco truck that's parked near the hotel. Armed with lunch, we grab a bench and settle in to people-watch. Even in the middle of the day, the sidewalks are full of shoppers and buskers, everyone from the hippiest college students to smartly dressed older women who look like they own art galleries.

"There's something to be said for food that comes from trucks," Noel says around a mouthful of chicken taco.

"You should have them at the orchard, like the craft breweries do. Are craft cideries a thing?" I turn the word over in my head, liking the sound of it. "If they're not, they should be. People could make an afternoon of it, go get lunch and cider." I bump his shoulder with mine. "I can do savory hand pies for you, maybe dose them with a little brand loyalty and a craving for appley goodness."

He laughs. "I like it."

I'm about to expand on the plan when I realize there's someone watching us watch the throngs of pedestrians. A man in a medium-blue suit and a red tie is standing on the sidewalk across the street, just looking at us. There's something familiar about him. "Noel. I think that guy is watching us."

"What? Where?" he says.

Before I can point him out, the man nods and says something we can't hear. He turns and touches his ear, removing a Bluetooth earpiece that he drops in his jacket pocket. I shake my head at my own stupidity. Not a creeper, just a guy staring into space on the phone.

"Never mind, it's nothing. Seriously, though, pies and cider are a winning combination," I say, my voice trailing off when I clock a very welcome trio of men descending on our bench. I almost drop my jackfruit taco in shock. "What are you guys doing here?"

Juan beams, pulls me up into a hug. "Supporting our Pie Girl!"

Flanking him are his husband Eric and a cranky-looking Frank. A cranky-looking Frank who is wearing a bow tie and suspenders.

"You guys didn't have to do this," I say.

"Of course we did," Frank says gruffly. "Gonna be good for business to put this award in the window."

I laugh. "Well, I appreciate it."

I introduce them all to Noel, and we head inside together.

The ballroom is standing-room-only and, unlike the judging room, smells more like people than pie. It's a space more suited to weddings than pie contests, with an ornate chandelier and arched windows, but I kind of like the excess.

"All this for some damn pies," Franks mutters. Juan winks at me, and I bite back a smile.

A metal stage has been erected at one end of the room, with a podium off to one side and a trio of uneven boxes in the center, like they have for the Olympics. Each is draped with a thick ribbon.

When the door nearest the stage opens, a hush falls over the crowd. Mayor Ayanna Illiya steps up to the podium, a group of judges in chef coats behind her.

"I would like to thank you all for coming," she says, her voice as warm as pie. "Having lived in Hampshire County for most of my life, it is an honor to be judging this particular group of entries. There is something special about pie. It brings people together. That sharing, that connecting over something as simple and homey as a good piece of pie, is something everyone needs right now, more than ever. To the women who have entered, I know many of you have questioned whether you belong in this room or with the group protesting in Boston, and let me assure you that you can do both. One does not negate the other." She holds up a placating hand as some grumbles erupt in the corner. "I know you're all eager to get to the winners, so I won't belabor the point. But pie is more than dessert. It's love. It's comfort. It's home. Pie matters."

There's a smattering of applause, and Noel leans in. "Told you."

I roll my eyes at him, but he's right. He did.

"So without further ado," Mayor Illiya says, "let me introduce you to our winners. There were many amazing pies entered today, but our three winners stood out for their phenomenal flavor, technical expertise, and Massachusetts-inspired ingredients. I would like to welcome our third-place winner to the stage: Ms. Marjorie Athelny, whose cranberry-orange pie is something that belongs on every Thanksgiving menu."

Applause fills the room as a shrunken old lady with a wizened face like a raisin takes the stage. She shakes the mayor's hand and accepts the ribbon one of the judges drapes around her neck with a look of astonished wonder.

"Second place goes to Mx. Cory Barrow. Their entry was an exquisite maple sugar pie, made with maple syrup sourced from their family's very own farm in South Hadley."

The crowd erupts as Cory takes the stage, fists raised in triumph. It sounds like half the audience is here just for them. They accept their ribbon with an exaggerated bow, and I find myself cheering along with the rest of the audience.

As the applause dies down, fingers lace into mine. Noel's hand is warm, his grip strong and reassuring. I squeeze back, heart suddenly racing, although I'm not entirely sure whether it's more from anticipation or the feel of his hand in mine. Either way, it's the good kind of racing.

One thing I've learned is that there are moments in your life that change the course of it, and most of the time you never see them coming. But this time I'm staring right at it. One outcome, things go back to normal. Another outcome and I have a chance to make a new kind of difference with my pies.

"And finally," Mayor Illiya says with gravitas, "our winner. This pie wowed the judges with its originality, its interplay of elements, and its commitment to locally sourced ingredients. It is outstanding on every level. It is with great pleasure that I award first place and entrance into the finals to Ms. Daisy Ellery for her Hollow Hill Honey Apple Pie."

The applause roars in my ears like the sea in a shell, and I'm engulfed by the crashing wave of Noel and Juan and Eric's group hug.

"Guys, I have to go up there." I laugh, my head spinning.

They let me go, and I make my way to the stage, smoothing the skirt of my dress, and shake hands with Mayor Illiya. As cameras flash, she says, "You better believe I took a picture of that recipe."

"I'll make you one anytime," I tell her.

"I might hold you to that."

One of the judges comes forward to drape the blue ribbon around my neck and directs me to the blocks for photos. Cory Barrow fist-bumps me as I take my place on the first-place platform.

Time for the big leagues.

Chapter Twenty-Three

I don't have time to glory in my win or worry about the path it's set me on.

In the days following the contest, the PBG account gets spammed with messages from RememberRemember, and I know it's time to end this.

I pour through the list of names from UMass, searching for any I remotely recognize. If this guy claims to know me, it stands to reason that I know him, but no one jumps out at me.

I've sent another email to Emma, and while this one didn't get an out-of-office response, it hasn't gotten any other kind either.

I establish that Brittany Cline must be living with someone, is using a prepaid cell phone, and/or is going by a different name, because none of my extra search services turn anything up. Brittany Cline is either the most technophobic twentysomething in the country or she really doesn't want to be found.

My phone pings with another PBG message. *End them or I end you.* Another with a screenshot of a news article about the pie contest. *Finish this by July 4th or that contest will be your funeral.*

I'm tempted to throw the phone out the truck's window, but I don't. It won't help.

"Men are dumb," I tell Zoe. She thumps her tail in agreement.

Noel is waiting when we pull into Hollow Hill, and I can't help smiling at the sight of him. "Well, this one's not bad," I amend. I open the door and let her out. She waits when she lands, muscles quivering with excitement, and I flick my hand to release her. "Go play."

She rockets off toward the barn in an erratic path of zooming loops, tongue lolling out of her mouth. "Thanks for taking her again," I tell Noel.

"Happy to," he says, but concern creases his forehead. "You're sure everything is okay?"

"It will be."

* * *

I drive Noel's truck into town and past the diner for the third night in a row. I loop around until I'm on a residential street behind the diner, close but inconspicuous. I turn the engine and the lights off and settle in to wait.

The security camera has been a bust so far, but with the media coverage and increased messages, my gut tells me my mystery man is going to show up again.

And I'm going to be ready.

The camera is mounted on the back of the diner, pointed straight at Penny's door and set to activate if anything enters a sixty-five-foot area around it. When it triggers, I'll get a notification, and while I could do this surveillance remotely, I don't just want to see his face. I want to follow him home.

The night air is warm and still. Under other circumstances, say back at the orchard with Noel and Zoe, it would be quite pleasant. But the thing TV never tells you about stakeouts is how mind-numbingly dull they are.

The low growl of a motorcycle engine jars me out of my reverie. I tense, keeping the engine off. Just because it's a motorcycle doesn't mean it's my man. I wait, and my phone vibrates. A black-and-white photo of a motorcycle in range of Penny. The next shot shows him closer, then off the bike. I will him to take his helmet off, show his face, but he doesn't. The next photo is him approaching Penny's door, and something in me snaps. The patience and planning go right out the window. I don't even think; I just act.

Moving faster than I've ever moved in my life, I throw myself out of the truck and sprint through an empty yard into the diner's back lot. I rush him from behind, my soft-soled Keds almost silent on the blacktop, and shove him face-first into the side of the van. His helmeted head bounces off the thin metal siding, but having the element of surprise means I also have the upper hand, at least for a few more seconds.

I jab the narrow end of the rolling pin hard into his kidney, and a high-pitched yelp of pain is smothered by his helmet. I do it again, then spin him so he's facing me. I jam the rolling pin horizontally across his throat, where the big helmet offers no protection.

And I push.

Hard.

"Helmet off," I order. "Now."

Gloved hands fumble at the chin strap.

I keep the pressure on the rolling pin, one hand on each end, as he pushes the helmet up, tossing it aside to reveal a chin-length mop of purple curls.

I stagger back, the rolling pin falling limp at my side. "What the fuck?"

"I could say the same thing," Melly says, massaging her lower back. "Shit, that hurts. Did you seriously just assault me with a rolling pin?"

"You're RememberRemember?" I can't make sense of this. There's no way she could know about November fifth, no way a feminist as strident as her could want three women dead. No way. "What are you doing here?"

"What are you?" she asks. "I thought you were spending the night with your farm friend again. Which, by the way, kind of rankles me, because I thought we had a thing going on after that little museum date."

The rolling pin twitches at my side. Hurt and confusion are warring within me. "Was that real? Any of it?"

"Of course it was," she says, a rawness in her voice that I force myself to ignore.

"Then why are you doing this?"

She hesitates long enough for me to see the lies spinning in her mind. My fingers tighten, rage and betrayal prodding me to return the rolling pin to her throat. In the dull glow of the streetlight, I can see her looking between it and my face, and she sees something that makes her deflate.

"We should talk," she says. "Inside?"

The thought of her inside Penny makes my skin crawl. "No," I say. I point the rolling pin to the back door of the diner. "There will do."

"As you wish."

We each take a milk crate and sit facing each other, me nearer the door so she has to make it by me if she tries to escape. Above her head, the faint green glow of the camera's power light mocks me. I tuck the fabric of my skirt between my legs and lean forward, elbow propped on my knee, rolling pin still in my right hand, and for a long moment the only sound is the moths bumping against the dim light above the diner's back door. Finally, when I'm mostly sure I can do it without losing it on her, I say, "Talk."

The black leather jacket and dark pants make her nearly invisible below the neck. She studies me for several moments and says, "I know who you are."

"Elaborate."

"I know what you can do. With the pies. I knew about the magic before I invited you to the rally. I almost asked you to make ones that would convince people to take a stand, but I figured I could do that myself, no magic necessary."

She grins like it might be funny, but fury burrows into my chest like a pissed-off possum. This. This is why I don't let people in. This is why I keep moving. It was a mistake—Turnbridge, settling down, thinking I could have some kind of normal life. Of course I can't, not both. Not when I do the things I do.

I think about how close I came to telling her the truth when we were on our date, about the magic and my family, and feel impossibly stupid. She knew all along and let me believe I was just a normal girl on a normal date. A snake of fear grips my heart, because if she knows about the magic, she could know about the rest. "Tell me what you know about the magic exactly."

She shrugs. "That you can, like, cast spells on pies. They can make people happy or horny or wicked smart for a while. I don't know how, but I know it's cool."

"That's it?"

"That's not enough?"

It's not, but there's no way I can question her further without revealing the truth. I tap the rolling pin against my calf in frustration.

She pulls in a long breath and lets it go in a sharp burst. "Look, I didn't mean for things to get like this. I didn't expect to actually like you as much as I do, for one thing. And I think magic pies are badass. He said you come from a family of actual witches. It's amazing."

"He who?" I ask, fighting to keep control of my voice. None of this feels real. "Who told you that?"

"Daniel Cooper," she says. "My sister's husband. I mentioned something about the pie van on campus once—I was making fun of it, if I'm being honest, because it was before I knew you and I thought it was archaic—but he got real serious about it. Asked if a girl named Daisy was running it and if you were okay. He wanted to know what you were up to, all sorts of stuff. It's the most interested I've seen him in anything other than his own career."

"What do you mean, what I'm up to? Why does your brother-in-law care what I'm doing?"

She exhales knowingly. "He said you might do that—pretend he doesn't exist. He means well, though, in his stupid way."

I wait. The longer the silence drags on, the tighter my stomach knots. "Who. Is. He?"

She tilts her head and studies me in the dark. "You're really saying you don't know?" When I don't answer, she says, "Huh. Okay then. Shit. Well, aside from wanting to be the next governor of Massachusetts, he's also your half brother."

"That's not true. I don't have a half brother." Or a full brother, or literally any real family left in the world apart from Zoe, but I don't tell her that. She's lost the right to know anything about me, full stop.

Melly shrugs. "It's okay, I get it. I have family I want to disown too."

"Whoever he is, he's not my family," I insist, but I'm jolted by the memories of my father not coming home at night, even when Mom got sick. It's a possibility I don't even want to consider, so I focus on the more salient point. "But what, he has you spying on me?"

She shifts on the milk crate, not answering right away. "It's complicated. He's concerned about you, wants to make sure you're doing okay after everything that happened, and he knows you don't want to talk to him."

"I have no fucking idea who he even is," I say through clenched teeth. "Or what it is you're on about."

"The relationship. The shit with your ex," she says, her voice softening. "It's okay that you haven't told me; I get it. He told me all about it, and I saw you at the Saint Stan's meeting—"

Something halfway between a snort and a laugh erupts from me. I feel like I'm dreaming, like logic and sanity have lost all meaning. "You followed me to Saint Stan's and you think what exactly? That I'm a victim?"

"It's okay," she says again, in that same gentle tone that makes me feel like I might be the one acting crazy. "People end up in shitty situations all the time. Daniel just wanted to help make sure you were able to get out, and yeah, okay, maybe using me as a middleman wasn't his finest thought, but he's a guy. They're not exactly burdened with an overabundance of brains."

"And you're not burdened with any," I shoot back. "I don't have an abusive ex. I don't have a brother. I have no idea who this person is that you're talking about, but you're being played."

"You don't have to lie to me."

I can't fathom who could possibly have convinced her of this, but she says it with such complete conviction that I almost start to doubt myself. Instead of arguing, I embrace the chaos for the moment and try a different tack. "Who are the women to him?"

"What women?" She sounds genuinely confused, and for a second I feel wrong-footed.

"The names. The list he gave me."

"I have no idea what you're talking about."

I shake my head at the absurdity of this. "You delivered it. Stuck it right on my door where I couldn't miss it."

"Oh, the envelope?" She squirms a bit on the crate. "He said it was get-back-on-your-feet money, that you wouldn't take it if you knew it was from him but that you needed it. He said even if you didn't want him in your life, it was the least he could do to help you."

A new storm of rage sweeps through me at the mere thought that I might need help supporting myself, as if I hadn't been doing that very thing from the time I was a teenager, even before Dad died. It was my job at the bakery—working shifts from three thirty in the morning until six, then going back after school for another three hours—that kept our lights on and food in the fridge after Mom died.

If there is one thing in this world I don't need, it's help staying on my feet.

"This is my life," I snap, bringing the rolling pin up to point at her. "And you're playing in it like it's the goddamn Sims. I let you in my van, my home, and you violated that. You've spied on me—" I remember her at the farmers' market the day she argued with Noel, the camera draped around her neck. "And you're the one who took the pictures. Jesus Christ. What is wrong with you?"

An image of her standing at my sink, washing her fork and putting it away, flashes through my mind. The drawer she was closing wasn't the silverware drawer. "And you *stole* from me. You took my recipe box." I know in my very core that if I go check that drawer, the box will be there. She did her dishes as a diversion, an excuse to be in the area to slip the box back in.

"I gave it back," she says meekly.

"That doesn't make it okay!" I take several deliberately deep breaths, trying to calm down. "Why? Why did he want them?"

She hangs her head at this, folds herself right over her outstretched legs, speaks into her lap. "That was me. All me." When she finally looks up, there's enough anguish in her eyes that I almost feel bad for her.

But only almost.

"Why?" I can barely get the word out.

"I wanted to understand how you did it. The magic. I thought it would be in the recipes, but it wasn't. It was stupid, and I don't even know the words for how sorry I am." She twists a hand into her curls, and her voice is strangled when she says, "I didn't mean for it to go this way, I swear. I've known Daniel for years, and yeah, his politics are a bit shit, but he's actually one of the good guys. He is. I've seen how he treats my sister, and the money he gives to the shelters makes a real difference. He didn't want you ending up in a place like that. He wanted to help you, and after he told me about you, I did too." She pauses, as if weighing what to say next. "And okay, yeah, I liked learning about you for my own sake as much as his, and god, I realize how creepy that sounds now, but at the time I told myself it was just harmless, helpful even. And yes, now that

I know you and I care about you and I see how upset you are, I get how wrong it was. I get it. Fucking Daniel. I should've told him to mind his own business and get bent."

The anguish in her voice is too raw to be faked, but I don't care. I can't. "I want contact information for him. Phone, social media, all of it. You owe me that much."

She gives it without hesitation. "Daisy, honestly, I'm so, so sorry."

I ignore it. "I need to meet with him in person. When I'm ready, you're going to help make that happen. And you're not going to warn him."

Chapter Twenty-Four

Armed with the knowledge of Daniel Cooper's existence, I email Pinstripe again. *We need to talk. I can come to you or you can come to me, but it's urgent. Tomorrow if possible.* I include a list of places I'll be parked around town during the week, just in case she can't make it.

Then I put the kettle on and get to work.

I'm not stupid enough to think I can ignore Daniel until he goes away, and as much as I want to bake him his very own pie, I know I can't. But I can play the game. I can even use his rules.

Now that I have a name, Daniel Cooper is a breeze to find. He's on my list of UMass grads and all over the internet, largely through accounts and articles attached to his role at the Freer Future Foundation, a conservative think tank he helped start after doing campaign work in college with a self-proclaimed mission to defend liberty through the promotion of small government, personal responsibility, and free enterprise.

But his politics aren't what concern me. The photos do, because they all show a face I recognize.

Daniel Cooper is the weirdo who threw his pie away moments after buying it, the guy I thought I recognized in Northampton.

He may have Melly doing his legwork, but apparently he's the type who can't resist poking the bear himself.

He's about to learn this bear pokes back.

I make the first of what's likely to be way too many cups of tea tonight and set about confirming what I can from Melly's information. With my laptop on the counter and Zoe curled up behind my stool, I pull up his birth record.

She was right.

His parents are listed as Lorraine Masterson and none other than Shawn Cooper. Seeing my father's name listed there is like a knife to the ribs, but I tell myself it's just information, nothing more.

But still. A half brother.

How would my life have been different if I'd known about him before? When we were kids? According to the date on his birth certificate, he's twelve years older than me, so we probably wouldn't have been friends, but we still could've been close. He could've been a protective presence, someone to help with Dad when things got bad. Maybe everything could've been different.

Instead, he's the biggest threat I've ever faced. He's known about me and has made no effort to reach out until now, when he wants to exploit me.

What could've been doesn't matter. Not anymore.

I scroll through his social media accounts as far back as they go and am disappointed to find most of it is work related, photos of fund-raising galas and invitations to speaking events. If he has accounts he uses for private stuff, he has them well hidden.

I need more.

Time to make my databases earn those subscription fees.

Daniel Cooper is a common enough name, but with his birthday and mother's maiden name, I'm able to zero in on the one I'm looking for.

I don't know exactly what I hope to find, since there isn't going to be a proof-I'm-a-blackmailing-scumsack report, but at this stage, any information is good information. The more I know, the better.

Like, for instance, the fact that he has a firearms license. That's definitely good to know.

I scroll through his property history, noting his current address, and delve into the rest.

For someone capable of the things he is, he's almost squeaky clean on paper. The most scandalous things I find are a pair of dismissed DUI charges over a decade old and a list of speeding offenses. No criminal convictions and nothing from the civil courts. No prior marriages and no children he's paying support for. He's never filed for bankruptcy, has more vehicles than one man needs, and holds no professional licenses in any industry.

If only I had access to his email or phone records, something that was actually helpful. I wonder if it's possible to get my hands on his laptop. Melly owes me a favor, after all. She could help.

Zoe stretches with a mighty yawn and gets up from the floor, staring at me like she can't imagine why we're not tucked in bed yet. "Good idea," I tell her. "I'm not thinking straight anymore. Let's call it a night."

* * *

My alarm rings entirely too soon, but as much as I want to ignore it, I don't.

I have pies to make and a woman to see about a madman.

I spend most summer weekdays stationed at the public library, and it's been a good spot. It's nothing like the devoted college library crowds, but it gives me a steady trickle of customers throughout the day, mostly mothers with packs of kids in tow. The pies get infused with calm and curiosity, a combination perfectly suited to summer afternoons of reading.

When Pinstripe arrives, she's already armed to the teeth with curiosity and not a single ounce of calm.

"I have forty-five minutes for lunch," she says.

"You should probably come inside." I open Penny's door, and she climbs in warily. I offer her a stool at the counter and a pie that she picks up left-handed. Her right hand, which she keeps in her lap, is ensconced in a stiff black brace. Zoe sits at her feet in hopes of catching stray crumbs.

Emma gives the dog's ear a scratch and asks, "So what's so urgent?"

I lean against the serving window so I don't miss any approaching customers and say, "I need you to tell me about Daniel Cooper."

The pie freezes halfway to her lips.

"It's important," I say.

"How did you find out?"

"It's complicated. But he's the one who wants you dead. Still, apparently, along with Jackson," I say, nodding at her wrist brace. A scarlet blush crawls up her neck, and I feel like a shit. "I'm sorry." She doesn't need me to tell her it's a fucked-up situation. She knows that better than anyone. "But I really do need to know about Daniel."

"You know it's him, but not why?"

"Not yet."

She sets her pie on the plate and picks tiny flakes off the crust as she thinks. I can see her wrestling with whether or not to tell me.

"Please," I say. "It's important."

She sighs. "It was in college. It was stupid. I was stupid."

"I'm guessing that's not true," I say.

She shrugs. "It felt that way. I was at a party. I was drunk. We hooked up." She stabs the edge of her pie with a manicured nail. "I consented to that. As much as a drunk girl can, anyway. But I didn't consent to be recorded. Or to having it shared."

My stomach turns. It's not the scenario I was expecting when she said *drunk* and *college*, but it's bad. Really bad. "How did you find out?"

"One of my friends got it. Daniel didn't know we were friends, or he didn't care. I don't know. But I spent the rest of college worrying about that video." She gives a rueful shake her head and holds up her braced hand. "So obviously my taste in men has never been particularly stellar."

"Your taste in men is not the reason they're complete piss-gibbons to you. They're complete piss-gibbons because that's what they are on a molecular level." I'm seething with rage.

"The other two on the list, he did this to them too?"

"That's my guess." It would definitely explain why Brittany Cline has made herself virtually untraceable. I ask the shit question because I have no choice. "Did you report it?"

"And say what? Hey, look at this video of me willingly having sex with a guy?" She snorts. "No, I didn't report it."

I can't even blame her. Hell, just look at Kevin Beechum. Anna Hargrave reported him and he got to walk away, not only without consequence but with the sympathy of college sports fans across the country. Fuck that.

I would love a time to come where I don't need to make pies to eliminate these threats, but until the system gets its shit together, my ovens are staying on.

"I don't understand why he wants us dead, though," she says. "He's the one who did it."

"I don't know either, but I intend to find out. And he obviously won't be getting pies from me, but I can't promise you he won't try something else. So be careful."

"All I do is try to be careful," she says, and it's clear she's not talking about Daniel.

"You know," I say gently, "even if you don't want a pie, you don't have to stay."

She's quiet, and I know she already knows that. But sometimes hearing it out loud can help.

Chapter Twenty-Five

It's easier than it should be, which is exactly why I don't trust it. When I tell Melly I'm ready to see Daniel, she simply texts him and says she wants to meet in person because she has new information, and he invites her to lunch at his office the following day. Easy as pie.

Resisting the temptation to bring a pie is significantly less easy, but I doubt he'd touch it, and besides, I'm not sure a single pie could hold everything I want this monster to eat.

Melly insists on coming with me to see him, insisting that I won't get past reception on my own. The possibility that she may be right is the only reason I let her in the truck.

Every time she opens her mouth, it's to apologize, but I ignore it. While most of my anger is completely justified by her utter disregard for my privacy, there's a part of it rooted in my own stupidity. She crashed into my life like a tidal wave, and I never stopped to question it. I let her in, into my van and into my head.

But it doesn't matter now. She's crossed too many lines. Right now her only use to me is getting me a meeting with my half brother.

* * *

The Freer Future headquarters looks like it was made in the future. Tucked on the outskirts of an industrial park, the glass and metal building screams money.

There's nothing welcoming about the monstrosity. We have to get buzzed in and go through a set of metal detectors, and only then are we greeted by the frosty receptionist, whose circular desk is the only thing on the entire first floor. There isn't even a single chair or bench to wait on.

Melly takes the lead before I have a chance to. "We're here to see Mr. Cooper."

"Is he expecting you?"

"Would I be here if he wasn't?"

The receptionist's mouth puckers like she has a slice of lemon hidden in there. "Just a moment." She picks up the phone and after a moment says, "Miss Riggs is here to see you. Okay."

She hangs up and slides a pair of visitor badges across the bare, glassy surface of the desk. "Swipe for the elevator and keep them displayed at all times. Mr. Cooper is in his office."

Melly takes the badges and passes one to me. At the bank of elevators, she swipes hers through the reader and presses the up arrow.

I wait until we're inside to speak.

"You're not coming in with me."

"You're not going in without me." She studies the set of my face in the elevator's mirrored wall. "Look, I know you're mad at me, but I'm trying to help. Let me."

The bell dings for the fifth and top floor, and we exit into a plushly carpeted hallway. The frosted glass door immediately on our right says *Daniel Cooper, Director of Donor Development* in white script.

I don't knock.

"Daisy, wait," Melly says, but it's too late. I throw the door open and march inside.

"Melody, what—" Daniel Cooper's eyes meet mine from behind a gleaming mahogany desk, and for a split second it's like he's been electrocuted. Then those watery blue eyes narrow and grow hard. Keeping his gaze fixed on my face, he turns to Melly. The effect is eerily owlish, and if I were a different kind of pie girl, I might feel like a mouse.

"What is this?" he asks in a voice like a coiled spring.

"A surprise," I say.

And it is.

Because as I stand before him now, in person, there's a fact I can't ignore the way I tried to when he was just a picture on my computer screen or a passing customer.

I recognize him.

Not him, not exactly, but his ears and the slope of his nose and the shape of his nearly nonexistent lips.

They're photocopies of my father's.

I feel like I've been kicked in the stomach but refuse to show it. "We need to talk," I say, crossing my arms. I'm aware enough to know I can only look so intimidating in my cupcake dress, but I don't care. If he really knows what I can do, that should be all the intimidation I need.

"Close the door," he orders, and I hear it click shut behind me. I'm past caring whether Melly is here to witness this or not. He looks between the pair of us and pins Melly with a withering look. "What were you thinking, bringing her here?"

I need to take control of this situation and fast. "Actually, I'm the one who brought her here. I caught her breaking into my trailer the other day, which I know is something you put her up to. I want to know about the women."

"I don't know what you're talking about," he says, leaning back in his leather desk chair and folding his hands behind his head. He crosses one ankle over the opposite knee in the classic carefree corporate power stance.

"Bull. Shit." I snarl, slamming my palms onto his desk. I have to fight the urge to swipe everything off of it.

He considers me for several moments before nodding to the chair beside me. "Sit. We'll talk."

I push myself away from his desk, but I don't sit. Melly does, though, taking the chair on my right and pulling it farther off to the side. I can't sit, can't stay still. There are too many things crashing through me for that, and I hate it. I hate the look on his face and the way it's like looking at an old photograph.

He waves an arm dismissively before draping it on the arm of his chair. "Fine, don't sit. Whatever you wish." He turns to Melly. "I take it I should cancel lunch."

"No, have it sent up," she says blithely. "I'd like lunch. And an explanation."

I whirl on her. "Shut. Up. You shouldn't even be here."

"Nor should you," Daniel says.

"I know everything," I say. "I know you put her up to it, that you've had her stalking me, delivering your little blackmail notes."

A sneer pulls his top lip up, revealing his teeth. "You know nothing."

"Enlighten me. Start with your parents."

Something passes over his face that almost makes him look human, then hardens back into a mask. When he speaks, his voice is stony. "I was twelve when my father left us for that witch. He said he was in love, that he had a baby on the way, that he was starting over. He said he was sorry, but he wasn't." He shakes his head at the bitter memory. "He was under her spell."

I'm shaking too, all over, and I recross my arms as much to hide it as to stop myself from strangling him for using the word *witch* like a curse and blaming my mother for things she had no hand in. "He wasn't. That's not how it works."

"My mother cried all night, and then for weeks. She thought I couldn't hear, but I could. She found him eventually, shacked up with your mother, and she begged him to come home. He obviously didn't. When they got married, it broke her. He could never be bothered to marry my mom, no, but he married her like they were a real family." He spits the final words out like poison.

"We were nothing to him, a mistake left buried in the past, but my mother couldn't accept it. She kept tabs on him. It was like an obsession. You see, I didn't just lose my father when he left; I lost her too." Rage contorts his features into something monstrous, just for an instant. "And it only got worse when you were born."

I hear Melly's intake of breath. Whatever truth she thought she knew of him, it wasn't this.

"Keep going," I say.

"My mother always wanted more kids, but after me, she couldn't have any. Your birth was like a slap in the face. And your mother didn't even give you his last name." Contempt pulls his thin lips into a sneer. "Before you came along, my mother thought there was a chance of getting him back, but not after. After, she could barely get out of bed. She stopped working, stopped cooking, stopped getting dressed. It lasted for months. She was such a zombie we ended up on food stamps. That's when I tried. I left voice mails and emails begging him to come home and make her better, but he didn't reply. Not a single word." He leans forward, forearms stretched halfway across the desk. Rage radiates off him like desert heat. "And then one day in November, he disappears. Completely."

My blood turns to ice, and so does my voice. "Men go missing all the time."

"On the same day their daughters lie about a rehab program and run away? I don't think so. You killed him. First your mother took him away from us, then you took him away from the world. The pair of you destroyed my family. So yeah, when I needed a problem taken care of, I figured you were just the one to help. After all, you do owe me."

"I owe you nothing," I say, and the words are almost a growl. "I don't even know you."

Daniel acts like I haven't spoken. "This is how it's going to go," he says, voice low and threatening, with the hard edge of a man used to getting his way. "You're going to take care of that list, or I'm going to destroy you." He jabs a finger at Melly. "Thanks to her, I know where you live, where you work, and what you care about. If you refuse to comply with my demands, it's not just you I'm taking down. It's all of them. Starting with your little vigilante murder group."

Chapter Twenty-Six

I whirl on Melly, who's gripping the arms of her chair like it might run out from under her. She's staring at Daniel like she's never met him before.

"How could you?" I ask, barely above a whisper. I'm trembling beneath the weight of rage and betrayal. It's one thing to expose me, but at least she had convinced herself she was doing it for a good reason. But there's no justification for endangering the PBG customers. None.

When her eyes meet mine, it isn't guilt I see but confusion.

Daniel smirks. "Oh, she's not in on that part," he says to me. "No, she got me into your private life. But she wasn't the only one I had digging into you. See, we work with some sensitive clients here, and I know more than a few discreet investigators. For instance, I know that you've had the same phone for years now and that we can trace it to towns where men who were otherwise perfectly healthy have dropped dead of unknown causes. Men certain people may have wanted killed. Not to mention the GPS tracker on your truck confirms you were just at Victor Layton's house on the very day he died. I can't prove that it was magic, but I can prove you were there."

"What's he talking about?" Melly asks me.

I ignore her. It's taking everything I have to keep from killing him. Every instinct is screaming that it would be an act of self-defense, that he's coming for me and I need to act now if I want to survive.

He must mistake my silence for fear because he says, "I take it we have an understanding?"

"We have nothing."

"Actually, you have three weeks. I plan to announce my campaign on the fourth, and I would like this resolved before then."

"Resolved?" I itch to leap over the desk and throttle him. In this moment, I don't need a pie. I don't even need a weapon. I am dangerous enough already.

"Resolved," he repeats, kicking back in his chair as if satisfied our meeting is over.

I sit and count my breaths, willing my heart to slow its frantic flutter. "I want to know why."

"Because you owe me."

"Why. Them?" I have to force the words through clenched teeth. "I know what you did to them, with the tapes. But what have they ever done to you?"

"Tapes?" Melly asks.

He makes a dismissive sound. "They're loose ends. I don't need that mucking up my campaign, not when I plan to take it all the way to the White House one day."

I go rigid in my seat. The edges of my vision blur, blocking out Melly and the office and everything that's not this *thing* sitting in front of me. My voice sounds far away to my own ears. "What kind of loose ends?"

"The kind who might get vindictive and try to have a little #MeToo moment right in the middle of my campaign."

My lips curl like an angry dog's into an uncontrolled expression of contempt. "You violate them and expect them to pay for that with their lives?"

"I did nothing wrong," he says. "It was definitely consensual. But seeing someone move up in the world can make people spiteful, especially embarrassed drunk girls."

"What'd you do, spike their drinks?"

"I did nothing wrong," he repeats, "But I won't risk them jumping on a bandwagon saying I did. You're going to take care of this. To make up for what your father did to us."

"I'm not doing it."

"You are if you want to keep yourself and your little pie groupies out of prison."

Melly is on her feet before I can respond. "Is this true? Does my sister know you're blackmailing your own sister for murder?"

Daniel's eyes grow glacial. "I think you know better than to interfere with this, Melody. My *wife*"—he says the word like it automatically trumps sister—"is a very important part of my life, and I'm paving the way for the future we deserve. I will not allow *anyone* to jeopardize that."

"Fuck you," she spits. "I should've known. I never should've taken your offer."

"But you did," he says. "And beyond that, I happen to be on very good terms with the dean at Turnbridge U. It'd be a shame to miss out on your senior year."

Like most people, I've never given much thought to the ramifications of blackmail before, but sitting here as it is being inflicted, I realize it's one of the worst crimes a human can commit—and I say that knowing full well what I do. But I don't work my magic for personal gain. I don't use people's lives against them. Yes, I kill bad men on a regular basis, but I don't exploit their secrets for leverage.

"We're done," I say, surprised by my own calm. I stand and stare down at him. "I'm sorry for whatever pain my father caused you, but I had no part in it. Nor did my mother. He was a grown man and he made his own choices, same as you do, and same as I do. That's how the world works. I owe you nothing."

I turn and walk out without waiting for a response from him or to see if Melly follows. She does.

"I'm sorry, Daisy. Please, wait." She grabs my arms, forces me to look at her. "I didn't know it was like this, that *he* was like this. I had no idea. He made me think he really just wanted to help you."

I shake her off and hit the button for the elevator. "Just save it."

We're both silent on the ride down, and when the elevator dings for the ground floor, I march toward the receptionist and whip my visitor badge across her desk. "If you have any self-respect," I say, "you should find a new employer."

* * *

I want to leave Melly there in the Freer Future parking lot, but I don't. I can't, not knowing what kind of predator is in that building, probably watching from his perch.

As soon as we're out of visual range, I pull over and get out, slamming the door. I start at the bed, searching for a GPS tracker. Nothing. I feel under the bumper and along the wheel wells. My hands turn black with truck grime, but still nothing. Was it a bluff?

Melly gets out and watches me warily.

"Did you know about the tracker? Is it real?"

"I have no idea. It seems there's a lot I didn't know."

Without a care for my dress, I drop to the pavement and scoot under the truck. With the help of my phone's flashlight, I search the undercarriage. Even with the limited light, I find it quickly, a black rectangle no bigger than a credit card stuck below the passenger door panel, almost taunting in its lack of subtlety. I wrench it off, and the magnet gives with unsatisfying ease.

He's been tracking me for who knows how long, and I didn't have a clue.

The violation rips through me like a current. My heartbeat grows painfully erratic against my breastbone, and with a wild cry, I fling the device as hard as I can. Fuck him. Fuck all of this.

I take a couple ragged breaths as the vise eases on my chest, the adrenaline finally ebbing. I don't have the luxury of losing it. Not now.

The ride back is stony until we hit the highway, when Melly says, "Can we talk?" I glance at her. She's worrying the buttons on the strap of her bag, a bundle of coiled energy. She looks exactly how my brain feels.

"Fine," I say. "Talk."

"What did he mean, about the dead men?" She asks it like she's not positive she wants the answer. "I mean, I get the magic. And trust me, that was a head trip at first. I thought he was messing with me, but I get it. I know you somehow transfer feelings into food, but I thought it was harmless. Like the college study pies. It's not that simple, though, is it?"

Several miles pass in silence while I consider how to answer. Or if I even should answer. I consider the buttons she's playing with on her bag, the feminist slogans and her strident opposition to all things misogynistic. If anyone would understand, it would be her. And she's already in this far. Maybe it's time to move her from Daniel's side to mine. "No," I say. "It's not that simple."

I tell her the barest of basics: that Pies Before Guys is a service that helps wronged women out of bad situations.

"So you're like the Punisher with pie," she says when I finish. "That's so much cooler than magic emotion pies."

I take my eyes off the road long enough to fix her with a look that says we're not at the point of joking about this. Not by a long shot.

"Now it's my turn," I say. "I want to know why. Why you really got involved in this. What leverage does he have on you?"

She sighs. "My financial aid is shit," she says. "My parents make too much money to qualify, but my father refuses to help me cover my costs because he doesn't believe in what I'm doing. Or my politics. Daniel doesn't either, but he loves my sister, so he set up a scholarship through an anonymous entity that's paying my tuition. It's the only way I can afford school."

"You spied on me for *tuition*?"

She drops her head back onto the seat. "I'm not like you. I don't have a skill I can use to support myself. Not yet. My skill requires a degree. And my degree requires significant payment, each and every semester. It seemed like a good deal at the time. Help my sister's husband learn about his long-lost sister and get school money in exchange. No brainer. But yeah, now I realize how fucked the whole thing is, and there's nothing I can do to make it right."

There's a part of me that wants to reassure her, make her feel better, but I can't, because she's right.

"Wait," she says. "I can't change what's already happened, but I can help you stop him. We can talk to Aria."

"Is she in on it? Does she know about the girls? About what you've been doing?" It's too many questions at once, but I can't help it.

Melly chooses the easiest. "She knows he pays my tuition. Lords it over me as evidence of his supposed saintliness. But no, she doesn't know what I'm doing in exchange."

"And the girls he wants dead? Does she know about them?"

"No, I swear. She's not like that. She wouldn't be with him if she knew."

I want to believe her, but I can't. If Aria doesn't know what Melly's been doing on her husband's behalf, then it's equally possible that Melly doesn't know what Aria's doing. She could be knee-deep in this, and if she is, going to her could escalate things and put all the women I've helped at risk.

I remember Melly making a comment about Aria's vows including *obey* and realize that even if she doesn't know anything, she might not care even if we tell her. There are plenty of women who fall prey to that stand-by-your-man nonsense.

There's one other possibility, and it's the one that pulls me up short.

Daniel Cooper's wife might be innocent in all this. If I expose his secrets to her, I could be putting her in harm's way, and that's not something I'm ready to do yet, not without more information.

Chapter Twenty-Seven

I've decided the next best thing to information is leverage.

There are two women in Daniel's life that he cares about, and I have the names of both. Even as I plug Lorraine Masterson's name into my deep searches, it feels wrong, not like with Jackson Vance, where I at least had concern for Pinstripe's safety and well-being to guide me. This is personal and it feels gross, but I remind myself that Daniel set us down this path. His game, his rules.

I find the Lorraine Masterson I need on the second page of my search. I'm surprised to see the address is only a few towns over. A quick Google shows it's part of the Oakholm Active Retirement Community, a swanky-looking condo development with an eye-watering set of fees that Daniel is no doubt bankrolling. Donor development must be a pretty lucrative gig if he's paying this on top of his own expenses and his sister-in-law's tuition.

The nice thing about people with nothing to hide is that they're pretty easy to find. Especially Boomers on the internet. Lorraine has an overactive Facebook page full of pictures of an obese orange cat, marketing posts for a scammy-looking jewelry company, and check-ins for all of the many activities she does at Oakholm.

She's tagged in several knitting group photos that lead back to an album called *Stitch-n-Bitch*, which is a name I have to appreciate. The woman in the picture looks nothing like the broken creature Daniel described, and I wonder how much of that was about him. Or perhaps it was as simple as time healing old wounds. My gut twists at the thought of reopening them.

I click into the album owner's profile and those of a few of the other tagged women, familiarizing myself with their names and interests.

Then I get to baking.

* * *

Oakholm's welcome center is modern and bright and looks more like a hotel lobby than anything else. A woman in her late thirties sits behind a gleaming white desk, vases of fresh flowers flanking her on each side. "Hello," she says. "What can I help you with?"

I give her my sunniest Pie Girl smile. "I have a delivery for the Stitch-n-Bitch club."

The woman returns my grin. "Oh, lovely. They'll be in the solarium," she says, rising and reaching for the box. "I can take it over."

"I'm actually friends with Marisol's daughter," I say, referencing one of the women tagged in the photos. "I'd love to go myself and say hi."

"Oh, of course," she says, coming around the desk anyway. She leads me to a bank of windows overlooking the development and points. "It's attached to the clubhouse on the other side of the pool, just over there. You'll probably hear them before you see them."

She's right. As I approach the sun-room, I can hear cackling laughter. My heart jumps at the audacity of being here, but I carry on. I come around the side of the clubhouse to find a long room attached to the building, constructed entirely of windows. Leafy green vines snake across the slanted glass ceiling, filtering the light. Inside, the Stitch-n-Bitch–ers are spread out in wicker chairs, balls of yarn at their feet and drinks within reach. I smooth my dress, channel as much confidence out of Nana's seams as I can, and let myself in.

Several heads turn in my direction, and I hoist my pie box with a bright smile. "Pie delivery!"

"Set it here, dear," one of the women says, clearing a spot on one of the low wicker tables before asking the group, "Who ordered pie? What a nice surprise!"

I don't give anyone a chance to answer, and I have to fight not to stare at Lorraine, who's sharing a wicker love seat with Marisol. I slide the lid off the box to reveal a pile of cutie pies with heart-shaped vent holes cut in their centers. "I have apple cinnamon, blueberry, and double chocolate. Something for everyone!"

The women set aside their knitting and help themselves. Several split pies in half and swap with neighbors so they can try each flavor. Lorraine takes whole apple cinnamon and chocolates for herself.

"You made these yourself, dear? They're wonderful," one of the women—Alice, I believe—says.

"I did. I'm glad you like them."

"And that dress is just charming," Marisol coos, touching the edge of my skirt to inspect the hem. Lorraine nods in agreement. "Such quality work. Handmade?"

"By my Nana," I confirm.

I let them draw me into various conversations as they eat, and I find myself enjoying their company despite my real reason for being here. I genuinely hope the magic works for all of them, however they need it.

The pies are forgive-and-forgets, and the blend of magic is both highly specific and very general. The crust magic is specific and, for my own safety, the forgetting half. Everyone who has one of these pies will have no memory of my being here.

The forgiving part, that's different.

Baked into the filling is a magic that will affect each woman differently. I can encourage forgiveness, but I can't direct it beyond that. It may cause some to let go of old grudges or free themselves from past mistakes. It's an open-ended kind of magic, but in Lorraine's case, I hope it goes the way I want. I hope she's able to forgive my father and forget I exist, for his sake as much as hers. He might not have been perfect, but he was my father and I know he loved my mother. I want to believe he never meant to hurt this woman.

On the other hand, I want Daniel to believe very much that I might.

Before I leave, I gather the group together for a photo I "promise" to share on Facebook. Lorraine holds the Pie Girl box up, logo prominently displayed, smiling at the center of the shot.

I give the forgetting magic a chance to kick in before I send the picture to Daniel.

Now he knows I, too, can get to something he cares about.

Chapter Twenty-Eight

I wake up to a string of messages sent from Daniel that he started sending at 2:40 AM. I groan. The only people who send that many texts in the middle of the night are drunk or obsessive, and I suspect he's both.

You don't make the rules.
Go near my mother again and you'll pay.
The price?

The next message is a picture of Zoe, dozing beneath my pie table, that makes my stomach flip.

You can't threaten me. I'm the one with the real power. Not you.
I own you.
The 7/4 deadline stands.
Get it done.

* * *

The diner is hopping when I get in, and I'm happy to let the bustle of the kitchen temporarily distract me from my worries about Daniel. Frank doesn't even let me get through the door before demanding, "More chocolate cream ASAP. Goddamn Boy Scouts wiped us completely out. What kind of diner runs out of pie? Oh yeah, the kind that has a pie girl gallivanting all over town instead of making me my damn pies."

"Nice to see you too, Frank," I say. Juan winks at me from behind the old man's back.

"You know what, just double the usual amount. We're getting overrun with people wanting pie now that you went and won that damn contest." Frank's words may be dismissive, but I know better. He's not half the curmudgeon he pretends to be.

I give him a cheeky salute. "You got it."

"If people think we're gonna start gettin' all fancy with honey this and organic that, they have another think coming," he grumbles as he goes back out to the front counter.

I start with Frank's pies, just to make him happy, although a peek out front shows me we're not as low as he wants me to believe.

Once the first round of crusts is blind-baking in the oven, Juan slides me over a steaming bowl of fries smothered in mushroom gravy and melty cheese.

"Ooh, at least I'm somebody's favorite today," I say, forking up a mouthful.

"They're apology fries," he says.

I groan. "The universe hates me."

"I don't hate you," he says, "but Eric and I aren't going to be able to come to Boston for the finals. Our first home visit with the adoption agency is that Friday, and that means Frank can't go either, since he'll have to cover for me here."

I sag with relief. "God, I thought it was going to be something actually bad. You must be so excited!"

His grin is irrepressible. "We are. But I do feel bad that we're not going to be there."

I wave away his concern. "Don't even worry about it. Besides, you've seen me make more pies than anybody. It's not like you're missing anything."

In truth, I'm relieved. If things go sideways with Daniel, and there's every chance they might, the fewer people I have to worry about, the better.

* * *

Noel, apparently, is someone I do have to worry about.

"Of course I'm coming," he says. "If it wasn't for me, you wouldn't even be going."

I raise an eyebrow at him. "I think I had a little something to do with it."

"Well, I gave you the idea to enter. And you named your pie after my orchard."

"And you're already benefiting," I say, gesturing at his empty booth. Earlier this morning the local news came to interview me about the contest, and I made sure to stress the importance of Noel's honey and cider in the winning recipe. A clip went up on their social media account, and both of our stocks got decimated before lunch. We considered packing up but decided to stick it out, at least until I burn through my stash of cutie pie dough, since we're both getting enough orders to make up for the lack of stock.

Plus it's a gorgeous day, the band doesn't suck, and I can't complain about the company.

Until now.

The problem is, he's right. It's perfectly logical that he would come along, and I don't have a compelling reason to give him for why he shouldn't. Just an abundance of caution, the need for which may be all in my head.

"If you really don't want me there, I get it," he says. "I could even keep Zoe for the weekend if you want."

At the sound of her name, Zoe thumps her tail.

The soft *shoosh* of it against the grass makes my heart stop.

In all of the scheming, I forgot to take her into account. If things go wrong, what will happen to her? The mere thought of it makes my throat close up.

"Don't look so horrified," Noel says. "I'd take good care of her."

"I know you would." And I do. He would be perfect, and that makes the decision for me. "You really want to drive back and forth to Boston with us? It's gonna get repetitive."

Hope lights up his eyes. "I actually thought we could make a weekend out of it," he says. "Instead of driving back and forth. I found a campground twenty minutes outside the city. I thought we could set up there. I mean, I've never actually camped before, but I think it could be fun."

"Yes, because you'll really be roughing it in Penny," I say with a laugh. "You realize I live in the van all the time, right? Parking it in the woods doesn't automatically make it camping."

"But campfires and s'mores and feeling smug about being more comfortable than people in tents does."

I laugh and realize I quite like the idea of spending a few whole days with him. "Fine. It's a camping date. I'll protect you from bears and everything."

"Sweet," he says, looking so pleased I think he might pop. "Pie Girl and Farmboy, hitting the road! I'll buy gas."

"And snacks?"

"And snacks," he agrees.

"We should leave Thursday morning so we have time to settle in. I want to bake that night so the custard will have plenty of time to set."

I'm about to ask about meal preferences, but when I spot a purple head coming my way, the words die in my throat.

Melly is on a mission, marching toward us in a black tank top and tight jeans. She has boots on despite the warmth of the sun, so I figure her motorcycle is nearby. I haven't seen her since I dropped her off after our meeting with Daniel, and her face is set with enough determination to make me worry.

"I want to order a pie," she announces without preamble. "The special kind. For Daniel Cooper."

I'm off Penny's steps before I comprehend the motion. I'm shaking my head, eyes shooting desperate telepathic messages she ignores. Not here. Not like this. This isn't how it's done. Not in front of people.

Zoe, sensing a change in atmosphere, lets out a low whine and comes to sit rigid at my side. I pet her head, but panic stops me from even feeling her fur. "I'm afraid I'm sold out for the day," I say, willing Melly to stop, to see the mistake she's making.

"Hence the order," she says. "Shit, I'll even deliver it personally."

"Melly—" Her eyes glisten like a doll's, and the realization that they're full of tears throws me off-balance. She dives into my hesitation like it's water.

"I want to order a pie," she insists. "A murder pie. A Pies Before Guys pie. I started this mess; I'm going to end it."

"Lower your voice," I say, mine barely above a whisper. The table between us feels like a continent. Noel is a blur in my peripheral vision until he's beside me, a look on his face like he can't decide if staying or leaving would be worse.

"Do I want to know what a murder pie is?" he asks.

Melly and I answer at once.

"It's nothing," I say, just as she says, "What it sounds like."

Noel looks between the two of us, and I feel the world collapsing around me.

"That's hyperbole, right?" he asks.

I hesitate a fraction of a second because I don't want to lie to him. He is good and pure and the opposite of everything Pies Before Guys exists for, but in my silence, he sees the truth, and it guts me. He backs away, horror writ large on his kind face.

Anguish lives in the hollow between your ribs, just below the sternum, and when he turns away, it's like he's pulling all of my organs out through that spot. I reflexively clutch a hand there as if to keep them in, but the pain persists.

Zoe leans hard against my legs. An anchor.

Noel breaks down his booth with quick efficiency, and I see the Saturdays we've shared dissolve like sugar in a hot pan.

I turn to Melly as if from underwater. "What are you doing?"

"Fixing things," she says.

I shake my head dumbly. "Do you have any idea what you just did?"

"Ordered a pie," she says, but she squirms just enough to let me know that she does know, at least somewhat.

"You just outed me. Publicly."

"To one person," she corrects, jabbing a finger toward Noel. He's slinging his packed tent into the bed of his truck and studiously ignoring us.

"Publicly," I repeat.

"He won't tell anyone." She doesn't sound positive, though.

"But now he knows. And that's a problem."

"He's into you. He won't say anything."

"But now he knows," I say. "And that matters to *me*."

Noel's truck pulls away from the green with a quiet rumble. My insides feel like he's driven right over them.

A war rages behind Melly's eyes that I can't comprehend. "Are you going to make it?" she asks. "The pie?"

"No."

She's clearly taken aback. "But why not? He deserves it."

"Because that actually isn't how this works. You're not the wronged party in this. You don't have a say."

Defiance twists her face into something unrecognizable. "I'll get my sister to order it then."

"No," I bark. "You've done enough damage. I'm not a vending machine. You don't just put money in and get a pie; that's not how it works. There are protocols, routines. They exist for a reason."

"He deserves to die," she says, the words almost a moan.

"Probably," I agree, "but not like this."

"You don't understand," she says. "He's going to do it. He's going to destroy you."

"He can try."

Chapter Twenty-Nine

He is not going to destroy me, because I'm not going to give him a chance.

Threatening him didn't work.

Threatening his mother didn't work.

And of course, simply telling him no didn't work, because he lives in a world where consent isn't a concern.

It's time to go after him the same way he went after the girls in the videos: secretly and without remorse.

No one threatens my dog, my life, and my livelihood and gets away with it.

It takes nothing to pull up his address. He may be an aspiring politician, but right now he's the same as every average resident, and his personal details are only a few clicks away.

I lean into this distraction, this sense of purpose, because it's easier than thinking about Melly's betrayal and the fact that Noel will probably never speak to me again.

I plug the address into my map app and thank the technology gods for providing such easy intel. I zoom in on the aerial view, noting that the house is set at the end of a cul-de-sac with huge swaths of grass surrounding the house. There's a kidney-shaped pool in the back and a border of trees beyond that. I switch to street view and reveal a sprawling McMansion that's more roof than house and a garage that's practically fifty percent of the total footprint.

Now I curse the technology gods, because there's no way this thing isn't outfitted with alarms and video doorbells.

I consider options, discarding a UPS disguise and a stolen truck out of hand. It would work in a movie but not in real life.

The door on the back deck probably doesn't have a video bell, but if I'm right about an alarm, I'd still be screwed. Plus there's the issue of access to consider. There's no inconspicuous parking on a cul-de-sac. I zoom the map out and scroll beyond the property. It turns out the trees in the back barely count as woods at all, more of a simple barrier between Daniel's street and the condo development on the other side. Unless I'm way off, it should be easy enough to walk through.

And then what? It's not like his backyard is going to be teeming with secrets.

If I'm going to find leverage, I need to find a way inside.

Then it hits me. There are exactly two things Daniel Cooper cares about. Himself and his image.

I don't need a way inside his house.

I just need a way inside his life.

* * *

They say that every great man has a great woman behind him, and while Daniel may not be great, he has had more than his share of women.

They're going to be the key to his undoing.

It was his mother who planted the seed. The woman I met in that retirement community, with its expensive condos and thriving social scene, is a far cry from the broken woman he told me about that day in his office.

It's practically a different world. I check the Oakholm site again to confirm the cost of residence. It's as staggering as I remember.

Real estate records are a breeze to find, even without the databases I subscribe to, and I soon know what he paid for his own house as well.

Apparently you really can't buy happiness, even with more money than brains.

My next stop is the Freer Future Foundation's website. I scroll through their staff pages, noting the name of the frosty receptionist, Annabella Fiore, whose official title is executive assistant, and memorizing the biography of the youngest-looking staffer, one Jacob Harney, recent graduate of Amherst College and part of the finance department. Perfect. Finally, I make note of the human resources director's email address.

I create a fake email address in less time than it takes to make tea and start typing.

Dear Mrs. Abbott,

I'm a student at Essex Abbot Academy and the leader of the Young Republicans club. As part of an assignment for our Personal Finance class, I am researching jobs I might like to have. I was wondering if you could tell me what qualities you look for when hiring people at the Freer Future Foundation and what the starting salaries are for three different positions. The ones I think I would excel in are Policy Analyst, Media

Relations, and Donor Development, so if I could get information on those, that would be great. Thank you in advance for your help!

Sincerely,
Marcus Crouch

I press send and feel an almost electric buzz run through me. I could be wrong, of course. I have been before. But in Daniel's life, just like in the photos women send me with their PBG orders, the little details in the background are suggesting something more than meets the eye.

He is a man concerned with image to the point of excess. His mother, a woman he despises, lives in absolute luxury. He himself paid a fortune for his home despite also paying for his mother's retirement and his sister-in-law's education. If Connie Abbott responds to sweet Marcus's email, I'll bet my oven she gives him a salary range that doesn't support such extravagance.

So where is the money coming from?

It's possible his wife has the answers, of course, but it's equally possible she doesn't, and I have no intention of going to her with anything less than the whole works. And who knows, maybe I can dig up enough dirt that I won't even have to reveal my part in this whole saga at all.

But before I can do anything else, I have pies to bake.

Raspberry almond cutie pies, to be exact, full to bursting with the same blend of honesty magic I almost used on Noel.

The memory stings like lemon in a cut, but I don't let myself dwell on the way he drove off after the fiasco at the market or all the texts he's ignored.

Right now I have something more painful to face: shopping.

While the pies are cooling, I leave Zoe in the van with the AC on and head to the mall, because this is one occasion where flashy vintage dresses won't fly.

I head straight to Ann Taylor and buy a scoop-necked sheath dress and matching three-quarter-sleeve blazer in charcoal gray and try not to feel guilty that I'm going to return them the second I'm done with them.

I find a pair of black slingbacks on sale at a price I can justify keeping them for and a bag at a price I can't, and head back to the diner.

I take Zoe out to pee and box up the cuties before getting changed. It feels like donning a costume, the structured stretchy fabric so unlike the swingy soft cotton I'm used to. I take my hair out of its usual high bun and part it on the side, sweeping it back up into a French-ish twist.

Steeling myself, I leave Penny and let myself into the diner.

"Whoa, Pie Girl, look at you!" Juan crows. "What's the occasion?"

"Secret mission," I say, with complete honesty, knowing he'll assume I'm kidding. "But I have a favor to ask."

"Hit me," he says as pulls down the new-order tickets.

"So you know how you feel so guilty about not being able to come to the finals?"

He looks at me properly then, wary.

"Can I maybe borrow your car? Just for a couple hours. I'll be back before your shift is done, swear."

He's silent for a beat, and I know I have a fifty-fifty shot, at best, of this going my way. His little green BMW is his pride and joy. It's older but absolutely pristine, and most importantly, it won't look at all out of place in the Freer Future Foundation lot.

"You robbing a bank?" he asks.

I draw an X over my chest. "I am not."

He pins me with a stare and points his tongs at me like a sword. "You better take perfect care of her."

"You know I will."

With the exaggerated sigh of a truly beleaguered man, he points the tongs to the back door. "Keys are on the hook," he says.

"You're the best," I say.

"I know." He turns back to his tickets and says, "Be safe, Pie Girl."

"Always," I promise.

* * *

It's easier going into the Freer Future Foundation this time. For one thing, I know Daniel won't be there.

On the way over, I called the offices, pretending to be a friend of Jacob Harney's interested in setting up a recurring donation. I asked if it would be possible to meet someone at Alino's Restaurant, since I was in the area for business, and I was promised Daniel Cooper would meet me there personally.

From the safety of Juan's anonymous BMW, I watched him leave before I went inside.

Annabella Fiore is manning the front desk, same as before, but unlike the last time I was here, this time she looks at me like I matter. Whether it's the new clothes, tags tucked carefully out of sight, or the fact that I'm not accompanied by Melly, she almost smiles at me.

In return, I flash her my own most winning smile. "I was hoping to sneak in to see Daniel Cooper," I say. "I'm not on his books, but I was in the area, and I have some stock I was thinking of transferring to the foundation."

"He actually just left," she says. "Would you like me to schedule an appointment for you?"

"Oh, what a shame! I brought him pastry and everything. Suppose that's what I get, just dropping in. Yes, please, book me in. It's Carla Thompson," I say, placing the box of cutie pies on her desk. "Would you like one? They're no good unless they're eaten fresh. It'd be a shame to waste them."

I open the box, and with barely any prodding, she reaches in and takes one. I swallow a sigh of relief as she removes a tissue from a drawer and places the pie on it. She breaks it in half as she pulls something up on her computer screen. As she clicks, she takes her first bite.

"It looks like the rest of the week is fairly booked," she says apologetically, popping another bite of pie into her mouth. "Perhaps Wednesday next week?"

I take out my phone and feign checking my calendar. I just need to buy enough time for her to get a couple more bites in. "Ah, that's no good. Thursday, maybe?"

She breaks off another piece of pie with one hand while sliding the mouse around with the other. "How about Monday at four?"

I swipe randomly on my phone, making *hmm* sounds as she chews. "I suppose that will work. Four, you said?"

"Yes. I can give you a half hour."

"That'll work," I say.

She puts the last piece of the cutie in her mouth and chews while she types. "Okay, you're all set. Monday at four. My, those really are good," she says. "Where are they from?"

"A little shop in Turnbridge," I say, pushing the box closer. "Please, have another. I insist."

She takes it with the look of a kid sneaking candy before bed. I let her get halfway through it before I pounce.

"So," I say, leaning in conspiratorially. "What can you tell about Daniel's work here?"

Chapter Thirty

Aria Cooper is a teacher at a private preschool, a position she will no doubt be expected to abandon once her husband starts climbing the political ladder.

A political ladder that I now know will be built with dirty money.

It's not something I can keep secret any longer.

The school's website boasts about their exceptional summer programs that provide "enriching educational opportunities for young learners along with convenience and peace of mind for working parents."

The prices are staggering.

I know I have no hope of getting past the main office staff at such a school, but running Aria's name and home address through one of my databases revealed a silver Volvo SUV registered to her, so all I need is the parking lot. I find the vehicle, park as close as I can, and wait.

The bell rings just before three, and students pile not into the yellow school buses like I remember, but sleek black vans with *Clarkwell Day Academy* stenciled in gold along the side.

Once the vans leave and the line of parent pickups goes through, the parking lot around me starts to empty out. I keep my eyes on the Volvo. Part of me wonders if this would go better if Melly were here, but after what she did at the market, I couldn't bring myself to involve her.

I have to do this myself.

I spot her before she even gets to her car because the resemblance to Melly is so striking. Aria is willowy where Melly is strong, but even though they're built differently, the eyes and mouth are carbon copies of each other. I hop out of the car and head to her, trying to keep my expression as friendly as possible even as a frisson of nervous energy rips through me.

She notices my attention on her and slows, cocking her head in question. Her hair is cut in a glossy bob that frames her face, and I can't imagine Melly ever taking the time to tame her curls like that.

"Hi," I say. "I wonder if I could talk to you for a minute? I'm a friend of your sister's."

"Oh," she says, taken aback. Perhaps she thought I was a potential parent. "What about?"

"Could we go somewhere more private?" I know this sounds ominous, but I don't want to have this conversation in a parking lot. She hesitates for a moment, and I dive in. "Please. It's important."

"We could walk." She gestures at the playground and baseball field.

"Thank you."

She takes a moment to stow her overflowing tote bag in the Volvo, and then we set off. I wait until we're past the jungle gyms and out of earshot of anyone still leaving the building before I say, "This isn't about Melly, so please don't worry about her."

She slows at this admission, wary now. "Then what is it about?"

"Your husband."

She stops and holds a hand against her stomach like she's expecting a sucker punch. She must think I'm about to tell her we're having an affair, because in her world that's the worst thing possible, the only reason a strange woman would want to have a private conversation about her marriage.

Part of me hates what I'm about to do to her world.

But only part.

The rest of me knows it's necessary.

"He's not cheating, but this is going to be hard to hear." I start walking again, and she follows because she has to know now.

So I tell her.

All of it.

I start with the women he wants dead and why; then I tell her about the conversation I had with Annabella Fiore after the pies kicked in, while Daniel was safely away from the building. I tell her how Annabella has scheduled dozens of donor meetings for him and how none of them got the returns the company expected. I tell her that accounting is looking into his record keeping. I tell her exactly how much it costs to keep his mother at Oakholm and that HR confirmed that it was more than his official salary could support.

She listens in mute silence, an elegant hand pressed to her lips, like she has to physically keep the questions in.

"So there are three women," I say in summary. "That I know of. Three women that he filmed during sex that he now wants dead for no reason other than they *might* become a threat to his campaign. The very campaign he's going to fund with money he's embezzled from his job."

I give her a chance to digest this.

"That can't be," she says, more to herself than me. She stops abruptly, dropping herself onto the edge of the metal bleachers. She stares out over the empty baseball diamond, forehead creased with thought. Every so often her head twitches like she's having a silent argument with herself inside it.

I sit beside her, the ridged metal hot beneath the fabric of my dress, and wait.

"He said he'd never done it before," she says, still lost in her own head.

"Done what?" I ask gently. Surely she can't mean murdering innocent women.

"Filmed himself."

I blink away my surprise, not wanting to stop her from talking.

Her breathing grows louder, angrier. "That bastard. He said it was special, something he wanted to do just for us."

Out of everything I just told her, the fact that he made other sex tapes is her biggest concern? Relationships really do make people blind.

"But he doesn't want you dead," I remind her.

"No, but still." She shakes her head sharply, as if clearing out the war in there. "Why are you telling me this? Why not go to the police if you're so concerned?"

"Because he's a threat to me too, and the evidence I have isn't enough. The letters I have aren't signed, and the texts are from a burner number. He's used your sister as an intermediary on more than one occasion. The cops are more likely to find her fingerprints on the demand letter than his."

"So what exactly am I supposed to do about it?" She asks the question calmly and without rancor, but I want to shake her.

What is she supposed to do? Leave him. Expose him. Kill him! Do something other than just be pissed off about sex tapes.

But I don't say any of that.

Instead, I tell her what I need. "I think you can get him to see reason. To stop."

She's quiet for several moments, long enough that the bench cools beneath my thighs and I become aware of the ridged grooves tattooing themselves into my skin.

"He has plans. I can't interfere with that. His campaign work, Mayor Beckett's mentorship, the work connections—everything is in place to launch him on his path to the White House. We're supposed to be a first family someday," she says, and although her voice is unsettlingly calm, she holds her stomach like the thought is tearing her apart. "This could destroy us."

"Probably," I admit. "But do you really want to be with a man who's capable of this?"

There's another stretch of silence, and I'm struck by how different she is from Melly in this regard. Melly's mouth never stops moving, but it's like Aria has to turn over every possible thought before she selects one to share.

When she finally speaks, it's the last thing I expect to hear. "I'm pregnant. It's early still, first trimester. No one knows yet. Not Melody, not even my parents. Please don't tell her."

"I won't," I say. "But don't you think that makes it more important to get away from him? Do you want to raise a child with a murderer?"

I ask it as gently as I can, but it's still a cheap shot.

"He's not, though, is he? Not really." She sounds more like she's pondering some abstract philosophical puzzle rather than the stark reality I've just presented her.

"Because he's too much of a coward to do it himself," I say before I can stop myself. She looks at me like I slapped her, which might be fair, but I've had it. "Have you not heard a word I've said? The man you love is going to *kill* people because they're an *inconvenience*. I'm giving you a chance to stop this before it escalates."

She shrinks in on herself, curling protectively around her still-flat stomach. "It would destroy our family," she says, the words hazy with denial.

"It would. But it would also save lives. Maybe even yours. Probably mine, and definitely Brittany, Kerenza, and Emma's."

"But our baby . . ."

"Deserves to be raised without a monster for a father," I say, and again I am struck by the difference between this woman and her sister. I may be unspeakably angry at Melly, but at least she has conviction. A backbone. A belief in doing the right thing, even if it's for the wrong reasons. It's mind-boggling that these two had the same upbringing yet emerged so different.

And I realize that was the flaw of this plan.

I had expected to find an older version of Melly, someone who would hear what I had to say and leap into action, who would face an ugly truth with fire and focus.

Instead, I have an ostrich with her head buried so deep in the sand she's forgotten what the world even looks like.

I stand and smooth the back of my dress. Aria hardly notices.

"Please," I say. "Think about it. You can do the right thing. You can help stop him."

Perhaps it's an unfair burden to place on her, but she's all I have.

"I have to take care of my family. We exchanged vows."

"Just think about it," I repeat. "Taking care of your family doesn't just mean obeying your husband. It can mean taking a stand. Melly can give you my number if you want to talk again, but you can make a real difference for a lot of people right now."

She doesn't speak, and so I leave her there, locked in her private thoughts, and wonder what the hell else I'm going to do.

Chapter Thirty-One

I text Melly to let her know I met with her sister, and she responds with an unusually taciturn *I understand. And I'm also sorry.* I don't know how to respond to that, so I don't. I'm not ready to forgive her, not when there's a Noel-shaped hole in my life that I hadn't realized he'd been filling until he wasn't there.

After he ignored the first batch of texts, I stopped sending them. I'm not stupid.

Except that I am.

Colossally.

I might have set up shop in Turnbridge, but I don't belong here. I'm not a student like Melly; I'm not a local like Noel. I can sell pies in their world, but I should know better than to play in it.

I've always known my gift is different. I don't know if the magic broke when it got passed down or if I was already damaged, but it doesn't matter. My magic matters. I have more than most people will ever have: a purpose. I need to be content with that and stop trying to fit a normal life around it.

So I carry on. I make pies and I make plans, and I try to ignore the feeling that everything is going to hell.

I redouble my recruiting efforts at the meetings, hitting a different one each night. I get orders. I save women.

I email Kerenza Vallery that it's Daniel Cooper who wants her dead and that she needs to be careful. I suggest to her and Emma both that they can get ahead of this by telling their stories before his campaign even starts. After all, once that horse is out of the barn, he'll have no reason to burn it down.

I send a carefully worded email to the director of the shelter Brittany Cline volunteers at in Seattle, asking her to pass along a message to Brittany that Daniel Cooper isn't in her past just yet. She doesn't want to know, but she needs to. I give her all of my contact information. It's not a lot, but it's something.

At night I fall into bed and I tell myself that this is better. I'm more focused. I'm doing what I do best, without distraction, without having to worry about other people.

But sometimes I lie awake and worry about my never lines. Melly has already broken two: *Never divulge the identity of someone seeking a pie* and *Never expose myself as the face of PBG.* I consider the others.

Never choose your mark for personal gain.

Never kill a woman.

Never accept money for a murder pie.

Never get too deep to get out.

I get out of bed.

I have a pie to make.

* * *

I arrive on his porch just after one. The pie is still warm in its wooden box.

I knock hard, loud enough to wake the dead, and I wait.

The reckless sense of purpose I felt when I was baking is wearing off, nerves nudging in against the clarity and conviction.

Inside the house, the muffled sound of someone crashing into something is followed by a curse.

A light flips on.

My heart hammers.

Noel opens the door in a pair of sweatpants and nothing else. His hair looks like something is living in it.

Zoe's tail thumps on the wooden porch.

I hold the box out, and he squints at it in confusion.

"What is this?" he asks, rubbing sleep from his eyes.

"Humble pie. One hundred percent magic-free."

He stares at me for a long time. "Give me a minute."

He closes the door and I stand there, knees like marshmallows, and wonder what the hell I'm doing.

The never lines. They're already broken.

When he comes back, he has on a T-shirt and a guarded expression. "You realize it's one in the morning, right?"

"Consider it a midnight snack," I say, offering the box.

He doesn't take it, and the rejection hurts more than I thought it would. He strides past me and sits on the porch's sagging steps. Zoe happily plops down on the step below him and lays her head on his bare feet.

I set the pie on the porch and tentatively sit down beside him. "I think we should talk."

"I'm not sure I want to know," he says. "She was here, you know. Your friend with the hair."

I swallow a groan.

"She said she was just joking but that I still shouldn't tell anyone. Was she joking?"

"No," I say, plainly and without guile.

"So it's not just happy pie magic you do. You kill people."

"Yes, but probably not how you think."

He stares up at the starry sky as if it's going to have an answer for him. "Tell me," he says.

I put another cross through *Never expose yourself as the face of Pies Before Guys* of my never lines list. "It started with the pie that killed my father. I didn't mean for it to kill him, but it did. Things got real bad for a while after that, but I realized something good could come out of it. In a way, his death freed me. I can't save the world with pies, but I can save some. That's how Pies Before Guys started. The pies only go to bad men, really bad men, like rapists and abusers."

"That's why you give pies to that meeting at Saint Stan's," he says.

"The meeting pies are loaded with strength," I explain. "But yes, if someone is in a situation they can't get out of without help, my kind of help, then I let them know."

"How does it work?"

"They place an order. I verify the situation, and if it's something I think I can help with, I make a pie. They're always free, and they can only be ordered by the woman directly affected by the recipient. The magic is completely tailored to that person. There's no risk of transference."

"But it's still murder."

"It doesn't have to be." There's something heady about explaining this so frankly. The recklessness is intoxicating. "The magic isn't murder. Not specifically. The magic is exactly what went into my father's pie. I know it's safe because I ate it too, and I survived. The pies aren't infused with poison or malice; they're infused with an extreme plea to *stop*. The problem isn't the pie; the problem is the men. The only thing that can stop them is death."

"Always?"

"No, not always. This is the real magic part, the part beyond my control, where the magic does what it will," I say, even now awed at the power of it. "Sometimes—not often, but sometimes—a guy will eat a pie and he'll change."

"Then why don't you make pies that just do that?" The question is so plaintive, like he's desperate for a way to make this all make sense.

"Because I can't," I say, and it kills me that it's not the answer he wants. "I can't change someone's nature. They have to have it in them already."

He considers this for a long time, and I let him. It's a lot to process.

"I don't know what to do with this," he says. "I thought I knew you."

"This isn't really something you can just drop into a getting-to-know-you conversation," I remind him.

"When you left Zoe here those nights, that was because of this? You were delivering these pies?"

I shake my head. "No, that was something else."

"Related?"

"Yes. Someone was trying to exploit the system, to use pies to silence the women he wronged. I was figuring out who."

"And did you?"

"My evil half brother."

"But I thought—"

"So did I," I say, before he can finish.

He runs his fingers through his hair, making it stand up at even odder angles. "And Melly. Where does she fit in?"

I give him a brief rundown, and he goes quiet again. I wonder if this is the last time we'll be sitting together like this, but I don't ask. I don't plead my case. I'm not here to convince him of anything, only to tell him the truth.

He sighs. "I won't tell anyone," he says. "If that's what you're worried about. But I don't know how to deal with this."

Sadness squeezes around my heart like a snake. "I know."

"I'll drop a case of cider and honey at the diner," he says, his voice thick with emotion. "For the contest."

I swallow the lump in my throat. "Thanks." I stand, eyes burning with the threat of tears. "Come on, Zo."

She climbs to her feet with a yawn, and we leave him sitting there because there's nothing else to do.

Chapter Thirty-Two

True to his word, a box of ingredients is delivered to the diner the week of the contest.

It shows up when I'm not there, and stumbling across it in the walk-in causes a physical ache in my chest.

I try to ignore it for the time being, though, because I have no choice. I'm up to my eyeballs in diner pies because Frank is convinced he needs a month's worth to cover the four days I'll be gone. But while I bake, the hurt nags me like a toothache, and I curse my stupidity. I should know better than to get involved with people. Hell, up until just recently I was doing just fine on that front, then bam, not one but two disasters I could've avoided simply by sticking to my own damn rules. I'm the girl who makes murder pies, not the girl who gets to have normal relationships. I tell myself I can live with that and almost believe it until Juan asks if Noel is going to Boston with me.

I say no, without explanation, but the question is enough to send the bubbles of hurt bursting back to the surface like boiling fruit.

Juan doesn't let me off the hook that easily, though. "And why not?"

"He doesn't want to go," I say, and admitting it out loud is worse than keeping it in my head. "That's his choice."

"Is it?" Juan asks. "Or are you pushing him away?"

"Hey." I glare at him across the sea of pie pans. "I resent that."

"But do you resemble it?"

I roll my eyes. "That was awful. But trust me, this is all on him," I say, but as the words leave my mouth, I wonder if they're true. Could I have done more to make him understand? I grind a pile of graham crackers with more force than they need until I have a bowl that's more dust than crumbs. I drop melted butter in like it's a bomb and stir it together.

Juan lets a beat of silence pass while I brood. I have to concentrate to keep the negativity out of the crust.

"Well, if it really is all him," Juan says eventually, "then he's an idiot."

The front door swings open as Frank storms in. "I must be the idiot if I'm paying you two to wag your chins all day," he grumbles, ladling a cup of chowder from the pot bubbling on the stove.

"You don't pay me, Frank," I say automatically, but the words lack their usual zing.

Frank notices that too. He passes the soup off to a server and gives me a beady-eyed stare as I shove buttery crumbs into the pans like they've personally wronged me.

"Now what's got your knickers in a twist?" he asks.

"Don't ask her," Juan warns.

"Damn well ask what I want in my own diner. So? What is it? That stalker of yours back again?"

"It's nothing, Frank," I say, piling the filled pie tins onto sheet pans for the oven.

"Boy trouble," Juan says in an exaggerated stage whisper.

"You're never getting pie again," I tell him.

"Oh, Christ on a cupcake," Frank snaps. "That's what has you moping around like someone stole your dog?"

I slide the sheet pans into the oven. "Not moping."

"Kind of moping," Juan says.

Franks wags a finger at him, then the grill. "Less mouth and more cooking."

Juan salutes him with a spatula, checks the next round of orders, and gets to it.

"Now listen here," Frank says to me. "I may be an old man, but that means I've lived a long time and seen a lot of things. Known a lot of people too, and didn't like most of 'em, but I like you, Pie Girl, and if someone is messing you about, I want to hear about it."

"No one's messing me about," I say, oddly touched by his gruff concern.

He raises a bushy eyebrow. "It ain't that orchard fella we met in Northampton, is it?"

"It is," Juan singsongs from the grill.

"It isn't," I say at the same time. "It's nothing, really."

"He do you wrong?" Frank shakes his head. "Must be losing my touch. First impressions don't count for what they used to these days. I thought that boy had a head on his shoulders."

"He does," I say, setting a pot of cream on the stove to simmer. "I guess it's what's inside it that's the problem."

I grab two metal bowls and start cracking eggs, separating the yolks into one for the chocolate custard and the leftover whites into the other for meringue.

"And what might that be?" Frank asks impatiently. "Spit it out, girl, I ain't a damn psychic."

There's no way I can explain to anyone, especially not Frank, the truth of what's going on with Noel and me. I whisk a hefty load of sugar into the egg yolks until they're pale and frothy.

"He find out some deep dark secret about you?" Frank demands.

My hand freezes. "You could say that." I rest the whisk on the bowl's edge and fetch the pot of heated cream to temper the eggs, feeling horribly exposed.

"Well, tough titties," Franks booms, nearly causing me to drop the scalding pan. Juan and I exchange shocked looks as he goes on. "That boy's a moron if he thinks he's going to like every damn thing about a person. No one's perfect. My old Helena, for instance, I tell you, that woman could snore to beat the devil, talked in her sleep, and was mean as hell if you interrupted her nap, but that didn't stop me from loving her until the day she died. No sir. Was just part of the package. Sometimes you have to endure the bad to enjoy the good."

Unexpected tears burn my eyes, but I'm smiling. "Is that what we do with you, Frank? Deal with your grumpy-old-man act so we can get a glimpse of this?"

"I am a grumpy old man," he says, suddenly flustered, "but I ain't wrong. If that boy can't appreciate all of you, the good parts and the bad, then he ain't worth a minute more of your time."

He turns with an air of finality but pauses at the door to look over his shoulder. "And if that's the case, then I'll make sure nobody we know is buying his damn apples. We look out for our own around here, Pie Girl, and in my book, that includes you."

* * *

The rest of the diner pies get a little extra magic that night because I can't hold it back: a sense of family and deep, deep gratitude.

In all of my planning, it never occurred to me that Frank might actually care if I was gone. Not just that he'd be inconvenienced by a lack of pies, but that he would actually be worried. I haven't felt that kind of parental concern since my mother was alive, and dwelling on it makes my heart hurt.

Nothing will ever replace my mother, and even though my father was a train wreck of a man, I think in his heart, he was doing the best he could. I spent so long hating him for how hard he made it after Mom was diagnosed and wanting to blame him for things going wrong after she died that I couldn't really admit to myself that a lot of that was simply because he was hurting. Even now, it's a hard thing to admit, but it's true. We might not have been a perfect family, but we were one, and in a way, I kind of owe Dad as much for who I am today as I do my mother and the Ellery magic. Morbid as it is, without him going so far off the rails, I might never have discovered the depths of my power. It's a realization as bittersweet as the mountain of dark-chocolate curls I make to garnish the cream pies.

I have no way of knowing if my parents would approve of who I've become, not just with the magic but with everything. I hope they'd be proud, though. I might've dropped out of high school and evaded authorities during some of my formative years, but I think I ended up okay. I own my own business doing something that makes me happy. Even if the Noel and Melly situations are a mess now, I think my parents would've liked both of them. I think they'd be happy that I've found Frank and Juan and a community I feel at home in. And okay, yes, they'd probably be concerned that

I'm about to risk throwing it all away over a half-baked notion of what this pie contest could mean, but I think they'd understand, because that's what family is supposed to do.

I'm sure Frank would bristle at something as sentimental as being told he's part of my new, cobbled-together family, but I know he'll get it when he tastes the pie. And let's be honest, I'm more comfortable putting it into a crust than into words anyway.

Even though I know it won't be enough if things go wrong in Boston, I want to leave Frank the recipes for the most popular pies, just in case something happens and I can't get back.

I retrieve the recipe box from the drawer, flip the top open, and flick through the cards. They're like the rings on a tree, telling the story of my life. The cards are a jumble of white, pastels, and neons. The lack of order would drive some people crazy, but the rainbow edges please me. Many of the cards are worn soft with age and stained with any number of ingredients, the recipes written in unsure block letters or the looping inconsistent cursive from the time in high school when I was still experimenting with handwriting styles. Some are crisp, nearly new, the sharp corners sticking out above the rest, their surfaces unmarred by errant bits of butter or vanilla. They're all there, though, in perfect order, except for the mango mint mojito recipe that's still stuck to my fridge. I take it down and slot it back in the box behind the lychee raspberry coconut-crust pie. In a daze, I pull the chocolate cream, mile-high apple, classic cherry, and lemon meringue cards and set them on the counter. I return the box to its usual spot at the back of the drawer and try not to think about Melly doing the exact same thing.

I take the recipe cards and let myself back into the darkened diner. I contemplate the best place for them and settle on the stack of pie tins. I want them somewhere where they'll be found if the diner needs pie, but not somewhere where they'll be discovered too soon on the off chance everything goes according to plan and I make it back without a problem.

I really, really hope I make it back without a problem.

Chapter Thirty-Three

When I step out of the van, I find Noel sitting on a milk crate with my wooden pie box in his lap.

"You forgot this," he says, getting to his feet.

I take the box and immediately almost drop it, not prepared for its unexpected heft. I slide the lid back, wondering if he really left the pie sitting in there, and find that it's stuffed to the brim with candy, chips, and energy bars.

"I did say I'd buy snacks," he says sheepishly. "If you'll still have me."

From inside the van, I hear Zoe give an excited bark at the sound of his voice. I ignore her.

"What made you change your mind?"

"A lot of things. What you said about the magic acting on what's already inside. The fact that the thought of not seeing you again sucked more than facing up to some hard shit," he says. "I mean, I'm on probation for running illegal drug trials with magic mushrooms. I'm not sure my moral compass is as finely tuned as I'd like to believe."

Zoe barks again, and I open the door for her. She crashes into Noel's legs, tail wagging furiously.

"How long have you been waiting here?" I ask as he crouches down to pet her.

He looks sheepish. "Since five. I didn't know what 'leaving Thursday morning' meant to you, so I wanted to make sure I caught you."

"You could've asked," I say.

"And ruin a perfectly good grand gesture? Nah."

I laugh. Boys are dumb.

"Plus Juan gave me coffee and eggs, so it wasn't bad."

"You're lucky it was his day to open and not Frank's."

"I'm aware." He straightens up and sticks his hands in his pockets, suddenly the very image of a nervous schoolboy. "So, road trip?"

I consider letting him squirm in the beat of silence. Even Zoe is watching me expectantly.

"Let's do it."

* * *

The campground is packed, which I didn't expect, and I'm glad I booked our slot ahead of time.

"Think they're all here for pie?" Noel asks.

"At least some of them."

The semifinal round of the contest is set up the same way as the county round, but in addition to the pie that will be presented for judging and evaluated against the scorecard, we need to provide three extra pies to be sampled at the awards ceremony. The top three contestants will move on to the finals, which is where things will change. The finalists will be invited to the State House's catering kitchen, where we'll have to prepare the pies we're submitting for official judging under strict supervision from the kitchen staff.

The winner of that round will be awarded the $10,000 and have their pie entered into the official Miss American Pie recipe collection. The finalists' recipes will be submitted to the state's caterers early so that they can start preparing them in quantity to be served at the picnic.

Once Penny's hooked up to water and electricity, we take Zoe for a walk around the grounds.

"Standing is nice," Noel says, stretching his long frame to its limit.

"Indeed." The back of my dress is horribly wrinkled from the drive, but I'm not bothered enough to change it. My phone buzzes inside my pocket, and I grab it without thinking.

I regret it instantly.

A new message from RememberRemember: *Time is ticking.*

I put it away without comment.

"You okay?" Noel asks.

"Always," I say, pasting on a cheery smile. "Let's head back. I need food that doesn't come in a wrapper."

"Ooh, do we get to roast hot dogs on an open fire?" Noel asks.

I laugh. "If you want to go find someone with dogs and a fire, go for it, but I have salad stuff and a mac-and-cheese recipe that'll change your life."

"You're right, that sounds better."

In the van, I set a pot of water to boil and say, "You can grab the first shower while I cook."

"Or I can help," he offers.

"I know, but tiny kitchen, remember?" The thought of dancing around him and Zoe in the tight space is ridiculous. "Plus the hot water takes forever to regenerate, so it's either go now or get stuck with cold later."

That's enough to convince him, and I soon fall into the soothing rhythm of stirring and whisking.

My phone vibrates in my pocket, but I ignore it this time.

Noel emerges just as I'm dumping noodles into the cheese, his damp hair slicked back and the distinctly familiar scent of grapefruit body wash clinging to him. I sniff again, just to be sure.

"I forgot to pack soap," he says with a look of chagrin. "I borrowed."

I laugh. "At least you packed clothes. If your grand gesture had stopped at just the snack box, you'd be having dinner in a dress."

"I could rock it," he says, opening the fridge and taking out the salad fixings without asking. He carries them to the end of the counter, out of the way, and I slide him a bowl. "Do you have cider vinegar?"

"Secret ingredient of my crusts," I say, getting him the bottle.

"Yeah, that's your secret," he says dryly.

I throw a potholder at him. "It's one of them."

He goes back to the fridge for a bottle of cider, saying, "I have more in my bag," before I can protest, and sets about making a dressing. I pop the mac and cheese under the broiler to crisp and have a surreal feeling that we're playing house. It's nice.

We eat at the counter, side by side, and I watch him take the first bite. He moans on cue, and I grin. "Told you."

"It's magic, right? It has to be."

"Only in that it's made with nutmeg and a scandalous amount of good cheese," I say, digging in. I splurged on heaps of fancy cheese, just in case.

"I could get used to this camping thing," he says.

"I'm glad you came," I blurt out.

"I am too."

After dinner is cleared up, he sits at the counter and watches me make the contest pie, telling me about his dream plans for the orchard and cidery as the RV fills with the sweet scent of honey and apples. It's a completely lovely way to spend an evening.

I shower while he takes Zoe for another walk, and it pleases me how happy she is to go off with him. You can always trust dogs to have good taste.

I hear them come in just as I'm turning the water off.

"Your phone's vibrating," Noel calls. "You want it?"

"Negative." I try to remember if I left it facedown. I doubt Noel's the nosy type, but I don't need him seeing messages from Daniel. The thought is enough to make me rush, and I yank on sleep shorts and a tank top, leaving my hair twisted in its towel.

Noel bursts out laughing as soon as I come out of the bedroom.

"Oh, come on," I say, touching the towel on my head. "I know you don't think girls dry their hair as soon as they get out of the shower."

"It's not that," he says. "It's the shorts. I was just surprised. I've never seen you out of a dress. I figured you even slept in them, like frilly nightgowns or something."

"You've thought about it?" I say, arching an eyebrow.

Watching him fluster about for the right answer makes me laugh. Now we're even. "Not to sound like a pumpkin, but it's almost midnight and I'm beat."

"Same," he says.

"The submission window is between nine and eleven tomorrow, so I want to leave by eight thirty. If you're not up, I will one hundred percent leave you here."

"I'll be up," he says with a laugh.

I lower the blinds and lock the door before checking to make sure Zoe has enough water for the night. She's already waiting expectantly by the bed.

Which is when it hits me. The one logistical detail I didn't work out.

I look from Zoe to Noel, who's leaning against the counter with a knowing smirk.

"One bed," I say. "And one largish dog."

He laughs good-naturedly. "Wondered what we were doing about that. If you can spare me a pillow, I'm fine on the floor."

"Then you'd be sleeping in the kitchen," I say, shaking my head. I consider him, his height, his Noel-ness. This is new territory, but it's late and I'm tired. "Share? I don't have cooties if you don't."

"Officially cootie-free since the fourth grade," he says.

"Perfect." I hit the kitchen lights, and the van is plunged into darkness. I go first, telling Zoe to stay before climbing onto the bed and throwing the covers back. It's weird getting settled on one side when I normally start in the middle with Zoe on my legs. I put the real pillow on Noel's side, keeping the fluffy decorative one for myself. "All set."

Zoe takes that as her cue and leaps onto the bed, and I laugh. "Better hurry before she takes your whole side."

"Just a sec."

I hear the soft swoosh of fabric and the rustling sound of clothes being moved, possibly *re*moved, and my heart speeds up. He can't possibly think . . .

"There they are," he murmurs. More rustling.

"Do you need lights?" I ask.

"No," he says quickly. "I'm good. Just changing. Pajama pants are an important part of my sleep station."

"Good to know," I say, glad he can't see my stupid grin. I wonder what they look like.

The mattress shifts, and I freeze as he settles in. Zoe, on the other hand, goes bonkers, leaping around our feet and digging at the blanket like a maniac. I can't blame her; it's the first time she's had to share the bed with anyone other than me, but I don't announce this.

"Zoe, lay down," I say softly.

After a few more pounces, she does, smack in between us with a massive sigh. In the dark, our hands brush as we pet her head.

"This is cozy," Noel says softly.

"You mean cramped?" I know the mattress is too short for his lanky frame even without our having to share it.

"I mean cozy," he says.

I smile stupidly into the dark and fall asleep with my lips still curled.

Chapter Thirty-Four

I awake on my side with a dog stretched out along my back and a hand on my waist. I roll carefully and see Noel, still asleep, his arm draped across Zoe until it reaches me. She stirs at my movement and I shush her, climbing out of bed carefully so as not to disturb either of them.

I grab a dress from the closet—lemons for luck—and pull the curtain, dressing quickly in the kitchen.

It's only after I do my hair and makeup and have the kettle on for tea that I check the notifications on my phone. There's a text from Juan that I reply to, some social media stuff I ignore, and seventeen messages from RememberRemember.

"Your phone makes you cranky," Noel says, startling me. He's sleep disheveled, clad in plaid flannel pants, and it's such a strange thing to have another human in the van first thing in the morning that I just stare.

He shrugs. "You get crinkles every time you check it. Right here." He points at a spot between his eyebrows.

I'm torn between being touched and annoyed that he's noticed. I hadn't even noticed.

"You could probably ignore it," he says. "Just until the contest is done?"

"I wish," I say.

The RememberRemember messages are exactly what I expect them to be, threats and hyperbole, right up until the last one. A screenshot of a text file—his drafted statement outing me to the world. As I'm looking at it, my phone buzzes again. *Clock is ticking.*

For the moment, at least, I can ignore it. "Okay, Captain Commentary, shirt and shoes are required for our adventures. And preferably real pants." I grab Zoe's leash, and she jumps off the bed at the sound. "I'll take her out, you dress, then post-pie-delivery brunch?"

"Sounds like a plan."

* * *

Boston is a city designed by a committee of the pettiest and most vindictive drunk traffic gods, and we have to pay a small fortune to park the truck, but I'm too swept up in thoughts of the contest and clocks to care.

"This is weirdly smaller than I was expecting," I say when we get to the conference room where they want the pies. Instead of numbered spaces, there are two long tables with county names running down them in alphabetical order.

"You're among the elite now," Noel says.

I scope out the competition as we make our way to the Hampshire section. Every single one looks amazing. "This definitely isn't amateur hour."

"Nervous?"

"Nope," I say, mostly meaning it.

As before, people are stationed behind the tables to ensure the pies aren't tampered with and to whisk away the extra pies. On the table is a folder with my name typed on the corner label. I take it and place my contest pie, the prettiest of the three, in its place. One of the men behind the table takes the extra boxes from Noel.

Inside the folder are four tickets for the award ceremony, which is being billed as a Pies and Prosecco Reception to begin at six o'clock. The mention of the time sends a chill through me, which Noel mistakes for nerves.

"You so have this," he says.

"We'll see."

We get a late breakfast at the Mad Batter, an adorable little place that feels like a French bistro married a Victorian circus. The black-and-white awning called to me from the street, and the inside doesn't disappoint. The space is incredibly narrow but quite long, and mismatched chandeliers hang above equally mismatched tables with candles on them. A row of white built-in shelves line one wall and are filled with an array of international treats and trinkets that I goggle at on the way to the counter.

"If I ever have a pie shop, I want it to look like this," I whisper to Noel.

"It is pretty amazing," he agrees. "But I'm kind of fond of the van."

I laugh. "Me too."

We order and snag a tiny table for two by the window where we can people-watch. Our drinks—tea for me, hot chocolate for Noel—come in adorable swirly teacups, and I slip my phone from my pocket, feeling like a complete tool. "I hate to be this person," I say apologetically, "but this place is worth posting."

I snap a couple shots of the restaurant and upload them, tagging the restaurant, the city, and the contest. "It's weird that this is the only Pie Girl work I'm doing today," I say, tapping my phone. "I feel like—I have the van here, I should be selling."

"Or take a break," Noel says with a grin. "It won't kill you."

"Just not used to it is all," I say as our food arrives. Everything looks and smells amazing, and I commandeer half of Noel's side order of hash browns for myself. He steals a forkful of my mushroom crepe in retaliation.

It's nice, this being-normal thing.

We linger once the food is gone, enjoying the atmosphere and a second round of drinks while we consider and veto seeing the usual touristy sights.

"I'm cool chilling at the campground with the dog if you are," Noel says. "I feel like you could use a relaxing day before the craziness of tomorrow."

"That's assuming I make it to that round," I say.

He grins. "Which I am."

A growl of a motorcycle makes me glance out the plate glass window, and I do a double take. Noel turns to follow my gaze.

Dismounting from the bike is a statuesque figure who pulls off a helmet to reveal a purple tangle of curls. Noel and I exchange looks as she throws open the restaurant door.

"Thank god I caught you," Melly says, stealing a chair from a neighboring table and joining us. She looks at the tiny table and the two of us, and something hardens in her face. "Am I crashing?"

"Well, yeah, kind of," I say with a forced laugh. "What are you doing here?"

"You have a problem."

* * *

We meet back at the campground because there is no part of this conversation that I want to have in public.

Noel is quiet on the ride back, and I don't blame him. I'm tense and unsettled myself, and more than a little peeved when I see she has beat us there.

I unlock the van and put the kettle on, more as a distraction than because I need another cup, and Noel and Melly each take seats at the counter. Neither looks thrilled to be sharing the space, but they do it.

Zoe makes anxious circuits among the three of us like she knows something's up.

Melly barely notices her. She's sitting on one leg and has the knee of the other drawn up beneath her chin, practically vibrating with energy. "He's here, you know. Daniel."

She taps at her phone and turns it toward me. An Instagram page is open on the screen, and she swipes through a series of photos showing all the Boston landmarks Noel and I skipped. The final shot is like a knife in the gut. A selfie of Aria, pressing her lips to the cheek of none other than Daniel Cooper on the State House steps.

He's here. In Boston. On the day of the deadline.

"Thought you'd want to know," Melly says.

"You're not wrong," I say, although it's the very last thing I want to be true.

"Apparently he'll be accompanying her to the finals." She pauses to let that bombshell settle before asking, "What are you going to do?"

My fingers itch to be in pie dough, kneading a magic into flour that can fix this, but I can't. I know I can't. A murder pie for Daniel would be crossing the line. It would be personal. It would go against everything I'm trying to prove by winning this contest—that my magic can do good without damage.

But still. The temptation is there, and I sigh. "I have no idea. Has Aria said anything to you? About him?"

She shakes her head. "You can stop him, though," she says. "You have to." She turns to Noel. "Look, you already know about this stuff, and you care about her, right?"

Noel nods warily, and Melly pounces. "Well, this shitweasel is going to destroy her if she doesn't do something. Tell her she has to stop him."

Noel turns to me, searching my face. "Is that true?"

I bring my hands up in a frustrated *Who knows?* gesture.

"It's true," Melly says.

"Shouldn't we go to the police?" He directs the question at me, but Melly answers before I can.

"And tell them what? Our magic murder-pie girl is being blackmailed by a respected member of the community?"

Noel looks pained, and I remember he's only ever had positive experiences with the police. Even when he was arrested for the mushroom incident, he was treated well and pretty much got to go on his merry way. It would be different for me, with murder in the mix. With the years of running from my past.

"She's right," I say, as much as I don't want to. "I can't have the police looking too closely at my life. They could be as dangerous as Daniel."

"So what do we do?" he asks.

"I don't know yet." My mind is spinning, but there's only one option that seems realistic, and it's the one I don't want to consider. A murder pie. A line-crossing, self-serving murder pie.

"I think I need to have a chat with sister dear," Melly says, launching herself off the stool and stalking out of the van, already pulling her phone from her back pocket.

"Is there any way I can help?" Noel asks when she's gone. "Anything at all."

I'm about to say no, but I realize that isn't true. I take a deep breath, suddenly nervous. "If something happens to me, would you take Zoe?" I ask.

Concern crowds out any lingering anger and annoyance on his face. "What do you mean, if something happens to you?"

"Just what I said. She likes you and you're good with her." My throat closes at the mere thought of being separated from her. "Please?"

"Of course I will," he says, getting to his feet. "But you're scaring me. Is this about Daniel? I thought you said he wasn't a threat."

"It's just in general," I say.

He comes to stand in front of me, warm eyes searching my face. "You can let me in," he says. "I might not like everything you have to tell me, but I'm team Pie Girl all the way."

"I'm glad someone is," I say, giving him a wry smile, and even though we both know there's nothing funny, we pretend otherwise.

We kill the rest of the afternoon taking Zoe exploring around the campground and eating last night's leftover mac and cheese, but Melly's arrival and the news of Daniel being in town have thrown the day out of whack.

The problem is the lack of easy answers. Part of me wishes I'd just given Melly the pie when she asked for it and let things play out. I consider and reject the idea of trying to meet up with Daniel before his deadline, but there's still a chance he's bluffing, and I don't want to risk calling it like that.

At a loss, I bake. Not a contest pie, not a murder pie, but simple cinnamon raisin cuties that I infuse with as much calm and clearheadedness as humanly possible. I know I won't feel its effect, but just going through the motions helps, and by the time they're cooling on the counter, I do feel calmer.

While Noel's in the shower, I change, swapping my lemon dress for the solid navy one. "Taking Zoe out," I call, grabbing her leash. "We should leave pretty soon."

He's sitting on Penny's steps when we return, looking surprisingly dapper in a pair of blue pants, a white Oxford with the sleeves rolled up, and a pair of nubby blue suspenders.

He stands and holds his arms out to the side. "Think this is okay?"

"I think it's rather dashing for a farm boy," I say, and relief floods his face, washing away the awkwardness. "Although I'm somewhat concerned that you forget to pack soap but can whip out suspenders like it's nothing."

"Priorities," he says. "I wanted to cover all bases."

"Except cleanliness."

"I'm grapefruity fresh," he says, following me into the van.

I feed Zoe and make sure we have our tickets. When he takes a cutie pie for the road, I can't help but laugh. "You remember we're going to a pie reception, right?"

He shrugs. "I'm pre-pieing."

Chapter Thirty-Five

The hotel has gone all out on the reception. It's hands down the poshest event I've ever been to, and Noel and I both are bordering on underdressed.

Luckily, neither of us is bothered.

The room is crowded with people in suits and formal dresses, and black-jacketed servers circulate with trays of pie bites and sparkling flutes of prosecco. Noel smoothly snags two off a passing tray and hands me one. I take it with hopes that the bubbles will quell some of the rising worries at what I'm considering.

"To pie," he says, tilting the glass as me.

I clink it with my own. "To pie." Someone bumps me from behind as I sip, and I fumble the glass, barely keeping myself from spilling it down Noel's shirt. When I recover, I lean in closer and whisper, "Just between you and me, I think your cider is better."

He laughs. "Agreed."

He offers me his arm, and I link mine through it. We wander the room, searching out as many different pies as we can find. Not a single one sucks.

"Okay, *this* might be my favorite," I say for probably the fifth time. This favorite is a blueberry pie that has the brightest-tasting lemon streusel I've ever eaten.

Noel samples it, nodding thoughtfully as he chews, then leans into my ear. "Just between you and me, I think your pies are better than all of these."

A warmth floods through me that has nothing to do with the alcohol and everything to do with his breath on my ear. I give him a playful shove away, but my fingers linger on his chest a second longer than necessary. "You're such a dork."

"But I'm your dork."

I meet his eyes, the bubbles making me bold. "Is that right?"

"It is."

My phone buzzes in my pocket before I can react to that, killing the lightheartedness of the moment. I pull it out, dread heavy in my chest, but before I can get past the lock screen, Noel plucks it out of my hand and slides it into his back pocket.

"Enjoy. The. Evening," he says, enunciating each word clearly.

Part of me wants to be angry and snatch my phone back, but part of me is more intrigued by the twinkle in his dark eyes. I don't know if it's the spiffy clothes or the general atmosphere, but there's something different about Noel here, a confidence I wouldn't necessarily have expected.

What the hell. I drain my prosecco, feeling it warm my cheeks, and decide he's right. The bad news will wait. I accept a fresh glass from a passing server, and we continue working our way through the state's best pies.

The room is crowded, and we find ourselves pressed together enough that it becomes almost automatic to stay that way, attached by his hand on my back or my arm through his. While part of me knows I have no business getting involved with him like this, especially now, especially here, a larger part of me likes the contact, the companionship, too much to care.

Without warning, the main lights dim and a spotlight lands on a podium set up on a low stage. An Asian woman in a pristine white chef coat steps up to it and lowers the microphone. A hush falls across the crowd, and the room goes still.

"My name is Lucy Yang. I would like to thank you all for coming tonight," she says in a sonorous voice. "I would especially like to extend my heartfelt thanks and respect to all those who provided the wonderful pies that have been on sample this evening."

A polite wave of applause swells around the room.

An annoyed murmur erupts behind me, and for the second time I'm jostled hard enough to disturb my drink. I turn, expecting an apology, but find myself face-to-face with a grinning Melly.

"Wouldn't miss it," she says, bumping her shoulder into mine.

I can't help returning the smile and curse the prosecco. I put my finger to my lips to shush her before more people complain, but for the moment I'm quite content sandwiched between her and Noel, where I can pretend the only thing that matters is the words being spoken into that microphone.

"As the executive chef for the Beacon Hill Hospitality Group, it has been an honor to participate in this round of judging, and we look forward to preparing samples of the final three pies to share at the Fourth of July Picnic on the Common." Chef Yang says when the applause stops. "For this round, every entry exhibited the mark of a skilled hand and an attention to detail that made it difficult to choose any definitive winners. Every pie we tasted was well composed, well executed, and most importantly, delicious. With that being said, we were tasked with choosing the three pies that would advance to the final round, and that we did."

She pauses for effect, and it's like the entire room holds its breath.

Except for Melly, who stares at her dimmed phone, thumbs flying. Her sister's name is at the top of the screen, but the messages are piling up too quickly to see what has her so enthralled.

I don't have a chance to ask, because Chef Yang is opening a red envelope with deliberate slowness. She removes a sheet of ivory paper and says, "It is with great pleasure that I invite, in no particular order, our three finalists to the stage."

Noel's fingers lace into mine.

"Representing Norfolk County is Olivia Babineaux, with a spectacular reimagining of a Boston Cream Pie."

Applause follows the tiny Black girl with a hot-pink forearm crutch to the stage.

Noel's fingers tighten around mine.

"Next, from Franklin County, is Jacinta Torres, whose Strawberry Rhubarb Crunch Pie is a delight from crumb to crust."

A pretty Latina woman maybe ten years older than me takes the stage with her hands over her mouth, happy tears gleaming in her eyes.

Melly turns and takes my face between her hands. The grin is gone, replaced with a look of steely determination. "You're next," she says. "Do this. All the way."

And before I can react, she kisses me hard and fast on the mouth and disappears back into the crowd.

Noel's fingers are still tight around mine, and I squeeze back, head spinning.

"And finally," Chef Yang says, "I would like to welcome Daisy Ellery from Hampshire County, whose Hollow Hill Honey Apple Pie combines everything we love about the classic with a delightful honey-cream twist."

Noel throws his arms around me, and I lean into him, the blood rushing in my ears. He releases me with a look of pure joy, and I practically float to the stage. I stand beside the other finalists, blinded by the glare of the spotlight and absolutely reeling from the win, Melly's unexpected kiss, and the very existence of Noel.

I think of my mother, of all the Ellery women, and the magic they've passed down. The power.

I think of the scared seventeen-year-old version of me, the miles on the road, and marvel that they led here, to the state's capital, to a life filled with people I care about and a purpose that matters.

And I think, finally, that the magic didn't break and that I didn't either. If any of my foremothers could see me on this stage right now, I think they would be proud. They would understand. The magic is more than murder; it's my heritage. It's who I am on a molecular level. The pies don't just end life; they enhance it. Pies Before Guys is only a single facet of what I do. The other pies, they're no less worthy. They bring happiness and comfort and strength, and that's no different at all from what my mother did in her salon or what Nana did with her dresses. It's connected, all of it. The Ellery magic makes the world a better place by empowering those who need them, plain and simple.

The little bees that have been buzzing in my brain with worries of Daniel disappear as surely as if they never existed. In their place, a seed of an idea takes hold.

It's amazing, really, the magic pie can do.

Chapter Thirty-Six

I let Noel drive back to the campground, because the three and a half glasses of prosecco I had combined with everything else make me behind the wheel a less-than-stellar idea.

Noel is chattering away happily about the win and has given me my phone back so I can share the news. I text Juan, who responds instantly with a barrage of emojis that makes me laugh, and I am surprised when a few moments later my phone pings with a text from Frank. *Damn proud of you*, it says.

I didn't even think the old man knew how to text, and I'm unexpectedly touched.

I update the Pie Girl social media accounts with the win—Noel had the foresight to get a photo of me on the stage—and only then do I turn my attention to the rest.

There is only one message from RememberRemember—*You'll regret this*—but a barrage of social media activity.

He's tagged me in a post, a photo of Penny used for attention, that's captioned *Daisy Ellery, known as The Pie Girl, is a murderer. Her pies have been responsible for the deaths of dozens, if not hundreds, of men, including my father. Her method is unknown, but the results speak for themselves.* He links obituaries to Marissa's husband along with those of two other PBG recipients. My heart constricts. *She is a murderer. She is not to be trusted. She must be found, stopped, and prosecuted to the fullest extent of the law.* He's tagged several of the major news outlets.

I realize Noel has asked me something, is waiting for an answer.

"What?" I say dumbly.

"Everything okay?"

"I don't know." It's the most honest answer I have.

Then I do the one thing I know I shouldn't do: I read the comments.

And slowly, comment by comment, a smile spreads across my face.

Pie Girl pies are to die for! Best ever!!

To die for raspberry crumb! Highlight of the farmer's market!

The hazelnut cutie pies are KILLER!!!

Finals would've killed me without these pies! Life-saving!!

Give me pies or give me death! Pie Girl makes the best pies I've ever had—sorry mom!

I murder a dozen or more of these cutie pies every week! They're the only thing getting me through school!

One bite and it's like you've died and gone to heaven!

They go on, page after page of comments. Most of the usernames are unknown to me, but many I recognize as PBG accounts. Something swells in my chest that isn't fear or worry or concern. It's security. Peace. Calm. Maybe my own pies work on me after all.

Buried in the swell of positive comments are the detractors, the ones with questions, and of course, the ones with wildly inappropriate sexual remarks.

Oh, internet.

Back at the campground, we take Zoe out, but not before Noel snags another cinnamon raisin pie.

"How are you not pied out yet?" I ask with a laugh.

He shrugs. "There's always room for pie."

The moonlit walk is nice, a quiet respite from a roller-coaster day. I deliberately leave my phone on the counter, desperately wanting to hold on to the happiness of the night. Fifteen minutes of ignorant bliss might not change the reality of things, but I'll still take it.

Noel and I walk close enough that our arms brush, and when his fingers find mine, I'm not the least bit surprised. Even though it feels more real out here, in the dark and away from the bustle of the awards ceremony, it feels like the most natural thing in the world to take his hand in mine.

"I knew you could do it," he says. "Win."

"I haven't won yet," I remind him.

"You made it this far. That counts."

Something seizes me then, a fist from the past around my heart that sends tears to my eyes. "I wish my mother could see this."

He squeezes my hand. "She'd be proud of you." He says it like an absolute truth, like he knows her, and it's enough to break my heart.

"She'd have liked you," I say, because I did know her, and it is an absolute truth. Things I haven't let myself consider well up all at once, flipping through my mind like pages in a book. A future, a family, things she'll never get to see, never get to be part of. "Noel, do you think I've let her down?"

"Of course not," he answers without hesitation, like there's no question there. "Why would you even say that?"

"It's just something I've been thinking about, how the magic works for me. I don't use it the way they did; I can't. It's like it broke with me, or maybe I'm broken. I don't know."

He stops, and like dominoes, Zoe and I fall in beside him. He's barely more than a silhouette in the darkness, but I can feel his gaze on me.

"There is nothing wrong with you," he says. "You inherited something powerful, and you're using it the best way you can. There's nothing broken about that."

"But do you—"

"No. What you do is incredible." He chuckles softly in the darkness. "And okay, yes, kind of scary sometimes, but incredible. It's brave and it's righteous and it makes an actual concrete difference in the world. How could anyone not be proud of that?"

I want to go to him then, wrap myself around him, but I don't. I can't. Every nerve in me feels raw and exposed to the past and the present in equal measure. Zoe whines softly at my side.

In the dark of the night I reach up and touch his cheek. "Thank you."

"For what?"

"Being here. And being you."

* * *

When we get back to Penny, I see immediately it was the right decision to abandon the phone, because notifications are piling up.

I sigh.

"Care to share?" Noel asks.

I open one of the posts and hand him the phone.

He reads, confusion written in the furrow between his brows. “This isn’t that bad,” he says.

“The comments aren’t, but the original post is. And he’s tagged the media.” I pull the bobby pins out of my hair and shake it out before recapturing it into a messy bun.

“I think you were looking at something else, then,” he says.

Now it’s my turn to be confused. I take the phone back, and I see that he’s right. It’s the same picture, but the caption has been changed from the one I read in the car. *Huge congrats to Turnbridge’s own @PieGirl for making it to the final round of the* Miss American Pie Contest*! We can’t wait to try the @HollowHillOrchard Honey Apple Pie. #SupportSmallBusinesses #WomenBusinessOwners #GirlBoss #PiesBeforeGuys*

“I don’t get it,” I say. I scroll the comments, and every single negative one has been deleted. I search other platforms for Daniel Cooper + Pie Girl and find the same thing: congratulations and a carefully curated comment section.

“Well, maybe he had a change of heart. I mean, he is your brother after all.”

I raise an eyebrow. “You didn’t meet him.”

“Blood is blood, though. He’s still family.”

I shake my head. “No, blood isn’t family. Blood is just a liquid, like water or honey. It’s not special.”

“You really think that?” He sounds genuinely surprised.

“You don’t? Your uncle is trying to sell out the orchard that’s been in your family for generations,” I remind him.

“I never said family was necessarily good,” he says. “Just that it exists.”

“Not because of randomly shared DNA, though. It’s more than that. It has to be.” I take a deep breath. Part of me knows this should all stay in my head, but something makes me say it out loud anyway. "After my mom died, I had to redefine what family meant. My father fell apart—and trust me, it doesn't help my opinion of him knowing that the only reason he was even with my mom was because he cheated on someone else's—and it was just me and Zoe. I didn't have aunts or uncles, and my grandparents were already gone. So my version of family wasn't the TV version. It was me and a dog and a man I felt obligated to take care of even though every time I looked at him, all I could do was blame him."

I take a ragged breath, the past and the disappearing prosecco buzz doing bad things to my brain. But Noel is watching me calmly, like I'm not as unhinged as I sound in my head, so I go on.

"And then he was gone too, and it really was just Zoe and me, for a long time. We had a home, we had each other, and it was enough, even if we were on the run. But then something happened that I never saw coming: our family grew. By staying in Turnbridge, we added Juan, and by extension Eric. We added Frank, who might come across as an ass but really isn't at all." I meet his eyes, and they're so steady and reassuring that I say, "And I'd like to think we've added you too, in a way."

"What kind of way?"

"Any kind. This kind." I'm flustered, my face hot, but I'm in too far to stop. "I can't explain it, but you just fit. You get the pie thing, all the pie things, and accept it for what it is, even if you don't like it all. I mean god, you know the very worst of me and you're still here. That matters."

"I told you I was team Pie Girl."

"And that matters. I know it's stupid, that we haven't known each other long enough for me to be saying this, but it's like a gut feeling. You fit, and I don't want you to go away."

"I'm not planning to," he says.

I'm about to continue rambling, but then he's in front of me with his hands on my shoulders and a gentle smile that shuts me right up.

"Everything is going to work out," he says. "You'll see. It always does, in the end."

I want to argue because I know firsthand that it doesn't always work out, not really, but it's like he reads my mind.

"It might not seem like it while you're in the shit of it, when everything feels like it's falling down around your ears, but at some point you're going to really like where you are and you're going to look back at the mess and realize it was one of the stepping stones that got you there."

The words are soothing and cinnamon scented, and I think he's talking about himself as much as me.

"This thing with Daniel," he says. "Whatever one-eighty he did, I'd say it's one of those don't-look-a-gift-horse-in-the-mouth things. Let it go. You can't control his actions; you can only control your own."

Cinnamon-scented, soothing words.

I steal a glance at the counter.

Only two cutie pies are still on the rack. No wonder he's suddenly Insight Boy.

I don't care. Pies or not, it's Noel. My Noel. I close the distance between us, and in that instant, everything changes.

"What are you doing?" he asks, voice thick.

"Controlling my actions," I say, but the words are lost as my lips find his.

* * *

Later in bed, I lie awake for a long time with that aphorism still rattling around my head: *I can't control his actions, I can only control my own.*

In the small hours of the night, with Zoe and Noel sleeping soundly beside me, I decide exactly how things are going to go tomorrow.

Chapter Thirty-Seven

The morning after might've been awkward if we hadn't already been friends, but we are, so it isn't. Plus, I've realized there's a world of difference between being with someone you actually care about and being with someone for the sake of ticking a box, and that makes the morning just as nice as the night before. I have too much in front of me to worry about what already happened, and besides, I don't regret it. At all. The fact that Noel has Zoe walked and tea ready and waiting by the time I get out of the shower makes me think he doesn't either, so we're five by five in my book.

Therefore, I'm comfortable in the silence that follows us into the heart of the state capital, because even though it's tense, we both know it has nothing to do with us and everything to do with what's coming.

Because no matter how confident I am in my plan, in the light of day, without the pleasant glow of prosecco's false optimism, I can't help worrying that there's more to Daniel's social media Jekyll-and-Hyde-ing last night than an actual change of heart. Maybe it wasn't enough to take me down online. Maybe it has to be in person.

At least I know that, for a few hours, I'll be safe. The baking part of the finals is restricted to contestants and judges, and there's no way Daniel will pull something during that time. It would be too obvious, even for him. The picnic will be different, though. There will be crowds and commotion and plenty of opportunity.

But that's later. Right now, I have a pie to make.

The instructions in the finalist folders tell us that we will meet at the State House and Chef Yang will oversee our baking in the catering kitchen off the Great Hall, where members of her team will be at work on food for the afternoon's festivities.

I'm stopped at the main entrance for security, and despite knowing I have nothing incriminating on me—even my phone, with its Pies Before Guys messages, is safe outside with Noel—the mere idea of being searched makes me uneasy. The security guard makes quick work of it, though, and I'm escorted to a cavernous Great Hall where Jacinta is already waiting. We exchange nervous smiles under the watch of a second security guard stationed by the wall. I can't help staring up at the domed glass ceiling where rows upon rows of flags hang. I feel impossibly small beneath the clear blue sky.

When Olivia is brought in, arrival heralded by the echo of her crutch on tile, our watchful agent touches a hand to his earpiece and murmurs, "All here."

Moments later, Chef Yang bustles in, chef coat already stained with the evidence of a busy morning. "Welcome," she says with a smile that instantly makes my shoulders relax. "Let's make some pies, shall we?"

She leads us to the kitchen with the security guard tailing a discreet distance back. It seems like overkill, him being here at all, and I wonder if he resents being on pie duty. It's not like he's going to catch any of us tipping a bottle of arsenic into our crusts.

We hear the kitchen before we see it—the rattle of sheet pans against metal racks, whisks banging the sides of pots, heavy oven doors being thrown shut. I relax even further. It's the sound of the diner on a busy shift.

Inside, though, it's nothing like the diner. For one thing, it's the size of the diner, easy, dining room and all, and it heaves like a living thing, a hive in full gear. White-coated cooks move with brisk efficiency, checking pans in ovens, chopping massive piles of veggies on stainless-steel prep tables, and whirling around each other, arms laden with pots and pans, *Hot behind!* punctuating each pass like a prayer.

Jacinta, Olivia, and I exchange astonished glances. In this moment we're not opponents in a contest but three pie makers given a glimpse of something few see.

"It's not always like this," Chef Yang says, leading us through the fray. "But putting on a picnic for a few hundred people kicks things into high gear. You'll be working at this table here."

There are bowls, rolling pins, and pie tins already piled on the table, along with a trio of open cardboard boxes, neatly labeled with our names. Bars of chocolate and cream for Olivia, strawberries and rhubarb for Jacinta, and apples, cider, and honey for me.

"Staples are in the bins below the table," Chef says, "Take what you need. I'll bring the butter out now. Jacinta, your lard should be in your box, and all spices are on that rack there. You may use the bottom rack of that oven to bake and those burners if you need it. Any questions?"

We all shake our heads.

"Julian will be keeping an eye on things," she says, tilting her head at the security guard. "But feel free to shout if you need anything else. Happy baking."

For a moment we all stand looking at each other, then, almost as one, we're sucked into the energy of the kitchen. We pull our boxes closer, inspect our ingredients. We weren't allowed to bring in any outside food, and I wonder how their cider and honey choices are going to affect my final pie. It doesn't matter, though.

I peruse the bins below the table, finding an array of flours: bread, cake, all-purpose, semolina, and pastry. The sugar bins are just as impressive: granulated, powdered, light and dark brown, turbinado, muscovado, and Demerara. Not roasted, though, but for the small amount I need, it won't matter.

I measure out my all-purpose flour, add my salt and sugar, and take a measuring cup to the sink near the spice rack for cold water.

Below the spices, bottles of vinegar stand like sentinels, and I take the apple cider, tipping a splash into my cup.

One-pound blocks of butter have been brought to the table, and I use a bench scraper to cut one in half. I set one section aside for my apples and chop the other into rough chunks that go into the bowl of flour.

And when I start to mix, everything in the kitchen falls away until it is only me and the pie and the magic.

* * *

Hours later, the chaos of the kitchen is transformed into something almost calm as trays of finished food are moved out to the tents on Boston Common.

Chef Yang turns her attention back to the three of us.

It's time.

Any camaraderie we've established vanishes in a swell of nerves.

We're spread out now, each at a separate table, our pies beside us like obedient puppies.

The kitchen door swings open and two security guards come in, stationing themselves on either side.

My heart hammers against my ribs.

Senator Elsa Bailey walks in with an arm looped through her wife's, the pair of them in coordinating linen sundresses. They're trailed by Governor Cora Strand and one of her staffers, Mayor Ronny Beckett and his wife, Julie, and finally, Aria.

Alone.

Something like a peach pit lodges in my chest. Daniel should be with her. Aria's whole presence is his doing, her spot bought through his company's sponsorship and his work on Mayor Beckett's reelection campaign. There's no way Daniel would miss the opportunity to schmooze. I was counting on him being here.

A small coterie of press people arrive last, and the one with the camera immediately starts moving around the kitchen, checking angles and getting close-up shots of the pies. Aria, looking ghost-like in an ivory sheath, watches them work, studiously avoiding my gaze.

No matter.

Chef Yang makes introductions, and Daniel still doesn't appear. It seems I'm not the only one noting the absence, because Mayor Beckett turns to Aria and asks, "How did that sly fox of yours manage to slip out of this? I wanted to hit the green myself, but alas, this old bird wouldn't hear of it." He chuckles and pats his wife on the arm, but there's a condescension there that keeps the gesture from looking truly affectionate. "Lucky man, your husband."

Aria gives a polite smile. "He had another engagement. He'll be along for the picnic, I'm sure."

Chef Yang claps her hands together, refocusing the group's attention on her. "All right, let's taste some pies, shall we?"

They start with Olivia. She introduces herself and her pie, explaining how she reworked the misleadingly named Boston cream pie into an actual pie while she cuts and serves slices. "Instead of cake layers, I used a lard-based crust filled with vanilla bean pudding, topped with dark-chocolate ganache, and I brought the cake element back in as a garnish."

Everyone murmurs appreciatively as they chew.

"These little cake croutons you have on top are amazing," the senator says. "I could eat these by the bagful."

Olivia grins, clearly flattered. "They're vanilla bean pound cake cubes that I rolled in sugar and caramelized. Sort of like crème brûlée, but with cake instead of custard."

"Well, it's genius," Senator Bailey says. "Just divine."

They come to me next, and Mayor Beckett immediately signals to the photographer. "Make sure you get a shot of this one. She looks like a fifties housewife. Does it get any more American this? It's like *Leave It to Beaver*. And is that apple pie too? That's perfect!"

I want to remind him that I'm standing right here, that I'm not a zoo animal, but his wife is already shushing him.

"Please excuse him, dear," she says. "You know how these old goats can be."

You mean awful? I want to ask, but don't. Instead, I focus on why I'm here. "This isn't your ordinary apple pie. It's has a honey-cream base with a cider caramel and honey crunch streusel." I smile as I cut slices, even though my heart is pounding.

I serve Aria first, because she needs this pie more than anyone. It's her pie. She hesitates, and I'm gripped by panic. What if she doesn't eat it?

But she accepts the plate.

Next, I pass slices to the Baileys, Governor Strand and her sidekick, and Mrs. Beckett, before turning to the security guards. "You guys want in?"

For a moment they look taken aback, but the one on the left shakes his head. "No, ma'am, but thank you."

"Your loss," I say.

I serve Mayor Beckett last, because if I can't be outright aggressive, I'm not above being passive.

"You know, I have to say, I have a soft spot for those McDonald's apple pies, those fried ones, and this is a little more complicated than I think a good apple pie should be," he says. "But if I were judging the whole package, you in that little dress and this pie looking almost as nice, well, I'd say you have a shot."

"Ronny," Mrs. Beckett hisses. "Leave the girl alone."

"She just reminds me of you way back when," he says. "Those were some good times."

Mrs. Beckett shakes her head. "Oh my," she says. "This is fabulous."

"Thank you," I say. Even though I should know better, I can't help looking at Aria, searching her face, waiting for a flicker, a sign that the magic is in there. Still, my heart is hammering, anticipation making my nerves sing. She finishes the whole slice, though, and I'm wondering if I can offer her a second without being conspicuous when Chef Yang bustles the group along to Jacinta's table.

On my left, Jacinta has her pie already sliced and plated, and she distributes the samples as she introduces herself. "For my entry, I went with a classic strawberry rhubarb, because there's always room for the classics. My original entry used fruit I grew myself, and the crust and streusel were made with flour milled in Northfield and butter from Rock-n-Oak Farm."

I barely hear her, though, because my eyes are on Aria now, watching, waiting for a change. The pie was overflowing with magic, filled with enough strength and conviction to set things right, and I expect her to rush out in search of her husband. Instead she praises Jacinta's pie and agrees with the other judges that they have a tough choice to make, as if she doesn't have a care in the world. As if her husband isn't a monster.

It's because he's not here. It has to be. If he were here, she would've felt the magic, the urge to take him aside and put an end to things. Instead he's going to announce his campaign at the picnic, and the wheels will be set in motion. The women I swore to protect will still be in danger.

I will still be in danger.

Chapter Thirty-Eight

When I leave the State House, it's with a sense of failure that has nothing to do with the contest and everything to do with the future. I find Noel waiting on the steps, an anxious furrow creasing his forehead.

He stands, conflicting emotions flitting across his face, before landing on something that looks like relief and happiness. "How'd it go?" he asks.

"Good, I think," I say, and put on a sunny smile, not wanting my sense of dread to show. "The mayor's kind of a dick, but everyone seemed to like the pie."

"Of course they did," he says. "There was never a question."

Not of that, anyway.

Before I can say anything, though, Noel's face grows serious.

"I think we have a problem," he blurts. He hands me my phone. "I wasn't snooping, I swear, but I saw when it popped up. It came right after I dropped you off."

I take the phone, a new dread crowding out all thoughts of Aria and failed magic.

With good cause.

On the screen is a photo of a man duct-taped to a chair, a silver slash across his mouth.

Daniel Cooper.

I shoot Noel a look.

"Read the texts," is all he says, taking my arm. "But do it walking."

I let him propel me down the sidewalk as I scroll through Melly's messages.

You don't have to worry about him anymore.

I was wrong, pie can change the world, and you're going to do it.

I'm sorry I got you caught up in this. I don't know if fixing it means you'll forgive me, but I owe you this much.

Pies Before Guys saved a lot of women, now we're saving you.

I told my sister everything. She's on our side now. She brought him to us.

That last one is like a physical blow. Aria knew. She set her husband up so I could kill him. No wonder she couldn't look at me.

My heart drops into my stomach, and I'm glad Noel is holding my arm, because it feels like the entire planet tilts beneath my feet.

"Finished?" he asks.

"This is everything?"

"Yup. I tried calling her, but she won't answer. I even tried from your phone, but when she heard it was me, she hung up."

"Shit." People and their goddamn grand gestures. I text her—*It's Daisy, answer the phone*—and immediately press call.

She picks up on the first ring. "Hello?" she says warily.

"What the hell are you doing?"

"Saving you," she says simply.

"Is he alive?"

"He shouldn't be," she says.

So he is. "Where are you?"

"Somewhere safe," she says. "You know, the Pies Before Guys crew are some seriously loyal chicks."

"I need an address." I have no idea what I'll be walking into, but I know that whatever they have planned isn't going to happen the way they think it is, and I need to be there. The pies are one thing; magic isn't the same as taping a man to a chair, killing him in cold blood.

"So you can help?" she asks.

"Yes." Help keep them from having blood on their hands, at least. I follow Noel into a parking garage, and the call gets staticky. "Where are you?"

Silence.

"Melly, I need an address."

At the truck, Noel mimes driving, but I shake my head. He hands me the keys and goes around to the passenger side.

Melly gives me an address and I repeat it, making sure it's right. Noel has his own phone out and is pulling it up on GPS. "Twenty minutes," he says.

"I'll be there in fifteen minutes," I tell Melly. "Don't do anything until I get there."

I hang up before she can argue and get behind the wheel.

"Sure you're good to drive?" Noel asks in that even way of his that carries no judgment.

"Yes." I follow the signs out of the garage, pay the ransom, and hit the road. For several minutes the only sound is the automated voice of the GPS directing us out of the heart of Boston.

I can see Noel watching me out of the corner of my eye. "Go ahead and ask," I say.

"You're not going to kill him, right?"

"I'm not going to let them kill him," I say, knowing it's not quite the same thing. The Arlington address can only mean Melly has roped Adelaide Brown into this. Adelaide's pie was for her uncle, a rich, well-spoken man who made a fortune selling girls like her to other rich men.

The house is modest by Arlington standards, but still nice, with a neatly manicured lawn and rows of tall hedges marking the property lines. I'm thankful for the privacy they offer.

The side door opens before we're even out of the truck, and Adelaide Brown waves us inside.

"It's so good to see you," she squeals, like this is a social visit. She throws her arms around me, and I return the hug somewhat automatically.

Over her shoulder I see Melly standing with a woman I recognize as Adelaide's referral—Courtney Martin, grasshopper pie for her abusive father—and someone I don't know. The stranger steps forward, hand outstretched.

"I'm Brittany Cline," she says. "And I need to order a pie."

* * *

She tells me her story, and it matches Emma Rogers's almost exactly, except for one important detail: she knows for sure the video went online for the world—and her family, and her church—to see. Because they did.

"I lost my scholarship over it," she says. "I was studying to be a teacher. My parents were humiliated, and instead of supporting me, they sided with the pastor and disowned me. They said if I chose to walk on that path of sin that I had to find my own way off of it. I was used as an example, a preaching point."

"Isn't religion supposed to be about forgiveness?" I ask.

"Not mine."

"And now you want a pie." It's not a question, and it's directed at Melly. "Who was your referral?"

"My what?" Brittany asks.

I swallow a sigh. I already know this answer. And I don't like it or the position it's put me in.

"Your referral," I say, trying to keep the strain out of my voice. This isn't her fault. She's a pawn in a game she doesn't know she's playing, and yes, she's also a victim. But that doesn't make her a client. "The person who gave you my information."

"Oh, that was Melly," she says. "It was crazy when Candice at the shelter passed along your email. I felt like the world was ending all over again, but then I got the message from Melly with the plane ticket, and it felt like a gift from God."

I dig my fingers into my forehead, hoping to chase away my burgeoning headache, and I hate myself for how this is going to go. "Brittany, tell me about your life now. You had to fly here. Where from? What do you do?"

A self-conscious smile lights up her face. "Seattle," she says. "But you know that; you found the shelter. I volunteer there at night a few times a week, mostly helping the kids with their homework or reading to the younger ones. I'm a wicked book geek. I work at the coolest little indie bookshop, and I know it's just retail, but I love it."

The headache grows fingers that wiggle into my brain. I meet her eyes, this girl I tried to hunt down, to warn, and know in my heart that I should've left it alone. "Brittany, you don't need a pie."

The smile falters. "But Daniel did that to me," she says, eyes darting between Melly and me. "I swear he did."

"I know," I say gently. "But that's not enough. This isn't how Pies Before Guys works. There's a system. Each new client has to be referred directly by a previous client, and I don't fill every request I get." I hold up a hand to forestall Melly's interruption. "Don't. A pie is the last resort for women who have no other way of making things right. And Brittany, you *did* make things right. You got away, all on your own, and you made a life that may not be what you planned, but that you love."

"But he should be punished," she says in a small voice. "It's not fair what he did."

"I know. But it's not worth killing him over and having that on your conscience for the rest of your life, not now. Now it will just be revenge, and I don't think that's who you are."

Tears are bright in her eyes, and she shakes her head.

Melly pushes herself away from the counter, a desperate look in her eyes. "He's not going to let this go," she says, grabbing my arms. "We made him change the posts, but as long as he's alive, he's not going to let this go. He's going to come after you."

"I know," I say. "And that's between me and him now."

Chapter Thirty-Nine

They have him in the basement, taped up next to the washing machine, and I have to admit, they did a solid job of it.

His eyes narrow when he sees me, but he seems to have learned that struggling against the bonds is useless.

I rip the strip of tape from his mouth with neither ceremony nor warning, and he grunts in pain.

"I need to piss," he says.

"Life is hard."

"This is kidnapping."

"No shit," I snap. "But fun fact, I'm not the one who did it. From what I understand, your own wife hand delivered you to this mess."

"It's that little bitch's fault," he rasps. "The two of them. Fucking set me up."

I fold my arms and lean against the washer. "It's your fault, Daniel. You brought this all on yourself. If you had treated those girls with the respect they deserved, none of this would be happening."

"If you hadn't killed my father, this wouldn't be happening."

"That's faulty logic, and you have no evidence that ever happened."

"On November fifth he went into that house and never came out," Daniel says, chest heaving in its duct-tape cocoon. "Never. The investigator I hired could turn up no trace of him after that day, not a single sighting. It's like he just vanished. So I got to thinking, if he hadn't left the house, he must still be there."

The scent of dryer sheets seems to swell in the air, sending me back in time. Another basement, another washing machine. A window. And through it, the hidden space beneath the porch.

"So I went to look."

I go very, very still.

"I searched the yard, and I searched the house but I found no sign of him. What I did find, in the basement next to the washing machine, was a shovel. Now, I couldn't have done it, not at my height, but you? I bet you fit under that porch no problem."

He smirks like he has it all figured out, but he's wrong.

It wasn't no problem.

It was cramped and dark and full of spiders. For stretches of time, I could put my brain on standby, the digging happening on pure autopilot, but then eight legs would crawl across my hand or up my neck and the horror would rush back in full force.

I ached for days afterward, while I drove for hours without any destination in mind other than away.

And I made it.

Away.

And now this man, this sleazy, fucked-up scumsack of a man who thinks recording women without their consent is acceptable behavior, wants to send me back.

Fuck.

Him.

I slap the duct tape back over his mouth and leave him there.

I have a pie to bake.

* * *

I go straight to Noel, bypassing Melly's questions and the others' silent stares.

I take his hands, the concern in his eyes making them almost hard to meet. "Can you go get the van and Zoe, meet me back here?"

"What's going on?"

I hold his gaze. "Do you trust me?"

He tilts his head, and a surprised little half smile pulls at the corner of his mouth like he's just realized the answer. "Strangely, yes."

I bring his hands to my lips and kiss his rough knuckles. "Thank you. I'll be ready to go when you get back."

He leaves, and I turn to the rest of them.

"Here's how it's gonna go," I say. I've been toeing the never lines since this whole thing started, and now I'm going to stomp all over them. I start with Adelaide and Courtney. "You may have figured this out already, but in case it's not clear, I'm not a delivery girl for Pies Before Guys. I *am* Pies Before Guys."

The glances they exchange suggest Melly has already revealed this particular nugget of truth, but they have the sense to keep quiet. Melly has this triumphant look on her face, though, an expression skating the edges of something like adoration. I pin her with a stare.

"You and him"—I stab a finger to the door where Noel just left—"you're like the goddamn angel and devil on my shoulders." Her full lips curl into a mischievous grin, and I shake my head. "Don't. Right now, I need to know exactly what your sister's part in this is. When I talked to her, she was like a Stepford zombie. Why the change?"

"Sometimes people need to hear things more than once," she says. "Like an intervention. She's not stupid, just stuck. She told me about the baby, and we talked about how she'd feel if someone treated that child the way Daniel treated Brittany and the others. Talked about the rest. Made it personal. You've seen me at rallies; you know I can be persuasive."

"Did you tell her you were setting him up for murder?"

She hesitates long enough that I'm not even a little bit surprised when she says, "Not exactly."

"Exactly what, then?"

She scrunches up her face, a sure sign she knows I'm not going to like the answer. "I might've framed it as more of a restorative justice thing. You know, meeting with the wronged parties, being given a chance to make amends, you know, all that jazz. Maybe with a possible side of violence as a treat."

I close my eyes and inhale deeply. I steeple my fingers against my lips, as much to keep myself from speaking as a signal that I need a minute. In the ensuing silence, I work the problem, factoring in this information.

And I find the answer.

I open my eyes, meet the gaze of each of the women in the room in turn. A weight has settled in the silence, as clear a sign as any that there's no uncrossing these lines. "There is a man in the basement that you put there. All of you." I give them a moment to absorb the absolute gravity of that truth. "So we're in this together now, and you each have a role to play. Adelaide, first, I'll need to use your kitchen."

She nods quickly, eyes wide.

The rage and fear from the basement are gone now. I'm back in control and I have a plan. I give them their assignments and get no arguments. "Now I'm going to bake a pie, and after this is over, every single one of you is going to forget this ever happened."

* * *

In the end, I bake two separate pies.

The one I put in Adelaide's only proper pie pan gets left out on the counter for the girls, and the other, a tiny single serving baked in a Mason jar lid, I take downstairs.

When Daniel sees what I'm holding, he finally fights, thrashing and rocking so the chair scrapes the concrete floor.

"Stop," I say, standing quietly before him.

After a time, he does, nostrils flaring with the effort to catch his breath.

I'm aware of the tableau I present, the sinister calm at odds with the cheerful little pie, the swingy dress belying the monster within. "We can do this the easy way or the hard way, but we are going to do it."

He chooses the hard way, because a man like him can go no other way. But in the end, the pie goes down.

Daniel Cooper—blackmailer, amateur pornographer, and all-around piss-gibbon—is soon slumped lifeless against his bonds.

I go upstairs.

Courtney and Adelaide jump when I enter the kitchen, pie-filled forks clattering to the table.

"You're up," I say.

They scurry downstairs, clutching knives, a pair of kitchen shears, and a trash bag.

"You talked to Aria?" I ask Melly. She nods. "Then prep the car."

"Already done," she says, grinning like we're in a movie.

I turn to Brittany. "You're sure you're good to drive?"

She nods, a hard set to her face. "I want to help. Plus, it's my rental."

"Straight to the hotel, then the airport. Under no circumstances can you miss your flight."

She nods again.

From the basement, Adelaide calls, "All set!"

"Pack yourself some pie," I say to Brittany. "We'll meet you in the garage."

Melly and I go downstairs, where the girls have freed Daniel from his bonds. He's slumped half off the chair in a boneless sprawl. Courtney stuffs the last of the discarded tape into a garbage bag while Adelaide gives Daniel a once-over, making sure they didn't miss any pieces.

"He's going to be heavier than you think," I warn them, "And a lot more awkward."

They nod like they understand, but two hundred pounds of dead weight is a lot harder to move than two hundred pounds of helpful human.

Melly and I are closest in height, so we take the top half while Adelaide and Courtney each grab a leg. "Ready? Lift."

There's an initial scramble while they adjust to the reality of truly inert flesh, then we move as a unit and we make it up the stairs in one slow slog without incident.

Brittany holds the door to the garage open, and I can't help noting the look of grim satisfaction on her face as she watches Daniel pass.

From outside, I hear the familiar rumble of my truck and hope Noel has the sense to just wait for me out there. This is the last thing I need him to walk in on.

Brittany's car is parked so the open passenger door is right in line with the steps, and it's a good thing, because I don't know how much farther we could carry him.

Maneuvering a lifeless body is a lot harder than it looks on TV, but after a lot of shoving and pulling and propping, we get him arranged in the reclining passenger seat.

"Okay," I say, shutting the door. I look at Brittany. "Melly is going to be right behind you the whole time. If anything goes wrong—"

"Give the signal," she finishes.

"Exactly."

"I'll have eyes on you the whole time," Melly confirms.

I turn to her, look deep into her blue eyes. "Do not, under any circumstances, fuck this up."

"I got you," she says, the words seeming to encompass more than those three words should. She gives me that trademark grin and slips her helmet on.

"Oh, wait, the pie," Adelaide exclaims. She disappears into the house and returns a moment later with a tinfoil-wrapped slab that she gives to Melly. "Enough for you and your sister."

She nods and zips it into an inner pocket of her leather jacket.

For a moment we're quiet, a quartet united by impossible circumstances.

I turn to Courtney and Adelaide. "Thank you for helping with this, and for forgetting," I say. "I mean this in the best way, but I hope our paths never cross again."

They know what I mean.

"Brittany, that goes for you too. Do this, then go home. You have a life that you built from scratch, just for yourself. Go enjoy it."

"I will," she says, and I believe her.

Melly flips the face shield up on her helmet. "Do you hope we cross paths again?"

I shake my head. "Not like this." I don't tell her there's a part of me that wishes we'd crossed paths sooner, before this became the one we had to travel, because I know it won't do any good. We can't change the past. The best we can do is forget it.

"I'll take that as a solid maybe then," she says. "Because I think that shoulder might get a little cold without a devil on it."

I meet each of the women's eyes in turn. "Pies before guys?"

"Pies before guys," they echo.

Chapter Forty

The look of relief on Noel's face when I come out of the garage is so profound that it could be used as a textbook example of the emotion.

I pray the others don't do anything to jeopardize it as I walk to the truck, resisting the urge to run.

"Everything good?" Noel asks with a sidelong glance when I slide into the passenger seat.

Zoe scrambles all fifty pounds of herself into my lap before I can answer or do anything other than acknowledge her wonderful existence.

"It is," I say. "But we should get moving."

"Did you kill him?" He asks it like he's not positive he wants the answer.

"I did not," I say, smug with the knowledge that it's not a lie. "But seriously, faster would be better with the getting-moving thing."

Instead of putting the truck in gear, Noel gives me a worried look. He cocks his head to the house. "Did they kill him?"

"They did not." Less smug, but sometimes the simple answer is the best.

Noel considers for a moment, then turns, puts the truck in drive, and eases onto the street. "If we hurry, we should be able to make it for the final awards," he says.

From behind us comes the roar of a motorcycle starting up, and it triggers in my head the singsong melody of "Que Será, Será."

Whatever will be, will be indeed.

In all the drama of the afternoon, the awards slipped to the very bottom of my priority pile, but I realize he's right. We need to be there, if for no other reason than it would be suspicious if we weren't.

"What about Penny?"

"Sorted parking while I was waiting," he says proudly. At my incredulous look, he says, "What? I can be on top of things!"

"I'm just impressed. Arranging parking for a truck and pie van on short notice in the heart of Boston is practically magic."

"Yes, I'm the magic one here," he says, completely deadpan.

I lean against the window, forcing my thoughts away from the car and the motorcycle somewhere in our wake. The plan will hold.

It has to.

"You okay?" Noel asks.

"I am."

* * *

The picnic is still in full swing when we get back, and we've barely had time to round up an appetizer when Mayor Beckett calls everyone to attention. He thanks the attendees for being there, the band for performing, and God for giving us such a glorious day for the event.

"And now, to introduce the contestants and their creations, I am pleased to welcome one of our fine judges, Aria Cooper, whose husband is not only a dear friend but one of our sponsors today."

Aria comes forward and accepts the microphone from the mayor. She's traded the ivory sheath of earlier for a cap-sleeved scarlet sundress, fitted through the bodice with an A-line skirt. It's a good look. She's topped it off with a matching wide-brimmed hat swaddled with a grosgrain bow that would fit right in at the Kentucky Derby or a posh English wedding.

The power of a good red dress can't be underestimated, because she no longer has the shrinking look she started the day with. Aria Cooper stands tall and confident as she faces the crowd gathered on the common and gives an overview of each entry, using the recipe cards for reference and holding each pie aloft in turn so the media people can get their shots.

"The wonderful chefs from Beacon Hill Hospitality have prepared plenty of each flavor so you can all get a taste of just how hard it was to select a winner," Aria says. "But select we must, so without further ado, let's welcome our three finalists in the Miss American Pie Massachusetts competition to the stage. Please give a round of applause for Olivia Babineau, Daisy Ellery, and Jacinta Torres!"

I give Noel Zoe's leash. Everything feels fluttery and full of possibility, and before I can think better of it, I stand on my toes and pull his head down, kissing him quickly. He tastes like apples. I leave him with a cheeky grin and set off for the stage.

Jacinta, Olivia, and I converge as one and climb the stairs in unison, letting Olivia set the pace with her crutch. Governor Strand comes forward, and we join her by the pie table. Beside each of our pies is an envelope, our names written in elegant cursive, but there are no ribbons, no indication of who placed first.

Unexpected nerves grip me, whether from anticipation or stage fright, I don't know. I scan the crowd for Noel and Zoe, but the sea of faces is vast. I know they're out there, though, and that's what matters. I take a breath, remind myself it's just a pie contest.

Aria's own inhale is audible on the sound system, and in the static I hear her make a decision. "Before I hand the microphone over to the governor, I would like to say a few words. I'm sorry to do this here, but we live in a country where shitty men are allowed to run things without consequence or oversight, and I've had enough. My husband, Daniel Cooper, intended to announce his plans to run for governor today, which is an insult to Governor Strand, akin to proposing at someone else's wedding. Until today, I intended to let him, because I'm a supportive wife, and I believed he knew best. I was wrong."

The meek and dreamy tones of our playground talk are gone. Instead the woman before me is fierce, determined, and more than a little pissed.

"But in the past few weeks I have come to know my husband in a way I never did before. I have learned he is a dangerous man. A selfish man who cares solely about his own ambitions, who will stop at nothing to get what he wants. We are already a country in turmoil, and we don't need another criminal getting a seat at the table. And my husband is most assuredly a criminal."

She stops in the middle of the stage, giving this time to sink in, and my chest fills with pride. It's working. The pie is working. Even after everything we did in that basement, she's going to take him down the rest of the way.

In the stillness, it's like the entire audience is leaning in.

"For the past five years, my husband has been embezzling money from the Freer Future Foundation. I have a ledger proving that, as the head of donor development, he funneled nearly as much money into his own private account as he did the coffers of the company. It is my belief he was going to use this money to fund his campaign for governor and that he was cultivating personal connections to high-value donors with the express intention of using them to fund a presidential campaign down the road."

There's a commotion from the back of the stage, and the microphone dies in a sudden hiss of static. Daniel storms across the stage, red-faced with rage. For a moment, panic grips me, but to Daniel I might as well be invisible. As I should be, thanks to the pie. With fists clenched at his sides, he zeroes on in Aria, but before he can reach her, he's intercepted by Mayor Beckett, who looks ready to hit the younger man. It can't be easy finding out one of your protégés is an utter creep, even when you're not exactly a hero yourself.

Aria Cooper doesn't acknowledge the interruption, just drops the microphone to her side and continues, voice raised to be heard across the common. "It is my intention to cooperate fully in any investigation into my husband's wrongdoings."

There is a swell of voices as the crowd reacts to this unexpected drama and as Daniel is removed from stage. The microphone crackles to life in Aria's hand, but she just waits, letting the crowd digest the news. When they settle, she raises the mic and says, "Again, I apologize for derailing the proceedings of this event, but it felt safest to make these allegations in a public setting, where my husband couldn't silence me. I offer my sincerest apologies to the talented bakers anxiously awaiting their awards."

She steps back, and when she hands the microphone to the governor, her hand is completely steady. She is a woman at peace with her decisions.

Governor Strand addresses the audience with a broad smile. "Well, I think we can safely say that the Miss American Pie Massachusetts would win the most unexpected excitement award," she says, and there's laughter, a palpable easing of tensions, like she's given everyone permission to relax. "A little pie, a little justice, all in a day's work, right? So, let's get on to the real reason we're here.

"Judging this contest was not easy," she says, "Although it was undeniably delicious. Each pie was a master class in excellence, and while we can only crown one baker Miss American Pie of Massachusetts, I am thrilled to announce that a generous donation to the contest has made it possible to reward each of your efforts with the full ten-thousand-dollar first-place prize money. You have all more than earned it. I would like to thank you all for being here, and I sincerely hope you will continue to use your gifts to make the world a better place with your baking."

A ripple goes through the crowd, and I glance between Jacinta and Olivia to find my own disbelief and joy mirrored on their faces. Ten thousand dollars may not be much to the Daniel Coopers of the world, but for the three of us, it's life changing. I turn around, searching for Aria, wondering if it's possible that she's behind this, but before the news can even sink in, a drumroll starts from the bandstand, and Aria reemerges with a satin pageant-style Miss American Pie sash adorned with glittery pies. It's gaudy and ridiculous and somehow completely perfect.

"That being said, we must still declare our winner," Governor Strand says, a broad smiling splitting her face. It's clear she's enjoying this moment as much as we are. "It is with great pleasure that

I present to you our very own Miss American Pie Massachusetts, Daisy Ellery!"

Aria drapes the sash across my chest and mouths *Congratulations* at me before stepping back behind the governor.

The band launches into something patriotic, and without thinking, I clasp Olivia's and Jacinta's hands in mine, and we raise them in united victory. Cameras flash and applause roars, and I know it's the right image to end this on. We are, after all, united by our time in the State House kitchen, and by the truth of what happens in all kitchens, every day. Kitchens, more than any other room, see the best and worst of us. It's where we make birthday cakes when it's time to celebrate, soup when we need soothing, and where we can find the ice cream when we need a cry. It's where traditions are born, where people come together to celebrate good times and to create comfort for the hard times. Worlds can change in kitchens, and kitchens can change worlds.

I know now that my magic is not broken and neither am I.

As we stand before the audience, our hands raised in triumphant solidarity, we are joined not just as pie makers, not just as women, but as the shapers of worlds. My pies may stop bad men, but they're no more powerful than the pies Jacinta fills with so much love it bubbles over the edges, or the crystalline happiness that a bite of one of Olivia's pies delivers.

Pies are powerful.

All of them.

And so are we.

Chapter Forty-One

On the drive home, Melly calls to report that everything went according to plan, which I figured after seeing Daniel in the flesh.

They arrived at the hotel just as the drugs were wearing off, so Daniel was able to stumble himself back to his room with a serious assist from Melly. Aria was waiting, and together they stripped him and dumped him in the bed, and Melly left so Aria could go about pretending to wake him for the picnic.

He swallowed the cover story—he drank too much—easier than he swallowed the forgetting pie, which seemed to have done the trick.

He expressed no recollection of spending a day taped to a chair, no memory of being force-fed a pie, and most importantly, no inkling of my existence. Mentions of Brittany Cline, Kerenza Vallery, and Emma Rogers also failed to elicit even a flicker of recognition.

So it worked.

I avoided a cold-blooded, never line–crossing murder and still kept his intended victims and myself safe. And thanks to Aria, he's going to be going to jail for a long time, and even if it's not for all his crimes, at least it's something.

Job well done.

In a different world, an earlier one, I might not have been able to do what I did with the forgetting pie. After my father died, I thought that was the end of my family for good. My mom was gone, he was gone, and hell, I was gone, heading for god knew where. When I buried my father, I buried the idea of ever having family again, although I couldn't have articulated it at the time. I realize now that I was wrong. Family is so much more than blood. There was a time I would've been thrilled to discover I had a half brother, a remaining link, however tenuous, to my "real" family, but I barely hesitated when I erased myself from Daniel's memory. I don't need him, and frankly, he doesn't deserve me. It's been a long road, but I've built a life that matters, that has a purpose and people I care about who care about me too. A few shared strands of DNA will never be worth jeopardizing that.

I send Kerenza and Emma emails to let them know they don't need to worry about Daniel anymore, and I have a reply from Emma within minutes.

That's a relief. In other news, I need a pie. Can we meet when you get back?

I tell her where best to find me, and while I'm glad she's ready to move on, there's something about the request that takes some of the wind out of my sails. As successful as the weekend was, has it really changed anything?

Sure, I've freed three women, four counting Aria, from Daniel and garnered some very positive press for Noel's orchard and Frank's diner, but is it enough? Is my one-woman pie crusade really doing enough to help any of the dozens of women I've made pies for or the dozens more who will still reach out?

Maybe not.

But it doesn't mean it wasn't worth it, and it doesn't mean I'm going to stop making pies.

"Deep-dish thoughts?" Noel asks. In the darkness, the steady stream of headlights of oncoming cars is hypnotizing.

"Or none at all," I say, adding an airiness to the words I don't feel.

"Liar."

I sigh. "None that I can articulate, then."

"Try. It'll keep me awake."

So I do. "I'm thinking about the greatest good for the greatest number and what that really means." I stroke the soft inside part of Zoe's ear, trying to figure out how to phrase it. "Like there are these things that matter on a large grand scale, the kind of things Melly cares about, like stopping fascism and curing climate change, and that's obviously super important, but then there are the little individual things, like a woman who's getting hit at home or a girl whose rapist gets a free pass for being popular. Do you go for the big sweeping save-the-world changes that will help the most people, or do you chip away at the little problems, fixing one and another and another until you have this huge snowball of good deeds built up?"

Noel doesn't answer right away, and I appreciate that about him, that patience, like he's genuinely considering what he wants to say. "I think you do both, wherever and however you can. And that's the royal collective you, not individual Daisy you. Individual you is not responsible for fixing the world or the worlds in your path." Another beat of silence, and something shifts in the air. "But I like you because you try to anyway. When you first told me about your mission, about Pies Before Guys and what it really entailed, yeah, I was thrown. But I get it. You're doing something nobody else can or will do, and it's important. It's like being a vet."

A surprised bark of a laugh shoots out before I can stop it. "Like a what?"

"Stop laughing. You're ruining my speech," he says. "It's like being a vet. As much as I love animals, I could never be a vet because I couldn't handle having to put them to sleep or having to amputate their limbs or any of the really hard stuff. But someone has to in order to help them, and I have nothing but respect for the people who can and do. You're kind of like that."

It might be the oddest compliment I've ever received, but my throat closes up around the sincerity of it, and I'm grateful that he can't see the heat spreading across my cheeks in the dark cab of the truck.

"So yeah," he says, "I think you're doing the greatest good for the greatest number you can, however you have to. And I think that's plenty. It's just like what your mom and grandmother did, just on a different scale."

He says it like it's the most obvious thing in the world, and I wonder if everything is always so clear to him.

"I'm glad you came along," I say, the dark somehow making honesty easier. "On the trip and just in general, into my life."

"Me too," he says.

Miles roll by in easy silence, Zoe snoring in a contented ball between us.

"There is one thing I have to ask, just so I know," Noel says, the words tumbling over each other in a rush, like he's been holding them back for too long. "About Melly."

"Yeah?"

"The two of you? Are you a thing?"

I can practically hear him blushing, and it makes me smile.

He barrels on. "I mean, at the pie reception, she did kiss you, and you didn't seem to mind and she's exciting and cute and I mean, I think it's great, I really, I mean, I was just wondering."

"Noel," I say, and the one word is enough to stop his nervous ramble. In the dark I find his hand, anxiously petting Zoe's flank, and still it with my own. "You're allowed to ask. But no, Melly and I are most definitely not a thing. In different circumstances, sure, maybe, but not anymore. She dropped me headlong into a pile of shit, and there's only so forgiving I can be."

"You like her, though." It's not a question.

"Somehow, yeah, I do. Even after everything. I guess it's sort of like you liking me. Logically it doesn't make sense, but there it is." I squeeze his hand, his fingers warm and reassuring beneath mine. "I like you too, you know."

"Yeah?"

I bring his hand to my lips and kiss the rough skin of his knuckles. "More than you know."

* * *

I practically sleepwalk into the diner the next morning, the long days, the excitement, and the lack of sleep having thoroughly caught up with me.

But the bleariness vanishes the instant Juan sweeps me into a hug and swings me around the kitchen before parading me through the dining room for a hero's welcome.

The servers and customers smother me with congratulations, one old regular insisting I autograph the article the local paper ran under the questionable heading *Local Pie Girl Takes the Cake*. Even Frank turns from his stepladder by the front window to offer a curt, "Well done."

I grin. High praise indeed.

But then I see what he's doing up on that ladder, and my heart swells.

He too has a copy of the local paper and is taping the article and its accompanying victory photo of me, Jacinta, and Olivia to the window for passersby to see.

I'm overcome with the urge to hug him and am about to when he turns, pinning me with his beady gaze. "You better see about getting that orchard to send over some of this cider and honey everyone keeps squawking about. Seems I'm gonna be needing this fancy-ass pie on my menu after all this damn commotion."

I give him a two-fingered salute. "Will do."

"But for now, see that we're stocked with the regulars. Can't believe you were gone that long. In my day we didn't get no vacation time."

"I still don't work for you, Frank," I say in a singsong, but I head to the kitchen and take an apron from the pile on my way by, tying it on over my cherry-print dress.

There are always more pies to make.

* * *

When the kitchen door swings open an hour later, Frank catches me with the forkful of cheesy fries halfway to my mouth.

"Pie Girl," he barks. "Some chick here to see you. Am I paying you to eat or make pies?"

"Neither," I chirp, brushing by him.

Sitting at the counter is Emma Rogers, dressed for work in a sleek navy skirt suit. She's tracing the rim of a half-full cup of coffee with a manicured finger.

"Hey," I say.

"Hey." A smile lights her face. "I'm sorry to ambush you here, but I wanted to say congratulations about the contest. You must be thrilled."

"It was a good time," I say. Understatement. Of. The. Year. "So, what can I do for you?"

She speaks more to her coffee cup than to me, but I can't miss the grin pulling at the corners of her mouth. "I need a pie."

I trust her to be discreet, but I still glance around to make sure no one is paying us too much attention. "For Jackson?"

"For me," she says, glancing up. Her eyes sparkle with life. "The most extravagant, decadent, over-the-top pie you can make."

This is one hundred percent not what I was expecting. "Explain?"

"I'm celebrating," she says simply.

"You're celebrating what, exactly?"

"That I've left my philandering, good-for-nothing fuckweasel of a fiancé," she crows triumphantly. Heads turn to us at this, but I don't care. I squeal and reach across the counter to hug her.

"I can totally make a pie for that," I say. "And I'll cancel the wedding order, but I'm keeping his deposit."

"Of course you are," she says. "He's lucky that's all this is costing him."

I tell her to come see me here tomorrow, but she suggests we grab dinner instead. After the barest hesitation, I agree. Old me would've said no, balked at letting her get too close, but I like it here in Turnbridge, I like being Clark Kent with a rolling a pin, and Clark could do with more friends.

Epilogue

Autumn erupts in an explosion of color just in time for the grand opening of Hollow Hill Craft Cidery.

The riotous colors bring in waves of leaf peepers from all over New England and beyond, and Noel plays right into the cozy New England fall vibe.

Groups have been arriving in droves for weeks in search of picture-perfect apple-picking trips, and every single one has left with an invitation to the cidery's grand opening.

It's possible we should've been a bit more selective with the guest list, because there's no way we're going to keep up with demand.

Penny is parked by the farm stand, and I'm doing brisk business in handheld chicken pot pies, Cornish pasties, and of course, fresh-picked-apple pies.

I take more Thanksgiving pie orders than I ever have in my life, and more than half of them are for the Hollow Hill Signature Apple, the very same honey-cream cider-caramel concoction that is featured in the new Miss American Pie cookbook. There's already been talk of a second book for next year, and FoodTV has expressed interest in making it a televised competition, something like the Great British Bake Off with an American twist. I'm pretty sure that just means cutting out the charm and replacing it with cutthroat challenges, but Noel was so excited I promised to think about it.

Right now, though, it's Noel's turn for the spotlight.

Live music, courtesy of a local band, pours from the cidery doors as people flit between activities like Noel's bees.

Noel, for his part, appears to be overwhelmed and overjoyed in equal measure. He hasn't stopped moving all day, and when I get a break in customers, I grab a warm chicken pie from the oven, stick my *Be Back Soon!* sign in the window, and set off to find him.

The cidery is housed in one of the falling-down barn buildings that's not quite so much falling down anymore, and it's packed with bodies. The original concrete floor has been left in its original pitted condition, and instead of tractor parts, picnic tables now fill the space. In one corner of the room, a pair of college-aged guys with a guitar and an accordion provide backing for the raspy-voiced singer. They play something upbeat that skirts the line between rock and folk and is infectiously good. A group of kids are dancing in a circle in front of them, and I spot Juan's daughter among them and have to laugh at her whirling enthusiasm. I make my way through the crowd and find Juan and Eric sitting hip to hip on a picnic bench, Juan's arm slung around his husband's shoulders, watching their daughter with such unabashed love that I don't want to intrude.

But then Zoe gallops into the spinning and leaping fray and lets the kids absorb her into their mob.

"She'll sleep good tonight," Juan says when he sees me.

"Zoe or Ana?" I ask, grinning.

He laughs. "Both." He looks around the crowded barn and nods his appreciation. "Hell of a good turnout your boy's getting."

"It's crazy," I say.

"I'm surprised you were able to get away from the van long enough to make an appearance. You've had a line a mile long since we got here. Let me know if you need any help slinging pies," Juan says, but I can't imagine pulling him away from his perfect family even if my oven was on fire.

"Keep an eye on her for me?" I ask, inclining my head to Zoe, who is busy twirling herself around little legs in an effort to get as many pets as possible.

"Will do."

A long reclaimed-wood bar runs along the back wall, and that's where I find Noel, completely in his element in plaid flannel and a white apron, moving easily between customers. He's more animated than I've ever seen him, his face lit with the excitement of a new beginning. If this is a sign of things to come, he won't have to worry about losing the orchard ever again.

He stops at the end of the bar to pour another sampling of ciders to a white-haired man who says something to make him laugh.

I catch his eye and his smile widens, starbursts of laugh lines crinkling at his eyes. He raises a bottle to me in salute, and I make my way over to him.

"I come bearing food," I say, holding out the pie.

The old man turns and snaps, "It's about damn time we got some delivery around here. I was just telling this chap that it's no way to run a business, making people wait in line outside. What he needs is some pretty waitresses around here, have 'em dress like you do."

"Frank! You came," I say. I'm oddly touched. I told him about it when I invited the rest of the diner staff, but I didn't think he'd make an appearance. "I can go grab you a pie. I would've brought two if I'd known you were here."

He winks at me. "I'm just messing with you, girl. I was really telling him that it's a damn fine establishment he has set up here, but he better not even think about stealing my pie girl."

"Oh, is that right?"

Noel laughs. "And I told him that I know better than to try to make you do anything you don't want to do."

"Smart man, right there," Frank says, nodding sagely. "You could do worse than that."

"I'm aware," I say with a little laugh, and I may be talking to Frank, but my eyes are locked on Noel's.

His mouth quirks up into a knowing grin.

"Eat something before you collapse," I say. "*Cidery Owner Succumbs to Fit of Exhaustion* is not the kind of headlines you're trying to make."

"I haven't had time," Noel says with such joy that I almost hate making him slow down. "There are even people from *Yankee* and *Bon Appetit* here. Actual still-in-print magazines. Can you imagine? What if they like it enough to mention it in an issue?"

"With great power comes great responsibility," I say. "Like my responsibility to feed these people." I turn to Frank. "Make sure he eats."

"You got it," Franks says, then with an air of his typical gruffness adds, "And I expect to see you tomorrow. We need to talk about our menu. I'm not about to have all my customers coming here for pies."

I give him a two-fingered salute. "It's a date." I meet Noel's eyes across the bar. "Find me later?"

"Of course." He grins widely and turns to answer a customer's questions about the different ciders he has on tap. I leave him to it.

A queue has formed at the van in my absence, and it's only when I'm almost close enough to join it that I realize it's moving.

I see hands stretch out the serving window, passing a waxed-paper-wrapped pie to a customer, and I run the rest of the way, dress tangling around my legs as I go.

I pull up short at the van when I realize it's Melly in the window, curls no longer purple but a striking teal, taking orders like she's been doing it for ages.

I let myself in.

"Don't get mad," she says, before I can say anything. She still has a customer-serving smile on her face as she finishes her current transaction. "You were in the weeds. I wanted to help."

I pull the oven open, check what's inside.

"Current stock only," she says. "I'm not dumb enough to try to bake something."

"That's good," I say, hip checking her away from my serving window. "Be bad for business if people start dying."

"Depends which business you're talking about," she says, then immediately puts her hands in the air. "Kidding, kidding!"

She edges back into the serving space, and we settle into an easy rhythm as we clear the rest of the line.

"Aren't you supposed to be on face-painting duty?" I ask, when we get a minute to breathe.

"Ran out of paint." She shrugs. "This ended up being a pretty big deal."

"It did," I agree. "It's good. He deserves it."

Something about Melly closes in a little at that, and when she smiles, it doesn't quite reach her eyes. "Yeah. He's pretty lucky."

I don't have a chance to question her about it, because we're interrupted by another customer.

"I need to order a pie," comes a cheeky voice I recognize.

I turn and see I'm right. "Emma! You came!"

"Of course I did," she says. "This is huge! And right up our alleys."

That's when I notice she has her arm linked through someone else's. I give her a look, and she grins like a schoolgirl.

"This is Rahul," she says, but I already guessed that. She's told me way too much about him for me to have any doubts. Still, I'm glad to finally meet him in person. He's every bit as handsome as she made him out to be, and if he's even half as nice as that, then she'll be all set.

"It's good to meet you," I say. "Can I get you guys anything? On the house."

I send them off with pecan cutie pies and orders to go see Noel for cider. I turn to Melly and find her perched against the counter.

"I shouldn't be here," she says.

"No, I'm glad you are," I say, and I mean it. "Really."

"You and Noel, though, you're like a thing now, right?"

I laugh. I can't help it. I recall an almost-identical question from Noel on that ride home from Boston that seems like a lifetime ago now, and I wonder what I, an orphaned, murder-pie-making semi-assassin, have done to be in such a contested position.

"Yeah, I guess we are," I say honestly. "It's nice. I'm happy."

"I'm glad, then," she says. I think she even means it. "Still, I wish it could be us."

"It might've been, maybe," I say. "In a different world."

"But not this one?"

"Who knows? This life is still young."

* * *

The grand opening continues far past its original closing time, and when the crowds finally disperse and I'm finished cleaning, I can't bear the thought of driving across town and decide to stay put. Zoe, exhausted from her day of socializing, is already asleep on the bed when I get out of the shower.

She barely stirs when there's a knock on the door.

"Just a sec!" I call, bundling my wet hair into a bun. A glance out the window reveals nothing more than a faceless shape at my door, but it's okay. Gone are my fears of mystery men in the night. Now I know there are only so many people it can be.

Before I can answer, my phone chirps twice—one signature PBG tone and an email. I scan the first message, a straightforward order request, and I forward her a contract. I almost delete the email, then realize it isn't spam. It's an invitation to audition for FoodTV's upcoming *Winner Bakes All: America's Bake Off.*

If I were to be selected, filming would only be a two-week commitment, and the prize money . . . well, that makes Miss American Pie look like pocket change.

I could completely change how Pies Before Guys operates with that kind of budget.

The idea is more than a little intriguing, but I don't have a chance to read the fine print before the knock sounds again, lighter this time but the pattern familiar. Noel. Zoe offers a sleepy woof of greeting as I answer.

"Hey," I say, smiling into the dark. "I think we have another road trip in our future."

"I like the sound of that," Noel says, coming inside. His hair is damp and his eyes are tired, but he looks happy, content in a way that I haven't seen yet.

"Is that right?" I ask teasingly. "Now that I said it, I don't think you'll even have time for a road trip, Mr. Busy Cidery Owner."

"Not the road trip part," he says, lowering his mouth to mine. "The future part. I like the future part."

When we kiss, he tastes like apples and honey and home.

And you know what?

I like the future part too.

Recipes

Buttered Up Pie Crust

I know the prospect of making pie crust gives people the wiggins, but there's no need to fear the crust! It's more forgiving than you think.

Ingredients

1¼ cups all-purpose flour
1 teaspoon sugar
½ teaspoon salt
8 tablespoons butter (can sub plant-based butter if preferred), cold and cut into small cubes
¼–½ cup cold water
Splash of apple cider vinegar

Method

1. Combine the dry ingredients in a bowl.

2. Add butter and mix with your hands or a pastry blender until incorporated. You should be able to feel and see flakes of flour-coated butter.

3. Add a splash of cider vinegar and enough of the cold water to form a cohesive dough.

4. Form into a disc and wrap in plastic. Let dough rest in the fridge for a half hour or up to two days.

Note

Recipe easily doubles for a two-crust pie or quadruples if you want to make extra to freeze.

Honey Crunch Apple Pie

This pie has several components, but the end result is worth it. (And the apples and crust can be prepped ahead to make things easier.)

Ingredients

Crust

One batch from previous recipe

Cider Caramel Apple Layer

7–8 medium apples, peeled and cut into cubes
1 cup cider (Down East is my favorite, but use what you like best)
½–¾ cup honey (exact amount needed will depend on the sweetness of your cider—don't be afraid to taste as you go!)
½ teaspoon cinnamon
Pinch of mace or nutmeg
Generous pinch of salt

Honey Crunch Topping

1¾ cups granulated honey
1 cup flour
1 cup chopped pecans
8 tablespoons butter, very soft
Pinch of salt

Cream Layer

8 ounces cream cheese
2 tablespoons honey
2 tablespoons light brown sugar
1 egg

Method

1. CRUST: Roll out the pie dough and transfer to a pie pan. Roll the overhanging excess along the rim to form an edge and crimp as desired. Freeze for at least 30 minutes or until ready to use.

2. APPLES: Combine all ingredients in a medium pot or skillet and cook over medium-high heat until cider is reduced and apples are tender. Set aside to cool.

3. TOPPING: Combine all ingredients in a bowl and mix with a fork until combined, then use your hands to form clumps.

4. CREAM: Beat cream cheese, honey, and sugar until smooth. Add egg; beat until combined.

5. ASSEMBLY: Pour cream layer into prepared pie shell, top with a layer of apples, and cover with the honey crunch topping.

6. Bake at 375 for 40 minutes or until filling is set and crust is golden brown.

7. Cool on wire rack, then refrigerate until filling is firm.

Notes

The apples can be prepped up to a week in advance—once cooked, simply refrigerate in an airtight container until ready to use.

Many grocery stores carry granulated honey, but if you can't find it, you can sub 1 cup granulated sugar and ½ cup brown sugar for the topping. It won't be quite the same, but it will still be tasty.

The topping recipe makes a large batch, because let's be real, half the point of baking is to sneak bites out of the bowl! If you prefer things in moderation, feel free to halve.

Raspberry Almond Cutie Pies

These are perfect for when you want pies in a hurry.

Ingredients

Double batch of Buttered Up Pie Crust (or for REALLY fast pies, use store-bought)
Raspberry Jam
Marzipan
1 egg, beaten
Coarse sugar

Method

1. Preheat oven to 375 degrees and line a baking tray with parchment.

2. Roll out pie dough and cut with 3-inch circle cutters (can also use a glass, mason jar, or cookie cutters of choice)

3. Gently reroll scraps together to cut more circles. The more pie dough is reworked, the tougher it gets, so be nice to it! Your goal is to have an even number of discs, since each cutie pie needs a pair.

4. Roll out the marzipan about ¼ inch thick (this is easiest if you keep it between two sheets of waxed or parchment paper), and use a 2½-inch circle cutter to cut disks.

5. Arrange half of the pie dough disks on the baking tray and top with a marzipan circle and a dollop of raspberry jam.

6. Take the remaining half of the dough disks, and cut vent holes in them. These can be simple Xs, or you can use a tiny cookie cutter for a single center vent. Either way, you want to do this step *before* you finish assembling the pies.

7. Arrange each top disc on top of the assembled pies and seal edges by pressing them with the tines of a fork.

8. Brush tops with beaten egg and sprinkle generously with coarse sugar.

9. Bake for approximately 25 minutes or until the tops are golden brown and the bottoms are crisp.

Note

Marzipan usually lives in the baking aisle, sometimes near the nuts, sometimes near canned pie filling. This recipe won't use the entire box, but don't throw away your leftovers! It keeps well in the fridge, and you can add it to muffins, streusel, or more pies.

Peanut Butter Murder Pie

Since we don't want this to be an accidental murder pie, feel free to sub SunButter for peanut butter if allergies are a concern. Mini chocolate chips make a cute swap for the chopped-peanut-butter-cup garnish.

Ingredients

Crust

30 Oreos
6 tablespoons butter
1 tablespoon sugar

Filling

1 cup heavy cream
¾ cup powdered sugar
⅔ cup peanut butter (can sub SunButter for allergies)
4 ounces cream cheese
1 teaspoon vanilla
Pinch of salt

Ganache

½ cup chocolate chips
¼ cup heavy cream

Garnish

1 cup heavy cream
¼ cup powdered sugar
2 tablespoon melted peanut butter
Chopped peanut butter cups

Method

For Crust:

1. Preheat oven to 350.

2. Crush the Oreos into fine crumbs, either in a food processor or in a zip-lock bag with a rolling pin.

3. Add sugar and melted butter to crumbs and stir to combine.

4. Press crust into pie pan, making sure to keep an even thickness on bottom and around sides.

5. Bake for 8 minutes and cool before adding filling.

For Filling:

1. Beat heavy cream and powdered sugar together to form stiff peaks; set aside.

2. Beat peanut butter, cream cheese, vanilla, and salt together until light and fluffy.

3. Fold whipped cream into peanut butter mixture and fill pie crust, making sure the top is smooth and there's enough room for the ganache. Depending on the exact size of your pie pan,

you might have a bit of extra filling—go ahead and lick the bowl!

4. Chill pie until filling is firm.

For Ganache and Garnish:

1. Heat heavy cream and add to chocolate chips. Stir until smooth. Let cool a bit and then pour over top of chilled pie.

2. Melt peanut butter and drizzle decoratively over ganache.

3. Whip heavy cream and powdered sugar to form stiff peaks and pipe around edge of pie.

4. Garnish whipped cream with chopped peanut butter cups.

Note

This pie can be served from the refrigerator or freezer, depending on texture preference. Both ways are great!

Acknowledgments

The first slice of thank-you pie absolutely has to go to Becca Podos, agent extraordinaire, for her immediate and uncompromising faith in my weird little murder-pie book. It isn't an exaggeration to say that without her help, this book might not have made it out in the world.

I was also exceedingly lucky to have added Faith Black Ross to Team Murder Pie. I couldn't have asked for a better editor—her belief in Daisy's mission and commitment to keeping the whimsy as high as the body count made this entire process a joy.

I am also endlessly grateful to the rest of the Crooked Lane team who helped make this book a reality, including Melissa Rechter, Madeline Rathle, and Rebecca Nelson. Rachel Keith's copyedits made sure it looked like I knew what days of the week fell when, and Trish Cramblet's cover design makes me happy every time I look at it. Pie for everybody!

I also owe thank-you pies to everyone who took the time to read and blurb. I'm thrilled that my book will be joining the shelves among such awesome company.

Thank you also to Sophie Hannah and Midge Gillies for giving me the chance to study at Cambridge as part of the Crime and

Thriller Writing MSt program. I wrote this book just before the course started and was querying from Madingley, so even though it's not my "Cambridge book," it feels linked. Hopefully when the pandemic is well and truly behind us, I'll get to return to actually finish the program! In the meantime, I'm very much keeping an eye out for books from the rest of the cohort (whom I definitely ghosted on WhatsApp because I'm a ball of introverted anxiety—oops!); Eliza North deserves special thanks for her support during that frantic querying phase when things were happening at lightning speed!

Erika Madden also deserves a special thank-you pie for her undying enthusiasm and the fact that her WIPs were a great distraction from obsessively refreshing my email while this book was on sub. I can't wait to watch her go through the same stress very soon!

And finally, thanks to Adam, mostly for continuing to eat the things I bake even after he knew what this book was about. That right there is true love.